SINISTER

by Jana DeLeon

Everyone wondered about Shaye Archer's past. Including Shaye.

Shaye Archer's life effectively began the night police found her in an alley, beaten, abused and with no memory of the previous fifteen years, not even her name. Nine years later, she's a licensed private investigator, with a single goal—to get answers for her clients when there aren't supposed to be any.

And maybe someday, answers for herself.

Chapter One

Thursday, July 2, 2015
Bywater District, New Orleans, Louisiana

Jinx LeDoux bolted upright, gasping for air, her heart pounding so hard she felt as if her chest would burst. The slightest movement sent shock waves through her head, and her stomach rolled. She felt the bile rise in her throat and took a deep breath, forcing the nausea away.

Something had happened. Something she couldn't quite remember.

She blinked several times, trying to clear her blurry vision, then realized it wasn't only her vision that was the problem. Wherever she was, it was almost pitch black.

Wherever she was?

She put her hands on the ground, feeling around for something familiar, something that told her she was safe in the abandoned apartment she'd been living in for the last month, but the floor she rested upon was concrete, not the aged, splintered wood she had grown used to. Slowly, she lifted her hands and reached out until her right hand connected with something hard and cool. She ran her fingertips on the surface, frowning as she felt the chilly, round metal rod. She moved her fingers to the side and felt another, then another as far as she could reach. Panicking, she reached upward and found the same bars about two feet above her head.

She was in a cage!

Then her memory came crashing back in like a tidal wave.

The shadow!

She'd left the docks where she'd been skating Wednesday evening and had been on her way to the apartment when she'd felt someone watching her. Jinx was only fifteen, but she had more acuity than most adults when it came to her surroundings. She'd scanned the street, looking at the shadows for movement, looking into the windows of vacant buildings for any sign that someone lurked behind one of the cracked, grimy panes, but she'd seen no one.

She'd been wrong.

As she'd reached the old abandoned drugstore, a shadow crossed the open door and inched onto the sidewalk. It was only for a second, but enough for her to know that the person who'd been watching her was inside that building. She spun around, ready to run as fast as her legs could take her, when she felt the needle pierce her neck. The last thing she remembered was falling onto the sidewalk.

That answered the question of how, but left a whole lot unanswered.

She got onto her knees and crawled around the structure, trying to determine its size and locate an exit. The door was located on the third panel she searched, secured by a heavy padlock. She tugged on the lock, but it didn't budge. The last panel yielded nothing more than a confirmation that she was inside an iron cage, approximately six feet square. The concrete floor was completely bare.

Her wrists ached a bit and she rubbed them, feeling the indentations where they had been bound together. Sections of her skin had been burned by the friction caused by the rope. The same indentations and burns surrounded her ankles.

What the hell was going on? Who had done this? And the worst question, why?

She brought her knees up to her chest and circled them with her arms. It was at least ninety degrees outside, but she shook from the chill running through her. Tears welled up in her eyes, and she felt them spill over and roll down her cheeks as she collapsed into sobs. In the eight months she'd lived on the streets, she'd never cried.

Now she wasn't sure she'd ever stop.

CHAPTER TWO

Friday, July 3, 2015
French Quarter, New Orleans

Shaye Archer waited until he made the first move, but the instant he raised the pistol, she sprang into action. She grabbed the barrel of the weapon with her right hand and yanked it forward, as she stepped to the side, then kicked the man in the groin as he moved forward, off balance. When he doubled over from the groin kick, she planted another knee in his face, dropping him to the ground and causing him to release the pistol.

She sprang back and took aim as he looked up at her and smiled. "You're improving," he said as he rose from the mat.

Shaye handed her sensei the plastic pistol. "You think so?"

"Definitely. Your response comes quicker than before."

"Yeah, well, taking on a serial killer tends to increase reaction time."

He sobered and nodded. "I'm sure it does. I read

about it in the newspaper a couple of weeks ago and assumed that's why you canceled training for a bit. I found it all, uh…shocking, I guess, although the word seems to fall rather flat given the facts."

Shaye nodded. Her first case as a private investigator had been a doozy, surprising her, her client, the New Orleans police, and a host of other people who couldn't have invented a story like the reality she'd witnessed, even if they'd tried.

"It definitely wasn't something I considered when I opened my agency," Shaye said.

"How are you handling it?"

Shaye gave him a rueful smile. She'd been asked that question at least a hundred times since the details of the case hit the news, sometimes by people who were genuinely concerned, but mostly by news reporters. They'd camped out on the sidewalk outside her mother's house in the Garden District and in front of her apartment in the French Quarter, shoving a microphone in her face every time she had to pass them.

She'd said nothing, of course. Years of experience had taught her that the quickest way to get rid of a media storm was to ignore it and pray that something else news- or gossip-worthy happened to redirect their attention. In her case, it required both news- and gossip-worthy, since anything that involved Shaye Archer, mysterious adopted daughter of heiress Corrine Archer, was both gossip and news. Fortunately for Shaye, a state representative had been caught in a less-than-desirable position with his daughter's nanny, and the reporters had flocked to his mansion several blocks from her mother's home.

Sensei Markham had been teaching her Muay Thai and Krav Maga for the last five years. He wasn't looking for the latest gossip to pass on. When he asked her a personal question, it was out of genuine concern.

"I'm doing good," Shaye said.

He raised one eyebrow. "You sure?"

"It was difficult, of course, and it took some time to process, but overall, I'm happy with the way I handled things. Even happier with what I accomplished. Emma Frederick can move on to the great life she deserves without looking over her shoulder and without thinking she's crazy."

He nodded. "That is definitely a good thing. Although when you told me you were opening your own agency, I thought you intended to continue the same type of work you did for Breaux Investigations. If you're planning on going toe-to-toe with serious bad guys, then I think we should concentrate more on close combat training."

"I think that's a good idea." Her brush with a serial killer had turned out all right, but the next time, she might not be as lucky. Any edge that she could gain might be the difference between walking away to take another case or leaving in a body bag. She'd thought she understood the risks from taking these types of cases, but if she was being honest with herself, she'd been unnerved by Emma and her stalker. The reality of digging into that kind of disturbed person hadn't been anything like it looked on television, and neither the classroom nor years of therapy had prepared her for the wave of emotions she'd experienced after it was all over.

"Good," Sensei Markham said. "We'll start on that next week. In the meantime, I want you to up your strength training. The stronger you are, the more effective the strike."

Shaye sighed. "You know I'm dying to spend more time at the gym."

He raised one eyebrow. "'Dying' is the operative word here."

"Low blow. I'll put in one more hour a week. Satisfied?"

"It's a start. You're doing good work, Shaye, like I always knew you would. Just be careful, okay?"

She nodded and grabbed her gym bag, giving him a wave over her shoulder as she exited the building. It was eight o'clock on a hot, humid summer night and the French Quarter was already alive with the sounds of the Friday night party crowd. That party would carry through to the wee hours of Saturday morning, leaving many regretting the night before and others itching to do it all over again.

A group of college fraternity boys whistled at her as she walked by. She smiled but kept walking. Most single women her age were probably on a date or getting ready for one, but dating wasn't on Shaye's list of things to do. Not on a Friday night or any other. Right now, she had a filing system to get in order and a new printer that still needed to be set up. That, microwave nachos, beer, and reruns on the

Syfy channel were about as much excitement as she wanted.

She rounded a corner and headed for her apartment. It was much quieter blocks away from the partiers down on Bourbon, but the streets weren't empty. Some of the faces, she saw on a regular basis and knew they lived in the area. Others were vacationers, sporting cameras and stopping every few feet to take pictures of the next historical structure.

The figure leaning against the lamp pole at the corner immediately caught her eye. He was tall and thin and wore a hoodie. Periodically, he glanced down the street, but she couldn't get a good look at his face because he was standing in a shadow. The skin on the back of her neck prickled, and even though other people milled around, she knew he was looking at her.

She shifted her duffel bag on her shoulder, putting her hand underneath it. That way she could unload it easily or use it as a weapon, depending on which made more sense. Increasing her pace, she closed the gap to the corner, poised to strike as soon as the man in the shadows made his move. But when she drew within ten feet of him, he stepped out of the shadows and looked directly at her.

"Hustle?" The boy's long blond ponytail was hidden under the hood of the sweatshirt, but there was no mistaking the light green eyes and gaunt facial features of the street kid she'd met when working Emma Frederick's case. "Is everything all right?"

He glanced nervously up and down the street. "You said if I ever wanted help…"

"Of course. Do you want me to call my mother?"

His eyes widened. "No. I mean, I don't want help for me. Not exactly. Shit. I don't guess I know where to start."

Shaye was all too familiar with that feeling. "Tell you what. There's a burger joint half a block away. It's got the best onion rings in the French Quarter and I'm starving. How about I buy us dinner and you tell me what you need my help with?"

He hesitated before answering, and Shaye could tell that his desire for help was warring with his inclination not to trust anyone. Finally, he nodded.

"Great," she said and started walking toward the diner.

Hustle fell in step beside her. "I heard you got the creeper. Is that lady okay?"

"Yes. Ms. Frederick has moved to another state and is making a fresh start."

"I'm glad. I wish someone would have been able to help my moms."

"So do I."

When Shaye had met Hustle during the Emma Frederick case, he confided in her that his mother had been murdered by an ex-boyfriend who'd stalked her. His father had never been around, so Hustle had become a ward of the court and had been placed in a home with a foster parent who'd beaten him. He'd been on the streets ever since. The fact that he'd sought her out for help told Shaye that whatever was bothering Hustle was no small matter. And it was personal. He wouldn't risk trusting someone else unless it was important.

She pulled open the door to the burger place and walked inside, heading for her preferred table along the back wall. The regulars were finishing up their dinner and heading out, so the tables nearby were empty. She pulled out a chair facing the plate-glass storefront and waited as Hustle glanced around the tiny restaurant, then pulled out the chair next to her and sat, tugging the hoodie off his head.

An older woman shuffled over with a pad and Shaye ordered a burger, onion rings, and a vanilla malt. Hustle hesitated and Shaye urged him on. "The burger is really good. Real beef. Not that fake stuff."

"Got that right," the waitress said.

"I'll have the same thing she's having," Hustle said, and the waitress headed off for the kitchen. Hustle watched her walk away, then glanced at the front door.

"Don't like your back to an opening?" Shaye asked. "Me either. That's why I always sit at this table."

He nodded. "You got street smarts." He looked down at the table and she could see a flush creeping up his neck. "I looked you up on the Internet. One of the kids from the neighborhood skates with us sometimes and he let me borrow his iPhone. I hope that don't piss you off."

"Not at all. I'm used to it."

He looked back up at her. "I'm sorry about what happened to you. I've seen some bad shit, but…"

Shaye felt her heart tug at the empathy in his voice. This kid had so many obstacles in front of him every day, but none of them had hardened him. It told her what kind of teen he was and hopefully what kind of man he would become. "Thanks. I was lucky. I mean, after."

"With the lady that took you in. Yeah, she sounds really great."

"If you want her to help you, she will. And she'll make sure what happened before doesn't happen again. You have my word on that."

A flicker of hope flashed in his eyes but it was gone so quickly, Shaye almost wondered if she'd imagined it.

He shook his head. "I don't need her kind of help. I need yours."

"Mine? As a private investigator?"

"Yeah. I mean, I ain't got no money or nothing, but I didn't know who else to ask."

"Don't worry about that. Just tell me what's wrong."

"My friend Jinx is missing."

"Is Jinx a, uh…" Shaye trailed off, not sure how to ask if Jinx was a street kid like Hustle without offending him. "Is she in the same situation as you?"

"She's on the street, yeah."

"When was the last time you saw her?"

"Two days ago. We skated at the dock until almost dark."

"Do you stay at the same place? I mean, at night?"

He shook his head. "You don't tell no one where you stay. That's the quickest way to get robbed."

Shaye took a minute to consider how horrible it must be for sleep to be the enemy. She had her own issues with the dark, but they never included someone robbing her in her sleep.

"Okay," she said, "so how do you know she's missing?"

"We was supposed to meet yesterday to skate but she never showed. Never showed today, either."

"Maybe she's not feeling well or something else came up?"

"I went to her place. She wasn't there."

"So she told you where she stayed at night?"

He shook his head and looked down at the table again. Shaye studied him for a moment, trying to figure out what was wrong, when she finally realized he was embarrassed. Jinx was more than just a friend. He had feelings for her.

"You followed her?" Shaye asked.

He nodded but didn't look up. "About a week ago. She said she thought someone was watching her at Jackson Square. She reads cards for people. I was worried so I hung out in the square all day. She didn't know."

"And did you see anyone watching her?"

"No. And she was careful going to her place."

"But not careful enough that you couldn't track her, which means someone else could have as well."

He looked up at her and gave her a single nod, looking miserable.

"Did you find anything at her place?"

"She wasn't there, and neither was her board."

"Maybe she got scared and changed locations."

"Her clothes was still there and her blankets. She wouldn't have left them. It's too hard to come by something decent."

Shaye wished she didn't have to agree with him and there was a simple explanation, like his friend had found somewhere she liked better, but Hustle was right. As hard as things were to come by, no one living on the street would leave them behind without a good reason.

"I know this is a stupid question," she said, "but I have to ask. Have you reported this to the police?"

Hustle gave her a disgusted look. "They won't do nothing. We're all missing already and they ain't looking for us now. What difference would my word be?"

Shaye knew he was right. Street kids were runaways or those left with no family to care for them, like Hustle. As long as they weren't causing trouble, the police didn't bother picking them up because they knew within a day or two they'd be right back on the street. And ultimately, the police couldn't launch an official investigation over someone who didn't really exist in the first place.

"Do you know Jinx's story?" Shaye asked. "Is someone looking for her?"

"I don't think so. Her moms is a junkie. Jinx ain't ever talked about her dad. She may not know who he is. For all I know, her moms don't either. What little Jinx said didn't paint a good picture of her, you know?"

"Did Jinx do drugs?"

"No way! She seen what it does to you. Her moms is wrapped up bad, though. She was hooking up with men to get a fix." His face flashed with rage. "I think some of them men came at Jinx. I think that's why she took off."

Shaye struggled to control both her anger and her disgust. As a social worker, Corrine had seen and heard most everything possible, and she discussed what she saw at length with Shaye, hoping to give her a better understanding of the things she could potentially run into as an investigator. Jinx's situation was an all-too-common one for a young girl with an addict for a mother.

"How old is Jinx?" Shaye asked.

Hustle shrugged. "My age, I guess. Fifteen. Maybe sixteen."

"Do you know her last name?"

"She never said."

"I don't suppose you have a picture of her?" She was certain the answer was no, but it never hurt to ask.

Hustle's shoulders relaxed a bit. "You going to find her?"

"I'm going to try."

He reached into his sweatshirt and pulled out a piece of folded paper. He unfolded it and passed it to Shaye. She lifted it up and marveled at the detail of the pencil drawing. The girl had a delicate face, pixieish, with big eyes and short spiked hair. Her expression was slightly indignant and had a bit of an edge—her tough look, Shaye guessed.

"Did you draw this?" Shaye asked.

Hustle nodded.

"It's incredible. Have you ever thought about pursuing a career in art?"

"Jinx said I should. I was saving for some art supplies, figuring I could make some money in the square. She's smart about things. That's why I know something's wrong. If someone got the jump on Jinx, it wasn't a last-minute thing."

"You think someone planned to take her."

"I'm sure of it. So what do we do now?"

Shaye leaned back in her chair and blew out a breath, trying to decide on the next course of action. "Two things. First, I need to see if anyone was looking for Jinx through the system. I know you don't think that's the case, but if someone was looking for her, the police could have picked her up and turned her over."

"Yeah. I guess that's true."

"Second. I want you to show me everywhere you know that Jinx spent time—where she worked in the square, where she hung out when she wasn't working, who she hung out with, where she stayed at night." Shaye looked directly at Hustle. "You have to be my eyes and ears on this. The street kids aren't going to talk to me, not without your help."

"I'll do anything you need. Just say the word."

"Okay. I need some time to work the system, and I have to have a convenient way to contact you. I'll pick you up a cell phone tonight and get it to you tomorrow morning. With the holiday, the square will be even busier than usual tomorrow. We can start there. I'll meet you in front of the Andrew Jackson statue at ten a.m. Does that work?"

Hustle's relief was apparent. "That's great."

The waitress pushed plates with huge cheeseburgers

and stacks of onion rings in front of them. Hustle's eyes widened and he grabbed the burger and took an enormous bite.

"It's good, isn't it?" Shaye asked, forcing herself to sound upbeat. The boy wasn't starving, but he wasn't getting enough to eat. She wished he'd let Corrine help him. If anyone could find the right situation for Hustle, it would be her mother, but Shaye knew she had a ways to go before Hustle trusted her with something that big, if he ever did. Still, there had to be a way to help without scaring him away. She'd work on that.

She slipped the drawing into her purse, wondering what had happened to Jinx and already praying that it was something simple and safe, even though she had a really bad feeling that it was neither of those things.

Hinges creaked and a block of light illuminated part of the room. Jinx sat up straight, squinting into the light, trying to make out her surroundings. The room was bigger than she thought but solid stone construction, even the ceiling. She heard footsteps and realized that the light was coming from overhead. She was in a basement.

She held a hand over her eyes and watched as a set of boot-clad feet appeared, every step echoing on the wooden stairs. Her hands started to sweat as the figure dropped lower and lower, first exposing his legs, then torso, and finally his face. It was the one thing she'd been desperately waiting to see.

Disappointment rolled over her in waves, taking her breath away as the mask came into view. It was a Mardi Gras mask, one of those Venetian ones with the split color. This one was gold on one side and purple on the other. Fear coursed through her and she scurried to the back corner of the cage, hiding in the shadows. It was only when he stepped onto the basement floor that she realized he had something slung over his shoulder. Something big.

He walked past her without so much as a glance and opened the door to a cage across from her. Then he flipped the bag over his shoulder and stuck it in the cage. Her heart pounded like a jackhammer and her vision blurred. Sweat rolled down her brow and into her eyes, the salt burning, but she couldn't tear her gaze away from the scene in front of her. She couldn't even blink.

He removed a rope from the top of the bag and pulled the ends of it, dumping a boy onto the floor. Leaning over, he cut the ropes around the boy's wrists and ankles, then took the rope and the bag and backed out of the cage, closing and locking the door behind him. He turned around and even though he couldn't possibly make out anything more than the outline of her body, he looked straight at her.

Lifeless blue eyes stared at her from behind the mask, and even though she couldn't see his face, she knew he was smiling. She pulled her arms tighter around her legs and dropped her head down, unable to meet his gaze any longer. She heard a low chuckle, then the shuffle of feet as he walked away. As the footsteps carried up the stairs, she opened her eyes and watched as the door above slammed shut, casting her into darkness again.

She waited a bit, until she was sure he was gone, then inched toward the front of the cage, staring pointlessly into the pitch black. "Hey," she said, "are you all right?"

The echo of her voice was the only thing breaking the dead silence of the room. He was probably drugged as she had been.

"Can you hear me?" she tried again, a desperate edge to her voice, but no answer was forthcoming.

The door above the room flew open once more and she scurried back into the corner. The man with the mask slowly descended, carrying a white paper bag. He walked directly toward her cage, and she squeezed herself tighter into the corner. Jinx wasn't afraid of a fight, but given the man's size and the fact that she was still woozy from the drugs, she knew any attempt to overtake him would be futile.

The man stepped up to her cage and pushed the bag through the bars. "That's food. You'll want to eat it. Where you're going, you'll need all the strength you can get."

He chuckled, and the hair on Jinx's neck and arms stood on end. Her body felt as if an ice storm had passed over it. He turned around and headed back up the stairs, closing the door behind him.

The smell of grilled meat wafted toward her and her stomach growled. She had no idea how long she'd been unconscious, but she was starving to the point of dizziness.

She crawled toward the front of the cage, her arm outstretched, her hand feeling the floor for the bag. Her fingers brushed the side of it, and she snatched it up from the floor and pulled something round and wrapped in paper from inside. A burger. Water pooled in her mouth as she pushed back the paper from the burger. She lifted it to her mouth, then paused.

What if it's drugged?

She lowered the burger for a couple of seconds, but starvation overrode her fear. If she passed out from drugs or from lack of food, the end result was the same. At least this way, she had an opportunity regain some of her strength and hope for a chance to escape. She shoved the burger in her mouth, almost choking on the huge chunk she bit off. She held her other hand underneath her mouth, making sure she didn't drop a single morsel. She had no way of knowing how long she'd have to wait before she got more.

Every bite counted.

CHAPTER THREE

Shaye parked in front of her mother's home and killed her car engine, but didn't make a move to get out of her SUV. Her relationship with Corrine had always been solid, but lately it showed some signs of wear. Corrine had made it clear that she didn't want Shaye to move out, but then Shaye was fairly certain Corrine would have had her living at home when she was ninety if she had a say. That one had been easy enough to get past.

The second item on Corrine's "I'm not comfortable with that" list was Shaye's choice to open her own agency rather than continue working for the established agency she'd been with for three years while she was finishing up her degree. But Shaye knew what she wanted to do with her life, and chasing down people committing insurance fraud wasn't the difference she wanted to make in peoples' lives. Even that disagreement was one that had been overcome. Corrine's profession wasn't exactly limited to paper pushing.

Then Shaye's first case blew everything out of the water. Not only was it a criminal matter that had put Shaye up against a horrific serial killer, but Shaye's representation of the victim had put Corrine directly in the line of fire. Her mother had been injured, and if it weren't for a huge combination of timing and luck, she'd probably be dead.

Which was really bad.

But none of that was the worst thing. The worst thing, as far as Corrine was concerned, was that Shaye hadn't told her why she was attacked, even though Shaye had figured it out at the hospital after Corrine was brought in. Shaye's argument was that Corrine was entrenched in her home with round-the-clock private security, courtesy of Shaye's grandfather, and New Orleans police parked on the street in front of her house, courtesy of her grandfather's status in the community. No one could have gotten to Corrine unless they could walk through walls.

And if Shaye had told Corrine the truth about her attack when it happened, her mother would have insisted Shaye give up the case. That was something Shaye couldn't do. Emma Frederick needed her help, and Shaye had given her word. And even though Corrine couldn't have forced her to quit, her mother would have worried herself to death and given Shaye so much grief that she would have wished she'd never told her the truth.

So she didn't. Not until it was all over.

Shaye had been guilty of a lie by omission, and it had been a doozy.

Thus the strain.

Not that Corrine was holding a grudge. Shaye wasn't even certain her mother was capable of doing such a thing. Corrine had never seen much point in investing oneself in the past. She'd always felt that today was the most important day. But now, Corrine knew firsthand what kind of risks Shaye was willing to take for her clients. She understood with a vengeance that her days of protecting Shaye were over.

Shaye pushed open the car door and headed inside. While things might still be a little uncomfortable, she needed her mother's help. The sound of the Beach Boys echoed through the cavernous front entry of the house, and Shaye shook her head. When Corrine needed to decompress, she always played the Beach Boys. She said the ocean was the most relaxing place you could be and the music reminded her of it. When she was younger, Shaye wondered why Corrine didn't cash in her inheritance, chuck her horribly depressing job, and go sit on a beach for the rest of her life. But as she got older, Shaye understood the calling Corrine had to help others. It wasn't easily ignored.

She followed the music into the kitchen where Corrine was wrist-deep in dough. Her second-favorite way to relax was baking. That one, Shaye would never understand. Domestic pursuits held absolutely no interest for her, but she would admit to liking the results of her mother's baking.

"What's on the menu?" Shaye asked as she stepped up to the huge marble-topped island counter and slid onto a stool.

Corrine looked up and smiled at her. "Raspberry croissants."

Shaye groaned. "My favorite."

"Moaning about it doesn't seem an appropriate response."

"Sensei Markham told me tonight I have to put in an extra hour of strength training every week. If you keep baking, I'll have to add another hour of cardio."

Corrine flipped the dough over and started working the other side. "Why more strength training?"

Crap. She'd walked right into the very topic she'd wanted to avoid. "We're going to work more on close combat." No use trying to hide it now.

Corrine's jaw flexed and Shaye could tell she wasn't thrilled with the news. "Well," Corrine said, "I'm not happy that you need the additional training, but I'm glad you're taking steps to better protect yourself."

"You should come to training," Shaye said, before she changed her mind. "I know this latest incident wasn't about your job, but you can't ignore the fact that it's getting more dangerous to do what you do."

Corrine sighed. "I'm not ignoring it. It's rather impossible to do so when your grandfather insists on calling every day to preach to me about quitting social work for a nice corporate office downtown."

Shaye grimaced. "Sorry."

Corrine glanced over at her, then flipped the dough, banging it on the counter. "You know how it feels from firsthand experience, don't you? God, I've become my father."

"Nah, you're not that bad. Look, Pierce loves his corporate games. That's why he works so many hours. You and I aren't made that way. We have different interests and unfortunately, sometimes they are dangerous. We can't change the environment that surrounds our work, but we can better prepare ourselves to handle an increasing threat."

Corrine stopped pounding the dough and looked directly at Shaye. "Do you know what his next idea was—when I finally got it through his thick skull that I wasn't quitting my job? A bodyguard. He wants to hire a bodyguard to stick with me while I'm working."

"It's not the worst idea."

"Really? So I suppose if I suggested the same thing to you, that would be fine?"

"I don't think I'd get very far questioning people with some beefy, imposing dude standing next to me, but if you had someone at least driving you, they'd be on hand if things got bad."

"I'm not Miss Daisy."

Shaye shook her head. "Look. I know you're thinking the attack on you was my fault, and you're right, but that doesn't mean you're safe doing what you do. People are…I don't know, meaner, have less to lose. I read this article that said one in twenty-five people are likely sociopaths. How many of them do you think you run across in a week?"

"One in twenty-five, huh? Socialites in the Garden District probably account for the bulk of them."

Shaye smiled. "Probably, but there are plenty more spread around."

Corrine sighed. "What am I supposed to do? Our office doesn't have the funding to send out two social workers for each case—we can't cover what we have now as individuals—and I'd feel funny having a bodyguard when no one else can afford that kind of luxury."

"No one else is heir to one of the biggest corporations in the state or daughter to a state senator. Has it never occurred to you that if the wrong person figured out who you are, they could hold you hostage?"

"Of course it's occurred to me, but I never considered it overly viable. I could say the same for you, you know."

"Since I try to stay out of the news and will do most anything to get out of those dress-up charity event things with the awful food and even worse people, my face is not as well known. Besides, I've been practicing martial arts for years, and I carry a weapon and am not afraid to use it. I'm not trotting through the Ninth Ward with a can of Mace as my backup."

"Fine. I'll start taking classes with you, but I'm not going to have a bodyguard."

"Just promise me no more walking into abandoned buildings. If something seems off, call for police backup."

"The city would love me for that—calling them every time I see something off while doing *my* job."

"Then call me. Hell, call Eleonore. She's not afraid to shoot someone."

Corrine shot her a look of dismay. "Don't even go there. She had me digging mints out of her purse the other day and I almost had a heart attack. I'm surprised the ATF isn't investigating that handbag."

Shaye smiled. "Speak loudly and carry a .45?"

Corrine waved a hand in the air. "Enough. If I start thinking too hard about the contents of that purse, I'll need Eleonore to write me a prescription for Xanax and she'll make me explain why. That's a level of exhaustion I don't need. Tell me what you came for. I know it's not a friendly visit. You have that look."

"What look?"

"Something's bothering you." She grabbed a bottle of wine from the refrigerator and poured them both a glass, then took a seat on a stool at the counter. "Is it work or personal?"

"Work."

"That's disappointing."

Shaye stared. "You want me to have a personal problem?"

"If it involves a man, then yes."

"Anything that involves a man is a problem, which is exactly why I don't have any personal involvement with them. I'll tell you what. I'll make an attempt to be nice to a man—on a personal basis—when you go on a date. A real date. Not a society event. And he can't be gay."

Corrine knew when she was defeated. "Fine. We'll both die crazy cat ladies. We'll knit hats and ride bicycles in the French Quarter, with kittens and flowers in those plastic bicycle baskets. If you'd like, we can do it wearing no pants. I actually saw that last week on Bourbon Street."

"I would rather be original."

Corrine smiled. "Evening gowns then, with combat boots." She took a sip of her wine. "So what's the work problem?"

Shaye gave Corrine a rundown of Hustle's story.

Corrine frowned the entire time. "This Hustle is the one who helped you with your last case, right?"

Shaye nodded. "I don't think he's making it up. Or exaggerating."

"I don't either. Someone with his background would avoid anyone connected to the system like the plague. The fact that he's reached out to you shows how worried he is. What do you need from me?"

"I need to make sure Jinx wasn't picked up by a relative, maybe even her mother."

"That would be the preferred solution. Maybe not her mother, but living with a relative, assuming they're a decent sort, would be better than the alternative. Do you have anything on her to help me search our records?"

Shaye pulled the drawing out of her pocket. "Here's a drawing Hustle did. It's all I've got to work on."

Corrine studied the drawing. "The detail is incredible. I'll put a description in the database and scan in the drawing and see what I get. I suppose this medical leave might come in handy after all. With so little to go on, this could take a while."

"I appreciate it."

Corrine bit her lower lip. "I don't have to tell you the things that can happen to a young, pretty girl on the streets."

"No. I'm prepared for the worst. I mean, as prepared as I can get."

Corrine nodded. "I hope Hustle is prepared as well."

Shaye shook her head. "He's tough and smart, but not as tough as he thinks he is. He still cares, and I think he cares about Jinx more than anyone. If something bad happened, he's not ready for it, even if he thinks he is."

Corrine frowned. "We never really are." She paused, and Shaye could tell she wanted to say something but wasn't sure she should.

"You might as well say it," Shaye said.

"Say what?"

"Whatever you're thinking you want to say but aren't sure you should. I can read looks too, you know?"

"Are you still having nightmares?" she asked quietly.

"Yes," Shaye answered. Corrine wouldn't like the answer, but Shaye wouldn't deliberately lie to her mother.

Corrine downed the rest of her glass and sat it on the counter. "Are you remembering?"

"I don't know."

Corrine narrowed her eyes at Shaye.

"I swear," Shaye said, "I don't know. I wish to God I did. They seem so vivid, so real, and then I wake up and try to remember, but it's just not there."

Corrine reached across the counter and put her hand on Shaye's. "Promise me you'll tell me when you know. I don't want you to try to protect me. This is not something you should deal with alone."

"Maybe not, but you shouldn't have to deal with it either."

Corrine squeezed her hand. "I've been waiting to deal

with it for nine years."

Detective Jackson Lamotte watched as the paramedic zipped the bag over the body of the boy a fisherman had caught in his cast net. The body hadn't been in the water long or it wouldn't be intact. The creatures in the bayou made quick work of a fresh meal. The fisherman had brought it up on his last pass of the day, and it was a lucky break for the police. The better the condition of the body, the easier identification would be.

Cause of death wasn't a mystery and unfortunately, it wasn't drowning. The single bullet hole through the boy's chest had eliminated the possibility of an accident. This was a murder investigation, and Jackson's partner and senior officer, Detective Vincent, wasn't going to be pleased. Jackson had been saddled with Vincent for a year now, and if the man didn't manage to kill Jackson's career before he sleepwalked into retirement, it would be a miracle. Anything that might result in real police work had Vincent running for his office chair.

"Fuck me," Vincent said as he stepped beside Jackson. "I needed to catch a murder case like I need my wife to discover another shopping channel on television."

"You could always put in for a transfer to traffic."

"And reduce my pay? Not a chance. You got some strange ideas about how to handle money."

No, I have credible ideas about being a detective.

Jackson wanted to say it, but it would only make matters worse for himself. Vincent hadn't liked him from the first day—Jackson was too eager, Vincent said, which meant Jackson actually wanted to solve cases. Then that whole mess with Shaye Archer had come up and Vincent had ended up looking the heel while Jackson looked the hero. It hadn't gained him any points. In fact, Vincent had gone out of his way ever since to find fault with everything Jackson did, even down to how he poured coffee. If Jackson gave him any reason to, Vincent would be calling for Jackson's demotion down to beat. And that was something Jackson had no intention of letting happen.

Jackson closed the door on the ambulance and lifted the plastic bag that held the card of fingerprints he'd taken off the body. "I'm going to head back to the precinct and run these. Do you want me to handle notification?"

Vincent frowned. Notifying victims' families was one of the worst parts of the job, but it was also a part usually handled by the senior detective. Right now, Vincent was mentally waging a war between wanting to pass off that particularly loathsome duty and maintaining his seniority by doing the tasks earned by his position.

"It's already after ten. No use waking people up with this kind of news. It can wait until tomorrow morning."

"Okay," Jackson said, even though he thought Vincent's logic was flawed. Someone with a missing child wasn't sleeping at all, but apparently Vincent didn't want to take his assessment that far. Unfortunately, there was nothing Jackson could do about it.

He headed for his car before he said something that would get him into trouble. His frustration with Vincent grew daily and sooner or later, something was going to give. He just hoped it wasn't his job, or worse, Vincent's jaw when he punched him.

At the station, he headed inside and nodded to the desk sergeant, an older gentleman who'd put in thirty-five years already.

"Pulling a late one," the desk sergeant commented.

"Yeah, some fisherman caught a kid in his cast net. Teenager."

The desk sergeant shook his head. "So many drownings around here. You'd think people would learn to be more careful around water."

"This one wasn't a drowning. It was murder—bullet straight through his chest."

"Hunting accident?"

"This time of the year? Not likely. The body wasn't in the water long. It's fairly intact."

The desk sergeant whistled. "I bet Vincent's shitting kittens that he caught an actual case."

"Yeah, but he's doing his 'thinking on it' at home for his own convenience. I'm going to run the print. Vincent thinks the family can wait until tomorrow for notification because they're already asleep."

"Yeah, sure they are. Let me know if you need anything."

"Thanks." Jackson headed for the forensics department and started the fingerprint trace, then headed to the break room for a cup of coffee. He finished one standing next to the pot, then poured another and headed back to the computer to see if anything had popped up. He bent over to look at the screen.

Jackpot.

He clicked on the link and an image of the victim displayed next to his vitals.

Josh Thibodeaux. Sixteen years old. Reported missing from his home six months ago.

Jackson frowned. A runaway. That complicated everything. His parents wouldn't know where he was or where he should have been when he disappeared. His movements couldn't be traced from school and home, and he wouldn't have friends who knew all the things he wouldn't have shared with his parents. No computer to hack. No gaming system to trace.

He blew out a breath. Even if they could find the area where Josh hung out, street kids wouldn't talk to the police. This case had just gone from bad to worse, and Jackson didn't even want to hear what Vincent had to say when he heard this news. Only one silver lining came from the information—after six months' time, Josh's parents probably *were* asleep. Waiting until morning to notify them wasn't going to make a difference.

He sent the information to Vincent, copying himself, then headed to his desk to print it out. After he did his duty with Vincent tomorrow morning with the parents, he'd head into the French Quarter and see if he could find a street kid who would talk. It was a long shot, and he was certain it was a shot he'd be firing alone, but it was probably the only angle he had to work. The advantage was that with it being the Fourth, Vincent would be in a hurry to talk to the parents, then get on with the holiday. He wouldn't stick around to waste Jackson's time with fruitless endeavors, so that left Jackson free to do what he wanted.

Like investigate the case.

He unlocked his desk drawer and pulled out an empty file to put the printout in. As he went to close the drawer, he saw the file in the back, labeled "S.A." He frowned as he closed and locked the drawer, then leaned back in his chair and blew out a breath. He'd promised Shaye that if she ever wanted to look into her past, he'd help, and he'd meant it. Unfortunately, his search of the police databases had produced nothing of relevance—no similar cases, no new leads.

At this point, they needed to start talking to everyone who was there when Shaye was found, starting with Detective Beaumont, the cop who'd found her and was now retired. Jackson had wanted to contact Shaye for days now, but every time he pulled out his cell phone, he hesitated.

It's because you're attracted to her.

He sighed. Of course he was attracted to her. Any man with a pulse would find her attractive. But it was more than that. He liked her. He respected her. And he didn't want to disappoint her.

Not that he'd expected to find much, if anything, with his search, but there was always that glimmer of hope, deep in the back of his mind, that something would pop out years after the fact, giving him the break he needed.

He rose from his chair and pulled out his car keys. Time to head home for a riveting night of microwave food and late-night television. He was pretty sure he'd watched everything viable on cable, but there was always a six-pack of beer and the hope of a new release in his future.

It might be boring and repetitive, but it was still a sight better than what he would face tomorrow morning.

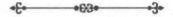

It was 11:00 p.m. when Shaye entered her apartment in the French Quarter. She locked the front door and pulled the dead bolts, then rearmed the alarm before heading through her office and into the kitchen. She'd picked up a phone for Hustle at one of the late-night shops and needed to call and get it added to her business plan.

She dumped the bag with the phone on the kitchen counter, then grabbed vanilla ice cream and root beer out of the refrigerator and made a root beer float, refusing to tabulate the additional minutes of cardio she'd have to add to work it off. It had been a long, taxing day, and since she'd left her mother's house before she'd finished up the baking, Shaye was going to indulge in her second-favorite sweet.

She stuck a spoon and a straw in the tall glass, grabbed her laptop off the counter, and plopped down on the couch. Nothing good was on television, so she switched to stored movies and turned on *Jaws.* Sometimes it was a relief to see a monster that had big fins and a lot of teeth. The news only showed those that walked on two legs.

She grabbed her laptop off the side table and started making notes from her conversation with Hustle. By the time she'd finished the notes, she'd polished off the root beer float and slumped back on the couch, thinking about the shower she needed to take, but too lazy to get up and do it right that minute. Maybe she'd just finish the movie, then shower and head to bed. It was already late, and she had a long day in the hot New Orleans sun ahead of her. The last thing she remembered before she nodded off was "Those bathing suits make all the women look like they have fat thighs."

The stone she lay upon was cold, but it was winter, so no cause for alarm…yet. Her head felt woozy as she lifted it up and blinked, struggling to see in the dark. A second later, a single candle ignited and her pulse surged. A second candle ignited, then a third, and a fourth, until she was surrounded by a circle of them. Her breath came faster and shallower and she struggled against the panic she knew was coming. She looked down at her body and her worst fears were confirmed.

It was the red dress.

She tried to get up, but thick ropes bound her hands and feet in place. The candles moved closer to her and she could see the shadowy, hooded figures holding them. One of the hooded figures stepped next to the stone table and sat his candle beside her. He pulled out a large knife with etched words that she didn't understand.

As he lowered the knife to her chest, she started to scream.

Shaye bolted up from the couch, gasping for air, her heart pounding so hard that it made her chest hurt. It took her several seconds to realize she was in her apartment, and only then did her panic begin to subside. Her body relaxed a tiny bit, and she sat on the edge of the couch only to jump back up as a bolt of lightning struck right outside her apartment, the blast setting off car alarms on the street. Thunder boomed behind, and she rushed to her bedroom to grab her big flashlight from the nightstand.

She hurried around the apartment, turning on every light in every room, then went back to the living room where she curled up on the couch and fought back the tears that threatened to spill over.

When would it end?

CHAPTER FOUR

Jinx jerked awake at the sound of thunder, reaching for her neck, which had stiffened in the awkward position she'd dozed off in. She hadn't intended to fall asleep, but exhaustion must have caught up with her. It was strange, she thought, how fear could tax your physical body as much as running for hours. She sat upright and blinked, but couldn't see anything in the darkness. Her head didn't feel woolly as it did earlier, so that was a good sign. The burger hadn't been drugged.

She inched forward until she reached the bars on the front of the cage and stared in the direction of the boy who'd been dumped there before. Was he still there? She shook her head. Of course he was still there. If the man had returned, she would have awakened. She wasn't that exhausted.

"Are you awake?" she called out.

She heard rustling and several seconds later, the boy replied, "Who are you?"

Her initial relief that the boy was alive fled at the sound of his high-pitched, shaky voice. He couldn't be more than twelve years old or so. His voice hadn't changed yet. "My name is Jinx. What's your name?"

"Peter Carlin."

"How old are you?"

"Ten."

"Are you hurt?"

"My head hurts, like I've been turning in circles. And my arms and legs hurt. Where am I?"

Jinx bit her lower lip. What in the world did she tell him? "I'm not sure where we are," she said.

"Why don't you know? You're here."

"I was brought her while I was asleep, like you."

She heard sniffling and her heart clenched.

"Was it…was it the bad man from before?" he asked, his voice breaking.

Her back tensed. "What bad man? Did you see someone?"

"Uh-huh. There was a man in the park. He was standing in the trees but I saw him."

"What did the man look like?"

"Big and scary."

"Could you see his face?"

"No. He had on a hat, and he was back in the dark behind the bushes."

Jinx felt momentarily disappointed, then put things into perspective. Even if Peter had gotten a good look at the man, a description from a frightened ten-year-old boy probably wouldn't get them much closer to identification. Besides, it wasn't like they had anyone to tell. They were both trapped here.

"Did anyone else see the man?" she asked.

"I told Mommy that he scared me, but when she looked for him, he was gone."

"Had you ever seen the man before that day in the park?"

"No. But I saw him outside my bedroom window that night, 'cept he was wearing something on his face. Like they wear in the big parade."

The mask. The man had been stalking Peter, looking for an opportunity to take him. "Like they wear in the Mardi Gras parade?" Jinx asked.

"Yeah. Mommy didn't believe me when I said he was out there. She said I had a bad dream because of the park, but I wasn't asleep. I was standing at my window."

"I believe you," Jinx said.

"Why didn't Mommy?" He sniffled again.

"She wasn't trying to hurt you. I'm sure she just didn't think anyone would be watching you. That's not normal, so people don't think it will happen to them."

Peter went silent for so long that Jinx worried he'd passed out. Finally, he spoke. "I think he's been watching me for a long time."

"I thought you said you never saw him until the park."

"I didn't see him until then, but I knew he was there. I could feel him looking. It made my arms itch."

She knew that feeling well. That feeling is what had kept her safe on the streets. Until now.

"How long have your arms itched?" Jinx asked.

"I don't know. It started at the school carnival. I was a

bear in the play. I got to wear a costume and everything."

"That sounds cool," Jinx said, although she'd bet anything that Peter was right—the bad man had locked in on him at that carnival. "What's the last thing you remember?"

"The babysitter took me to the park today. There was a party with fireworks and everything. Not the big kind, but the little ones. The fireman said the big ones might burn down a house so we could only have the little ones in the park. They just made different-colored smoke and weren't as good as the big ones that they do at night, but they were still okay."

"Did you remember leaving the park?"

"I think so…I don't know. I had ice cream and dropped it on my shirt. I didn't want to get in trouble so I went into the bathroom to get it off."

"Do you remember leaving the bathroom?"

"I, uh…no."

Jinx's heart dropped. He'd sneaked away from the babysitter to clean his shirt and that was probably when the bad man took him. From living with her mother, Jinx knew more about drugs than most people. Peter might not ever remember what happened in the bathroom, but Jinx would bet she knew what had happened.

The only silver lining in the situation was that the police would be looking for Peter. The missing child of concerned parents was something the cops wouldn't ignore. If the bad man had left any clues at all, they'd be tracking them down.

Unlike her. No one would be looking for her.

"I want to go home," Peter said, and started to cry.

"I know you do. I do, too."

Shaye clutched her enormous cup of coffee and headed into Jackson Square. It was her third already that morning, and she hoped this last cup was the tipping point that gave her sluggish body and mind the perk they both needed. After the nightmare, she'd tried to go back to sleep, but her overactive imagination wouldn't slow enough for her to drift back off. She'd tried warm milk, carb overloading, and even turning on a shopping channel, but nothing had been able to override her racing mind.

The dreams were coming more frequently than before. Ever since Emma Frederick's case. But why?

Eleonore had suggested that because Emma was being stalked by an unknown assailant, it had put a strain on Shaye's ability to keep her unknown past from affecting her present. That her subconscious mind was working out in her dreams what her conscious mind didn't want to address. Shaye supposed that could be true. Or the explanation could be an even simpler one—that Emma Frederick's situation had fired off memories that had been long buried. That the dreams she was having weren't fiction created by her subconscious but a flashback of her very real, very horrific past.

Shaye had put that theory to Eleonore and although

she tried to maintain the same expression, Shaye hadn't missed the flicker in her eyes. Eleonore had already thought it all through, and she knew that what Shaye said was a possibility, probably a better one than the theory Eleonore had set forward, but also a lot more dangerous one. If Shaye was remembering, then the person who'd done the horrible things to her would no longer be a mystery. He'd be exposed, and that could put Shaye in danger.

But none of that mattered to Shaye. She'd always assumed she was in danger—that the person who'd stolen her past could be lurking around any corner, waiting to finish the job. All of her martial arts training, her careful selection of a place to live, and the best security system she could buy were part of her acceptance and preparation for the day she always thought would come—the day she would meet her captor face-to-face.

"Shaye?" Hustle's voice sounded behind her and she turned around.

He walked up, studying her face. "You all right? You look kinda beat."

Someone like Hustle would be able to spot a lie a thousand feet away, so she just gave him the truth. "Rough night."

He frowned. "You drink?"

"Not much, but I'm going to start if I keep having nightmares."

His face cleared in understanding. "I get those sometimes…I see that man killing my mom. I wasn't there when it happened, but I know the details. It's like sometimes they play back in my mind."

"That sucks," Shaye said, both surprised and honored that Hustle had felt comfortable enough with her to share something so personal.

He nodded. "When you dream, are you remembering what happened to you, you know…before?"

"I wish I knew."

"I guess that would make figuring it out easier, huh?" He blew out a breath, and she could see his hesitation. Finally, he blurted out, "Do you ever think maybe you're better off not knowing?"

"All the time."

"Yeah. Well, coffee should help. I've lived for a couple days on stale coffee and biscuits."

Shaye's heart tugged. The thought of Hustle going hungry killed her even though she was more aware than most of the statistics on poverty and homelessness. "I think it's already doing the trick, but I think I need to eat something so I don't get tired too quickly."

She pulled some cash out of her pocket and handed it to Hustle. "Why don't you grab us some breakfast from that vendor on the corner? Make sure you get enough. We've got a long day ahead of us and if we catch a break, we might not be able to stop and eat again for a while."

He hesitated for a moment, then took the money. "What do you want?"

"I'll have a ham and egg croissant."

He nodded and headed down the sidewalk.

She'd lied, of course, and he'd known it. She had no

problem skipping meals when it was only herself to consider, but she wouldn't do it while she was working with Hustle. Still, she knew Hustle didn't feel right accepting handouts, and as far as he was concerned, she was already working for free. But as long as she pretended he was doing her a favor by dining with her, then Hustle would allow it to continue. That was a lie she could easily live with, especially since it meant feeding a hungry teen.

She walked out of the square and toward the corner where Hustle was getting them breakfast, making a note of the artists lining all four sides, setting up their wares for sale. Today was even busier than she'd expected. The bit of breeze that filtered through the Quarter had brought more people out into the hot day than usual. It would be hard to spot something out of the ordinary, especially when so many things in the French Quarter fell on the wrong side of ordinary to begin with. But she trusted Hustle's instincts and her own. If something was off in the square, they'd notice.

"Here ya go." Hustle handed her a wrapper with the breakfast croissant. "I've never had these before. They're really good," he said and took a big bite out of a ham and egg croissant.

"I love croissants," Shaye said. "My mom makes them from scratch sometimes. They're even better than these."

"I can't imagine that. Your mom sounds like a nice lady."

"She is."

"My mom used to bake sugar cookies. They were my

favorite. I haven't eaten them since…you know."

"You should sometime. Make it a special occasion and do it in her memory."

He almost smiled. "I like that. I think she'd like it, too."

Shaye polished off the rest of her breakfast and tossed the wrapper in the trash. "Okay, first things first." She pulled the cell phone she'd bought the night before from her pocket and handed it to him. "This is on my business plan. I need a way to reach you and vice versa…in case things get hairy. And this gives you an easy way to take pictures and make notes. I've put my number in your favorites so it will be easy to reach me."

His eyes widened in surprise. "You're giving me a smartphone?"

"I considered carrier pigeons, but I didn't want to clean the cages."

His lips quivered, and the smile he'd been holding back finally broke through. It was thin and tiny, but it was there.

"So," she asked, "where do you want to start?"

Hustle's eyes widened. "Me? I'm no detective."

"Maybe not, but you know where Jinx was working and you're more aware of your surroundings than the vast majority of people walking around. If something or someone is off, you'll know. Just trust your instincts."

He nodded but didn't look convinced. "Jinx usually set up across from the church."

"Then let's have a look."

They headed up the sidewalk to the west side where

Saint Louis Cathedral made up one side of the square. The street in front of the enormous church was blocked for automobile passage, so it provided plenty of room for artists to set up shop. Today, row after row of artists lined the street, filling the entire area with paintings, drawings, sculptures, and offerings of palm and tarot readings.

"What do we do now?" Hustle asked.

"Let's just walk around a bit and check everything out. If you see or feel anything funny, let me know." She looked directly at him. "I mean that. If you feel anything at all you let me know, even if you can't explain what you're feeling. Instinct saves lives—you know that. I don't want you to discount something important simply because I can't see it."

His shoulders relaxed some. "Yeah, that makes sense."

They walked among the vendors, Shaye stopping occasionally to look at a piece of art that she found particularly interesting. She picked up business cards from a few people, figuring if she ever had time, she'd commission some paintings for her apartment. She wanted to decorate with local artists' work. Even Corrine wouldn't be able to find fault with that artistic vision for her home.

Hustle glanced at the vendors and stood, shuffling in place, as she spoke with the artists, but his gaze constantly shifted back and forth across the street and the people. Shaye would bet money that if she asked him to draw what he saw, it would be as accurate as a photo. They were stopped at a table displaying decorative skulls when Hustle stiffened. He turned slowly and pulled his cell phone out, pretending to check something, but Shaye heard the *click* of the camera.

She wrapped up her conversation with the skull artist and stepped away from the table, Hustle falling in step beside her. "You got something?" she asked.

"Maybe. I don't know." He entered the park and headed behind a hedge, then showed her the picture he'd taken. "I saw that guy talk to Jinx one day in the Quarter. I was going to ask her about it, but I forgot. I saw him again a couple blocks from the dock the day Jinx disappeared."

Shaye looked at the image. "The man in the red shirt?"

"No," he said, looking uncomfortable. "The other one."

Her eyes widened. "The priest?"

"Yeah."

"Holy crap."

"That's one way of putting it."

Shaye took a couple of seconds to process the million thoughts she currently had. "Okay, let's not jump to conclusions. Priests are supposed to help people, especially children, right? So maybe he noticed Jinx was a minor and wanted to make sure she was all right."

"Maybe. But what if he's one of those crazies that hides behind religion?"

Shaye glanced at the image again and shook her head. "Don't worry. I'm going to find out which."

"Shaye?" The voice sounded behind her, and she and Hustle whirled around.

"Jackson," she said, feeling a bit flustered at the sight

of him. She'd been wondering when he would contact her, but wasn't really prepared for a chance encounter.

"How are you?" he asked, glancing over at Hustle.

"Fine," she said. "This is my friend Hustle." She looked over at Hustle, who'd stiffened.

Jackson extended his hand. "I'm Jackson Lamotte."

Hustle stared directly at Jackson and didn't move an inch. "You're a cop," he said, his tone making it an accusation rather than a statement.

"He's different than the others," Shaye rushed to explain before Hustle took off. "This is the cop who helped Ms. Frederick."

"Is that true?" Hustle narrowed his eyes. "You the five-oh that shot the creeper?"

Jackson glanced at Shaye and must have gathered that the boy was important to her and a flight risk if he said the wrong thing. "That was me," he said.

"You get in trouble?" Hustle asked.

"Not for shooting the creeper," Jackson replied, "but I caught a good amount of trouble for helping Shaye when the lead detective had told me not to."

"He sounds like a dick," Hustle said.

Jackson laughed. "He is."

Hustle gave him a single nod and finally shook his hand. "I'm glad you saved Ms. Frederick. She seemed like a nice lady."

Jackson's expression cleared in understanding. "You're the skater that brought her the scarf. I should thank you for helping Shaye with the case."

Hustle shrugged. "I didn't really do nothing."

"You gave her important information," Jackson said, "and a lot of people wouldn't have gotten involved."

"Like I said, Ms. Frederick seemed nice."

Recognizing Hustle's discomfort with the compliments, Shaye shifted the subject. "So, are you down here enjoying the holiday wares?"

Jackson frowned. "I wish I were. Unfortunately, I'm working." He looked at Hustle. "Maybe you can help."

Hustle put his hands up and stepped back. "I don't know nothing about nothing, especially no crimes."

"It's not like that," Jackson said. "A fisherman pulled a boy out of the lake yesterday."

"That's horrible," Shaye said. "And you think Hustle might be able to identify him?"

Jackson shook his head. "His prints came up. I talked to his parents this morning, but they haven't seen him since he ran away six months ago."

"He was on the street?" Hustle asked.

"As far as we know," Jackson said. "That's the problem. Since we don't know where he was, we don't have a place to start looking for information. I came to the square today hoping I could find some kids who knew him and were willing to talk."

Hustle looked over at Shaye, uncertainty written all over his face. She gave him an encouraging nod and he looked back at Jackson. "You got a picture or something?"

"Yeah. His name was Josh Thibodeaux." He reached into his back pocket.

"I don't know anybody with that name," Hustle said, "but people on the street don't usually go by their real name."

Jackson handed the printed photo to Hustle, who drew it close to his face and studied it. "This looks like Joker. I mean, Joker looks rougher, but if you grew this guy's hair out some and gave him a scar above his right eye, then it would be him."

Jackson looked excited. "The boy had a scar above his right eye. I noticed it myself."

Hustle nodded. "Somebody told me his stepdad clocked him—split his forehead."

"That explains a lot," Jackson said, clearly disgusted.

"What do you mean?" Shaye asked.

"Let's just say his parents didn't react the way you expect parents should when they find out their child is dead. Vincent said it was shock, but I didn't think so. I knew it was something else. I just couldn't put my finger on what."

"Did he drown?" Hustle asked.

Jackson glanced at Shaye, then shook his head. "Someone shot him. We don't think it was accidental."

Hustle's eyes widened. "You're talking murder? Joker was murdered?"

"That's what we believe. Can you tell me anything about him—what he did for money, where he hung out, who he hung out with?"

"Oh, man, murdered…I didn't know him, really, but I think he hung in the Tremé. He was an ace card player.

There's a bunch of musicians there that have regular card games."

"You never talked to him?" Jackson asked.

Hustle shook his head. "I only seen him once. My friend talked to him a couple times. She told me about him."

Jackson perked up. "Do you think your friend would talk to me?"

Hustle's expression grew dark. "Probably, but she ain't around."

Shaye instincts went on high alert. "Jinx knew Joker?" she asked.

"Who's Jinx?" Jackson asked.

Shaye looked at Hustle. She didn't want to betray his trust, but at the same time, Jackson's case had sent her instincts into overdrive. "Is it all right to tell him?" she asked.

Hustle glanced at Jackson, then back at Shaye. "I guess so."

Shaye filled Jackson in on the missing Jinx. He listened intently, glancing over at Hustle every once and a while. When she was done, he blew out a breath.

"I don't like it," he said.

"You think they're related?" Shaye asked.

"Don't you?" Jackson asked.

"Shit…yes."

Hustle stared at them. "You think the same guy that killed Joker took Jinx? Why?"

"Call it a feeling, intuition, instinct," Jackson said, "but

I bet we're right."

Hustle nodded. "I can buy that. You don't make it long on the street without instincts. Shaye's got good ones."

"Yes, she does," Jackson agreed.

"So how do we proceed?" Shaye asked.

"I'll keep working my homicide. With a body, identification, and a set of parents, however uninterested, my case will stay open until the chief deems it cold."

"But you can't do anything about Jinx?" Hustle asked.

Jackson looked pained. "No. Not officially. But if Corrine can come up with an identification, then I can try to make a case with my boss."

"You said not officially," Hustle said. "What about unofficially?"

"Unofficially," Jackson said to Shaye, "work the streets with Hustle. If you get a lead, let me know. If there's anyone you run across that makes you look sideways at them, let me know. I can run everything through our databases and let you know if I get any hits."

"How much trouble will you be in if Vincent catches you?" Shaye asked.

"A shitload," Jackson said, "but since Vincent's lazy, I can always pass it off as information-gathering based on things I picked up from street kids. Not like Vincent is going to get out of his chair and talk to them, so he'll never know the difference."

Shaye frowned. "Be careful. I don't want you losing your job. We need more people like you with the department, not less."

Jackson blushed a little. "Vincent won't catch on. I'll make sure of it."

They stood there looking at each other for a couple of uncomfortable seconds, then Shaye smiled. "Well, I guess we better get to work. I'll let you know if Corrine comes up with anything. Or if Hustle and I do."

Jackson nodded. "And this goes without saying, but you be careful, too. There's worse things out there than Vincent." He turned to Hustle. "Nice meeting you."

"You too," Hustle said as Jackson turned and headed down the sidewalk.

Hustle watched him walk away, then turned back to face Shaye. "He your boyfriend?"

"What? No!"

Hustle raised his eyebrows. "You sound kinda defensive."

"I'm not defensive. I just don't want anyone getting the wrong idea."

Hustle grinned. "If the wrong idea is that the dude is into you, then I'm betting if you're in the same room, people are gonna get it."

Shaye stared at Hustle in dismay. "You're as bad as my mother. Why are people always trying to set me up?"

Hustle held his hands up in the air. "I ain't trying to set up nothing. I was just saying what I seen."

Shaye huffed. "You think he's into me?"

Hustle nodded. "Totally. I don't blame him. You're cool and smart and you're a solid dime. That's not easy to find."

"A solid dime?" Shaye's smile finally broke through.

Hustle shrugged, looking a little embarrassed.

"Well, let's see if all these smarts can ferret out some information on Jinx."

"What do you want to do now?" Hustle asked, looking relieved at the change of topic.

"Let's cruise the square for a couple of hours and see if anything else catches your attention, then I want you to show me where she stayed at night."

CHAPTER FIVE

Jinx jerked awake when the door to the basement opened, and she ducked into the back corner of her cage, watching as the masked man's legs appeared on the stairwell.

"Is it the bad man with the mask?" Peter whispered.

"Yes, hide in the corner and be quiet," she whispered back. Not that she thought hiding or being silent would help the situation, but something about the man's voice haunted her, as if it contained his cruelty.

The mask appeared and the man stepped into the basement. Jinx let out a breath of relief when she saw his empty hands. No more prisoners. Not yet.

The man stopped at the bottom of the stairs and looked back, and a second set of legs appeared. This set wore black slacks. As the rest of him emerged, Jinx squinted, trying to get a good look at him. He was tall—as tall as the first man, but thinner, even though both had decent mass. Along with the black slacks, he wore a black long-sleeved shirt. His face was covered with the same mask the first man wore.

Black Slacks walked up to the cages and leaned over,

peering into both of them. Jinx tucked her arms around her legs and watched as his brown eyes studied her like someone would a rat in a cage, then he moved to the other cage and peered inside. Peter tucked his head in between his legs and covered it with his arms.

"Damn it!" Black Slacks straightened up and whirled around to face the other man. "This isn't the boy I selected."

"I know," the other man said, "but the client wanted this one. He paid double."

"It won't make a difference if he paid five times over if snatching this kid gets us caught."

"Nobody saw anything. We were careful."

"Careful like you were with the last one?"

"We used the regular dose. How was I supposed to know he'd need more? The second one took him out fine."

"And he's been out for a day and a half now. We can't keep him inside the house much longer. It's too risky. If he doesn't gain consciousness by delivery time on Monday, get rid of him."

"You want me to get rid of the boy, too?"

Black Slacks looked at Peter and cursed again. "And lose the fee? I don't think so, but he's got to go. He's seen too much. Put him on the delivery schedule for Tuesday night. I want him out of here as soon as possible."

"I don't know if the client will be ready by Tuesday."

"He doesn't have a choice." Black Slacks stepped right up to the other man. "If anything like this ever happens again, it will be the last stupid thing you ever do."

The first man was way bigger and Jinx figured he could have easily beaten Black Slacks in a fight, but Black Slacks must have been the boss, because the first man just nodded and they both headed back upstairs, slamming the door behind them.

"Jinx." Peter's voice sounded in the inky black. "What's a client?"

"I don't know," Jinx said, but her mind was filled with answers that she didn't want to think about. The kind of answers that began with someone paying for the abduction of a ten-year-old boy.

After several long, hot hours of cruising the square and coming up empty, Shaye and Hustle finally headed out of the French Quarter to check out Jinx's nighttime hideaway. Hustle had talked to a couple of street kids, but no one had seen Jinx in days, and no one could offer up any idea why she would have left or where she would have gone. No one else in the square caught Hustle's attention, so finally, Shaye decided to move on to the next phase of investigation.

Jinx's sleeping place was in the back apartment of an abandoned building in the Upper Ninth Ward. The area had sustained heavy damage from Katrina, and most of the surrounding buildings were crumbling. Every block or so, Shaye saw an occupied structure, but none of them looked safe enough to live in. The block Jinx's building was on contained no occupied structures, by either people or businesses.

Shaye looked up and down the street and a feeling of helplessness rushed through her. Most people looked at the damage and saw only rotting buildings and littered streets, but Shaye saw what used to be people's homes. Where people slept at night. Where people bought milk from corner stores. Now it was practically a ghost town. It was a good place to disappear. Unfortunately, it was also a good place for no witnesses.

"This way," Hustle said as he clicked on his flashlight and led her through the building to the rear. He stopped at the end of the hallway, moved a piece of plywood to the side, and opened the door.

Shaye stepped inside, shining her flashlight around the room. It had once been a studio apartment. No bigger than five hundred square feet, but it felt even smaller. The windows had been boarded up on the outside of the building, but someone, maybe Jinx, had nailed dark blankets over them inside the room. Shaye guessed it was so that light couldn't be seen through the cracks on the outside boarding. Light in an abandoned building would be a dead giveaway that someone was inside.

An old mattress was tucked into a corner, a stack of blankets on it. Next to it was a crate that looked like it contained some clothes. Hanging on a nail on the wall was a coat. An ice chest contained a partially eaten loaf of bread and a jar of peanut butter. Shaye pulled out a plastic bag and removed the jar from the ice chest.

"Can you get fingerprints off of it?" Hustle asked.

"Yeah, but the question is how many. I'd bet ten or more people touched that jar. If Jackson ran a bunch of prints, someone would notice and ask why."

She didn't add that fingerprints wouldn't do any good unless someone had reported Jinx missing, because she knew that between her and Hustle, that went without saying. No one had ever filed a missing report on Shaye, and she was hardly an anomaly. Plenty of people on the street weren't missed by anyone.

Shaye turned around, shone her light on the front door, and saw a new dead bolt in place. There was no other access point to the apartment.

"She wasn't taken from here," Shaye said. "This dead bolt is secure, there's no other entry, and there's no sign of a struggle."

Hustle nodded. "Jinx wouldn't have gone down without a fight."

Shaye walked over to the kitchen and checked the cabinets, but they were all empty. She flipped through the clothes in the crate, but no secrets lay between the couple of threadbare T-shirts and worn jeans. If Jinx was hiding anything that linked her to her previous life, it wasn't in an obvious place.

As she started to move away from the bed, Shaye paused and lifted the corner of the mattress up and peered beneath. A dark rectangular object lay just at the edge. "What's that?" Shaye asked and pointed to the object with her free hand.

Hustle dropped onto his hands and knees and reached

under the mattress to extract the object. Shaye dropped the mattress and looked at it.

Holy Bible.

Shaye looked up at a worried Hustle. "I think it's time for me to talk to that priest."

Father Michael.

It took Shaye a bit of searching images on her iPad to locate the church where the priest Hustle had identified worked. It was a smaller church located in Bywater, and had two priests assigned to it. Shaye spoke to a bored-sounding woman who informed her that Father Michael was busy with his street ministry that day and unavailable for a consultation, but he would be performing service the following morning.

Hustle had been disappointed when Shaye suggested they call it a day, but she'd promised him that she'd be at mass the next morning to talk to the priest and would let him know what she discovered. She made Hustle promise to be careful and to call if he saw anything that looked out of the ordinary.

She was leaving Bywater when her phone rang. Her mother. Hoping Corrine had found something on Jinx, she answered the phone.

"I'm so glad you answered," Corrine said.

"What's up?" Shaye asked. Her mother's tone hovered somewhere between slightly frantic and more than slightly irritated. Never a good sign.

"I need a date for the charity event tonight. It's the Freedom Auction."

Shaye's stomach clenched. "Noooooooooo! What happened to your gay artist friend? He lives for that crap."

"He got a better offer."

"Pizza delivery and *X-Files* reruns?"

"No. A talented masseur named Frank. Since I have neither the professional ability nor the requisite body parts to compete, I'm on my own."

"Can't you just stay that way?"

"Shaye Archer! Are you really suggesting I fend for myself in that jungle of pettiness?"

"Maybe?"

Corrine sighed. "I know these events are like fingernails on a chalkboard to you, and trust me, I'd pretty much rather be getting a root canal, but I need someone there to make excuses for me when I need to bow out. You know how that crowd is."

A twinge of guilt coursed through Shaye. Her mother still wasn't a hundred percent after the attack, and the event would be mentally taxing. If Shaye was there and insisted her mother cut out early in order to rest, the charity biddies would talk about what a lovely daughter Shaye was, looking after her mother. If Corrine tried to leave on her own accord, the charity biddies would accuse her of avoiding them and her civic duties.

The charity biddies were the worst.

"What time?" Shaye asked.

"It starts at six."

Shaye looked at her watch. "It's almost five already. I'm not at home and I have to shower and change into something awful. Can I meet you there?"

"You promise you'll show?"

"Unless I die or have a horrible accident before I can get there." One could always hope.

"No fair if you do either on purpose."

"You know me too well. Please tell me my black cocktail dress will work for this? I think it's the only dressy thing I brought with me when I moved."

"That works fine. You know, we could always go shopping sometime and pick you out a couple more items for these sort of events."

"Ha! Then you'd expect me to wear them and go. No thanks. I'll see you at six." Shaye disconnected before Corrine could think of anything else Shaye "needed" to do. Corrine tended to come up with those mother sort of things for Shaye—find a man, settle down, quit that dangerous job, move back home—it was a long list of things that Shaye had zero intention of helping her mother check off.

She headed home, took a quick shower, put her hair up, and slapped on a bit of makeup. The black dress was plain silk, nothing sparkly, so she put on a pair of dangly black-and-diamond earrings and a matching necklace. She looked in the bathroom mirror and smiled. The earrings and necklace had belonged to her grandmother, and even though Shaye hadn't had the opportunity to meet her, she'd heard enough about her from Corrine to know she would have loved her. Everything about her was casual elegance. No flash. Just class.

She tossed her license, a credit card, and lip gloss into a black evening clutch and headed out. Five minutes until six. She was going to be late, but hopefully by only a few minutes. She drove to the hotel where the event was being held and made her way to the Grand Ballroom. She'd barely stepped inside when Corrine hurried up to her.

And she wasn't alone.

"Shaye." Derrick Oliver flashed his million-dollar smile at her and leaned over to kiss her cheek. "It's been ages since I've seen you."

"Yes, it has," Shaye replied, and if she'd had her way, she wouldn't have seen Derrick again until the next life.

She glanced over at her mother, who gave her an encouraging smile, and held in a groan. Did Corrine honestly not see how horrible Derrick was? His overly white teeth. The fake blue eyes, and he didn't even need corrective vision. The perfectly groomed hair. The spray-on tan. The garish and ridiculously expensive watch, in case you didn't know he was one of *those* Olivers.

Derrick paused a moment, clearly waiting for her to ask him about his law practice and his bid for state legislature. When nothing was forthcoming, he tried a different tactic. "Your mother tells me you've opened your own private investigative firm."

"Yes." She smiled. One-word answers vexed people like Derrick. It gave them no opportunity to segue the conversation over to themselves.

"And how do you like it?" he asked, refusing to be stonewalled.

"My first case was a stalker who murdered at least four people that we know of. The police are still unraveling his background. The body count is likely to rise."

Corrine choked on her drink, and Shaye patted her on the back. The smile disappeared from Derrick's face and his nose wrinkled, almost as if he'd smelled something bad.

"Well, it was great seeing you again," he said. "I see my father motioning to me. We'll catch up more later." He gave them both a nod and hightailed it across the ballroom, in the opposite direction of where his father stood. Shaye managed to hold in her laugh until he was far enough away not to hear it, but then it spilled over.

Corrine frowned at her. "Do you have to be so rude?"

"Yes. Nothing else shuts down Derrick-I-am-one-of-*those*-Olivers. And don't even ask me to apologize, to you or to him. It serves you right for putting him in my face like some dating service."

Corrine's eyes widened. "I was not—"

Shaye held up one hand. "Don't even try it. We both know your ulterior motive. I can appreciate your desire, but your choice in men is so sadly lacking it's frightening."

Corrine sniffed. "Okay, so maybe he's a bit of a bore."

"And a huge snob. And an elitist. All of the things you claim to hate about New Orleans society."

Corrine sighed. "Fine. I won't try to set you up with anyone else."

"Ever?"

"I can only promise tonight. My willpower doesn't allow anything beyond that." Corrine looked past Shaye and groaned. "Margaret Babin is headed this way."

Margaret was the completely useless and overbearing daughter of one of the wealthiest men in the state. She was the head of every committee that would have her. Most didn't have much of a choice.

"Time for me to find a drink and some dinner," Shaye said and fled before Corrine could grab hold of her arm.

She hurried across the room to the drink station and gathered a glass of champagne, then snagged a plate of cocktail shrimp and two cookies and moved over to a corner of the room where no one could accost her without her seeing them coming. The usual crowd of big wallets wandered around the room, complimenting each other on their appearance, inquiring about children or a new vacation home, and generally trying to one-up each other.

Shaye did her best to stay tucked in the shadows, hoping no one would recognize her and want to talk. Once the sign-up for the silent auction started, she and Corrine could place their bids, then Shaye would insist her mother leave for the much-needed rest and the entire ordeal would be over. She glanced at the entrance, watching as people continued to make their way into the ballroom, then did a double take as Jackson Lamotte stepped inside.

He looked gorgeous and slightly uncomfortable in his black suit—a bit James Bond, a bit schoolboy. He looked around the room and frowned, clearly out of his element.

Shaye couldn't help but wonder why he was there. It didn't seem like the type of thing he'd be interested in attending. For a moment, she wondered if he was meeting someone, but then he looked her direction and when his gaze locked on hers, he smiled and headed straight for her.

"Thank God I found someone I know," he said as he walked up beside her.

Shaye smiled. "What? This isn't your idea of fun?"

"Hell no. I drew the short stick down at the police department, so I'm here representing New Orleans's finest."

"I'm sorry. It hardly seems fair that you get stuck with Vincent during the day and this at night."

He nodded. "I keep wondering what I've done wrong. This has to be a karmic thing, but damned if I know what's causing it. What about you? Your mother rope you into it?"

"How'd you guess?"

"I'm a detective."

Shaye laughed, then sobered. "Did you get anywhere on your case?"

"No. I talked to the parents again, but they weren't any help. I put out feelers in the Tremé to run down the card games. Hopefully, I'll get something I can check in the next day or two. What about you?"

"Nothing in the square, and none of the street kids Hustle talked to have seen Joker or Jinx. Jinx wasn't taken at the apartment she bunked down in at night. No forced entry. No sign of a struggle. But there was one thing."

"What's that?"

"A Bible."

"Doesn't sound like much of a lead. More people should be gone if it was the rapture, although, maybe not."

"Ha. Not in this group."

"So what's the significance of the Bible?"

"Hustle pointed out a priest today in the square. He said this priest spends a lot of time talking to the street kids." She shrugged. "Maybe it's nothing, but I'm going to hit him up after mass tomorrow and ask him some questions."

"Text me his full name and anything else you get on him and I'll run a background."

"I don't want you getting busted by Vincent."

"For what? I can say the same thing you did—that someone told me the priest spends a lot of time talking to the street kids. I figured I'd run a cursory check to see if any alarms go off before questioning him."

"Okay. I appreciate it."

He smiled and she smiled back, then an awkward silence ensued. Shaye was just about to start a discussion on the weather or something equally banal when Eleonore stepped up.

She looked Shaye up and down, then tilted her head back, so that she was looking at Shaye down the bridge of her nose and sniffed. "You look lovely, Ms. Archer. Is that *last* year's Valentino?"

"Actually, it's this year's Macy's. You look delightful as always, Ms. Blanchet. Have you had work done?"

Jackson looked back and forth between the two of

them, clearly trying to decide whether to speak or make a break for it.

Before he could make a move, Eleonore shifted her gaze to Jackson, studied him for several seconds, then frowned. "And who might this be?"

Shaye waved a hand at Jackson. "This is the dashing Detective Lamotte."

Jackson froze, so clearly uncomfortable that Shaye decided to put him out of his misery. She giggled and Eleonore put a hand on her shoulder and leaned over, laughing.

"I love it," Eleonore said. "This year's Macy's."

"I'm sorry, Jackson," Shaye said. "This is sorta a ritual we go through when we're forced to attend these events. We greet each other mocking some of the worst of the hypocrites in the room."

Jackson's expression went from confused and slightly frightened to relieved. "I thought for a moment I'd stepped into the twilight zone."

"Oh, you have," Eleonore assured him. "Most of the people here aren't really human. I would know. Did Corrine try to shove that douche bag Derrick off on you yet?"

"You knew?" Shaye glared at Eleonore, who held her hands up in defense.

"She didn't say anything to me until I got here. I told her it was a really bad idea."

"The worst idea ever. Where does she get the idea she knows anything about men?"

"Not from me, and if I were looking for one, this is the last place I'd do it." Eleonore glanced at Jackson and smiled. "Present company excluded, of course. I'm just waiting for the silent auctions to open so I can bid a ridiculous amount of money on some trinket that will go straight to Goodwill and get the hell out of here."

Jackson laughed. "I'm so glad I'm not the only one who thought this was horrible."

"Please," Eleonore said, "it takes a fifth of whiskey or a lobotomy to enjoy these things. I can't hit the bottle and I'm rather attached to my brain, so I settle for the bid-and-dash."

"I think they're setting the cards out now," Shaye said.

"Great!" Eleonore extended her hand to Jackson. "It was a pleasure, Detective Lamotte. Hang in there, Shaye." She whirled around and gave them a wave over her shoulder as she strode across the room.

"Old friend of yours?" Jackson asked.

"My mother's best friend. My friend, too, but Eleonore's also my psychiatrist."

Jackson's eyes widened. "That was Eleonore Blanchet? Holy crap."

"You know her?"

"Every cop worth his salt has heard of Eleonore Blanchet. Her expert witness testimony has put some of the worst criminals in Louisiana behind bars. She's practically a god as far as cops are concerned."

Shaye laughed. "She'd love that. I'll tell her next time I see her."

"Eleonore Blanchet," Jackson said again as he watched her grab the first bid sheet on the table and scribble something. "I would love to spend a day picking her brain. She's interviewed the highest-profile killers in the state. I bet she could tell me things that would give me nightmares."

Shaye took a sip of her champagne and nodded. Her own nightmares were enough to give people nightmares. She had no desire to poke into anyone else's.

Jackson looked back at Shaye. "You really hit the lottery with Corrine, didn't you? Not many people have the connections to get Eleonore as a personal therapist." He'd no sooner finished the sentence than his eyes widened. "I'm sorry. That was completely crass. I didn't mean to—"

Shaye waved a hand in dismissal. "You haven't offended me. Corrine is absolutely the lottery. I am positive I wouldn't be where I am today without her. Not even halfway."

Jackson's relief was apparent. "So Corrine and Eleonore are best friends. It seems a strange match, I mean, with Corrine so much younger."

"Eleonore was Corrine's tutor and nanny…after Corrine's mother died. Corrine was only twelve, and Eleonore was in medical school at the time. They've been friends ever since."

"That's cool. Not the part where Corrine's mom died when she was a kid. That part sucks, but it's cool that they formed a bond that's lasted all these years."

Shaye nodded. "It is."

Jackson studied her for several seconds. "You sound almost wistful. You don't have a BFF? Or whatever it's called?"

"No. I had private tutors for high school, and I kept to myself in college. I tried a couple times with people who seemed interested in being friends, but they all turned out to be more interested in getting the inside scoop on Shaye Archer, girl with no past, than getting to know the real me."

"That sucks."

Shaye looked at Jackson and smiled. "You know, most people give me the whole sympathetic routine while the entire time I can tell they're thinking 'what the hell does she have to complain about?' But you're always sincere."

Jackson shrugged. "So you're the only heir to more money than I can imagine. So what? That doesn't in any way make up for everything else that happened to you. Nothing could. The problem with society is that most people are too comfortable in their own lives to even try to imagine the difficulty of someone else's."

"If I give you a microphone, would you tell that to this group?"

"No way. I've only got one spare magazine in this suit."

She laughed and Jackson grinned.

"Shaye?" Corrine's voice sounded behind her. "The bidding has started."

Corrine stepped up beside Shaye and realized she wasn't alone. She raised an eyebrow. "Are you going to introduce me to your friend?"

"Yes, Mom," Shaye said. "If you'd given me a second, I would have. This is Detective Jackson Lamotte. Jackson, this is my mother, Corrine Archer."

Jackson extended his hand. "It's a pleasure to meet you, Ms. Archer."

Corrine shook his hand. "You're the detective who helped Shaye with Emma Frederick. I should be thanking you. Lord only knows how many people you saved."

A flush crept up Jackson's neck. "I was just doing my job."

Corrine raised one eyebrow. "I think we all know that wasn't the case. I'm just glad you have problems with authority."

Jackson smiled. "Only when it's wrong."

"Your mother must be exhausted," Corrine said, and smiled back.

"Eternally," Jackson said, "and she never misses a chance to remind me of it."

"Well, it was a pleasure," Corrine said, "but I've got to go place my bids. Shaye, are you ready?"

"Yep. Go ahead and bid for me, too. I'll come rescue you in a minute."

"I see," Jackson said as Corrine headed for the auction table. "You're here to insist she leave early because she needs to rest."

"You've caught us red-handed," Shaye said.

"Well, if the only interesting people in the room are all leaving, I guess I better make my rounds and slip out myself. Let me know what you get on the priest."

Shaye nodded as Jackson walked off for the tables. Halfway across the floor, he glanced back and Shaye shifted her gaze to the fake palm tree in the corner, embarrassed that she'd been caught staring.

"He's quite handsome," Eleonore whispered as she dashed by.

Shaye looked across the room as Jackson leaned over to place a bid for a basket of chocolates.

Yes. He is.

CHAPTER SIX

Jinx jolted awake, her arms and legs aching. The bare skin on her arms itched and she realized she was lying on straw, not the stone floor she'd been on before. She jerked upright, then grabbed her head as pain shot through it. She'd been drugged again. It must have been in the burger she'd eaten.

Peter!

She rose from the floor and gazed wildly around in the darkness, but couldn't make out anything except the shadowy shapes of objects, none of them human. She inched forward until she felt a wood wall with iron bars. "Peter?" she whispered through the bars. "Are you here?"

"We're the only people here."

The male voice sounded across from her. He wasn't young like Peter, but didn't sound like an adult yet, either. She squinted into the darkness but couldn't make out anything. "Who are you?" Jinx asked.

"They call me Spider."

It wasn't a name she recognized, but it sounded like a street nickname. "I'm Jinx," she said.

"You on the streets?"

"Yeah. I hang in Bywater. You?"

"Uh-huh. I mean, I was in the Tremé…before this."

His voice was melancholy, almost hollow. "What is *this*?" Jinx asked.

"The last dance."

A chill ran through her. "What do you mean?"

"This is it for us. Time's up."

"You're saying someone is going to kill us?" In the back of her mind, Jinx had always known that death was probably the closing chapter for whatever was happening to her, but voicing it made it more real.

"That's exactly what I'm saying," Spider said. "Those two sick fucks that have us here—it's some kind of game for them. They're keeping score."

"What are you talking about?"

"The guys who bought us."

"Bought us?"

"Yeah. Us and another one before us called Joker. Twenty grand apiece. I heard them talking."

Jinx's mind whirled with a million different thoughts. He couldn't be right. Why would people buy someone just to kill them? That didn't make sense.

She bit her lower lip. "Do you know…I mean how…"

"They turn us loose in the swamp and hunt us," he whispered and started to cry.

Jinx sank onto her knees, her arms loose at her sides. The thread of hope she'd been holding fast to vanished in an instant, leaving her with nothing but fear and regret.

Shaye studied Father Michael as he delivered mass. He was young, probably late twenties, and had an earnest look on his face as he talked religion that shifted to a smile as he spoke to parishioners after service. She kept her seat in the back of the church, waiting for the stragglers to finish talking with the priest and make their way out. Finally, the last of them headed past her with a nod and Father Michael came up the aisle.

He stopped at her pew and smiled at her. "Did you need to speak to me?"

"Yes, but not about my eternal soul." Shaye rose and extended her hand. "My name is Shaye Archer. I'm a private investigator."

The smile disappeared from Father Michael's face. "Oh, well, I can't imagine what I can help you with but please, ask your question."

Shaye pulled her copy of Hustle's drawing from her pocket. "Do you know this girl?"

Father Michael studied the drawing for a moment and frowned. "She looks familiar, but in my position, I meet a lot of children."

"You mean with your street ministry? I assume if she was a regular parishioner, you'd know."

His eyes widened slightly. "Yes, of course. There are so many young people living on the streets. The numbers keep growing, but no one wants to do anything about it."

"Except you?"

"I guess you could say I have a personal interest in the matter."

"Why is that?"

"Because a childhood friend of mine lived on the streets after his mother died and there was no one else to care for him. The system didn't work out well, as it sometimes doesn't. Finally, a retired gentleman who volunteered at a local shelter formed a relationship with my friend, and he and his wife took my friend in. They probably saved his life."

Shaye studied Father Michael's face as he delivered his story. He appeared sincere, and if she had his friend's name, it would be easy enough to check. "This girl goes by the name Jinx, and she's been missing for three days."

Father Michael took the drawing from Shaye and pulled it closer to his face. "Jinx…yes, I remember talking to a young woman near the docks in Bywater. Skater, right?" He looked back up at Shaye and frowned. "You said she's missing?"

"Yes. She was supposed to meet a friend of hers on Thursday and never showed. All her personal stuff is intact in the building where she crashes, but no sign of Jinx."

"This friend she was supposed to meet, are they on the street as well?"

"Yes. He is."

"Then how can he be certain Jinx didn't return home? Granted, most of these kids have horrible home lives, and they left for good reasons, but some come from decent families and are rebelling against their parents' rules.

Usually a couple of weeks or months on the street cures them of the notion that home was so bad."

Shaye nodded. "That's true enough. My mother is a social worker."

"So you understand the dynamics."

"Yes. But Jinx didn't fit that scenario. Her mother was a junkie, and there's some suspicion that she was trying to pimp Jinx for her next fix."

"Oh!" Father Michael's dismay was apparent. "That's horrible. Of course she wouldn't elect to return to such a… How can I help you?"

"When was the last time you saw Jinx?"

Father Michael pulled out his smartphone and checked the calendar. "I was in Bywater giving out Bibles last Tuesday. I visit a different area every day that I have availability."

"You gave Jinx a Bible on Tuesday?"

"Yes. She and two others were the only ones that would accept them. Everyone took sandwiches. I always bring food when I go, and blankets and coats if I have the donations."

Shaye recalled the coat hanging on the wall in Jinx's hideaway. "Did you give Jinx a coat?"

"Not that day. I didn't have coats, but I had a pile of them the week before and one of the secretaries here helped me hand them out. She could have gotten one then. That was in Jackson Square. It's summer now, but come wintertime, they'll be happy they took one."

Shaye nodded. "The last time you saw her, did you

notice anything unusual? Anyone new hanging around? Anyone who didn't seem to belong?"

"I, uh…" He shook his head. "I can't think of anything, but I've only been near the docks a couple of times."

"Were any other adults around the dock that day?"

"Not that I recall." He shrugged. "I'm afraid I'm not the most observant person. I spend a lot of time in my own thoughts."

He's lying.

She knew it immediately. His body language and pitch changed. It was subtle. So slight that most people wouldn't have noticed, but Shaye was trained to pay attention to those subtleties. The question was what was he lying about? Had he seen Jinx after she went missing? Had he seen someone at the docks that he thought didn't belong there? Or was it even more than that?

She pulled out a business card and handed it to Father Michael. "If you think of anything else or if you hear anything while you're working your street ministry, please give me a call."

"Of course." He slipped the card into his pants pocket. "I'll pray for Jinx and for you, Ms. Archer."

"I appreciate any help I can get," Shaye said and headed out of the church. She glanced back as she closed the door and saw Father Michael, still standing where she'd left him. He was staring out the window, a worried expression on his face.

That was a whole lot of angst for someone who

professed to know nothing.

Hustle dropped his skateboard on the pavement and gave himself a kick. He knew Shaye was doing everything she could do to find Jinx, but he was afraid it wouldn't be enough. The cop's story about Joker had freaked him out more than he'd let on. He tried to tell himself that Joker had probably taken the wrong guy at cards, but it didn't feel right. People got beat up all the time over gambling, but it didn't usually move to murder. If Joker had died from a beating and been found in an alley, Hustle would have passed it off as a card game gone wrong. But shot and dumped in the water? That didn't make sense.

A crowd of street kids was already at the dock, but none of them were skating. Instead, they were huddled in a group near the water, and no one looked happy. He skated over to them, kicked his board up, and stepped up to the group.

"What's up?" Hustle asked.

An older kid called Boots looked at him. "You ain't heard?"

Hustle's back tightened as he looked around at the grim expressions on all five faces. "No. I wasn't around yesterday. What happened?"

"Ain't nobody seen Scratch since Thursday," Boots said.

Hustle stared at Boots, trying to process what he'd

heard. Scratch was the oldest of their group. He was seventeen and had been on the streets for the last three years. Scratch had helped Hustle when he first showed up—gave him pointers on finding a night hideaway and how to find a niche for food and money. "Maybe he caught some overtime?"

"For two days?" Boots asked. "Besides, I went by the demolition site yesterday. That dude that runs it said Scratch didn't show up for work Friday or Saturday."

A kid called Reaper shook his head. "He ain't the only one. I heard two kids was missing from the Tremé—Joker and Spider."

"Joker's dead," Hustle said.

"What the fuck!"

"How do you know?"

"What happened?"

They all responded at once. Hustle scrambled to come up with a story that didn't include his involvement with Shaye.

"I was in the square yesterday looking for Jinx. There was this cop asking around about a kid some fisherman pulled up with a cast net. I saw the picture when he showed it to someone. It was Joker."

"Damn," Boots said. "Joker drowned?"

Hustle shook his head. "Somebody shot him. Least, that's what the cop said."

"Shot him why?" Reaper asked.

"I don't know," Hustle said. "I ain't ask no questions. I just tried to hear what he was saying, and that's what I got."

The kids all looked at one another. "What the hell is going on?" Boots asked.

"Street kids is disappearing," Reaper said. "That's what's happening."

Boots ran his hand over his shaved head. "Maybe we should all lie low for a while."

"Lie low where?" a kid named Shadow asked. "Ain't no amateur got the best of Scratch. He's been doing this longer than anyone. And Jinx might have been new, but she was smart. If someone got the jump on them, what chance do the rest of us have?"

"We gotta change things up," Hustle said. "Change everything we do."

"What are you talking about?" Shadow asked.

"He means change our routine," Boots said. "All of us have one—when we skate, when we work our gig, when we eat, and where we sleep. It's too easy for someone to know where we're going and when."

"We all skate here most days," Reaper said. "Ain't nothing gonna happen at the docks, not in the daylight and with all those construction workers around."

"Maybe not," Hustle said, "but it makes it easier for someone to find us and track us. It probably wouldn't be a bad idea to cut back on our time here, and don't go directly from here to your nighttime place."

"But if we change things up," Shadow said, "how will we know if anyone's missing?"

"We'll set a check-in place," Boots said. "One for now and then another when we check in at the first. A different place every time. If you want to come to the docks, then that's fine, but Hustle's right—you shouldn't leave here and go straight to your hiding place."

"That sounds good," Hustle agreed.

"Okay," Boots said, "so tomorrow, regardless of where else you decide to go, everyone check in at the corner drugstore on Saint Claude. Noon."

He looked around the group and everyone nodded.

"And it goes without saying that we all keep our ears to the ground," Boots said.

"And watch our backs," Reaper said.

Boots looked around. "Well, we're here. Might as well skate." He tipped his board up and set off for a series of ramps on the far side of the dock. The other kids slowly followed suit, but Hustle stayed where he was. He watched the skaters for a bit, then sat down on the curb behind him. Shadow sat down next to him.

"You find out anything about Jinx?" Shadow asked.

Hustle shook his head.

Shadow looked down at the ground, making a circle in the dust with his finger. Hustle didn't know him well. He guessed Shadow was fourteen, maybe younger, but his eyes had that haunted look that said he'd seen and experienced more than someone his age should have.

"What's happening to us?" Shadow asked.

Hustle's heart clenched at the fear in Shadow's tone. Living on the streets was hard enough when things were normal. "I don't know," Hustle said.

"I'm scared," Shadow said, his voice small and hollow.

"Me, too."

Shadow looked up at him, his expression slightly surprised. Hustle held in a groan. Even though it was the truth, his statement wasn't going to help alleviate Shadow's fear. It probably made it worse.

That's a good thing.

Hustle took in a breath and blew it out. "Look. Fear isn't bad. Lots of times, it's the one thing that keeps you alive. You know how sometimes you get a funny feeling about something—sometimes you feel it in your stomach or sometimes the back of your neck?"

"Yeah."

"Don't ignore it. If anything feels off to you, no matter where you are, get out of there and go somewhere with lots of people."

Shadow nodded and rose from the curb. "I gotta get to the animal shelter. They're paying me to help clean the cages. It's not much but it gets me food, and I like the dogs. They kinda remind me of us."

Hustle nodded. "Be careful. Be aware."

"Okay. I'll say a prayer for Jinx."

"Thanks," Hustle said as Shadow skated away.

A prayer for Jinx.

Hustle checked his cell phone, but there weren't any missed calls or messages. He wondered if Shaye had talked to the priest, and what, if anything, she'd discovered.

The man watched the skaters from the vacant building across the street. The one sitting on the curb was the kid from the square—the one he'd seen talking to the woman and the man the day before. The man was a cop. The posture, the walk, the way he studied the crowd…he might as well have been wearing a sign. The woman had confused him. She hadn't acted like a cop, but she didn't appear to be a typical holiday shopper either.

Maybe the woman was social services. That would explain her familiarity with the cop and her talking to a street kid. Either way, the woman was potential trouble, and the cop was definitely trouble.

He blew out a breath. For that matter, his clients were trouble, too. Most of them weren't from New Orleans and if they screwed up, the police would investigate in their area of the world, not his. Usually, the product was collected here and the clients arranged for transport. He had no idea where the product went or why it was purchased to begin with, nor did he care. He was in the procurement business, not writing a book. The out-of-town clients had never been trouble, but the local ones were a whole other ball game—this new one in particular.

They had promised him no bodies would ever surface, and now a cop was circling the square, asking questions. He should have known better than to sell to them. They had plenty of money but low intelligence—some of the many redneck millionaires that had cropped up when oil was found on their land years ago. The money they'd offered had been more than his normal asking price, so he'd given in. He should have known it was too good to be true.

Their agreement had been for five healthy teens, but he was cutting their agreement short. If the one that was still unconscious didn't make it, then they'd have to make do with three. They wouldn't be happy, but he didn't care. They were the ones who'd broken their part of the agreement—drawing the attention of the police.

Things like this were happening far too often. People were getting careless, some reckless even. And that included his own associates. He hadn't spent decades slowly amassing a fortune only to lose it all over carelessness and stupidity. Kidnapping Peter Carlin had been a huge mistake. He couldn't turn on a television set without seeing the boy's face plastered across the screen.

Product acquisition was harder as well. So many had relocated after Katrina and never returned. The Ninth Ward had provided easy pickings for over a decade. Plenty of people were the kind no one missed. Others were the kind that would sell a kid for the price of a hit. After the hurricane, product had been harder to acquire given the depletion due to so much relocation, but missing persons had been so common that he'd made several years of good hauls, waiting on the police databases to catch up.

The small bayou towns had been a stopgap for years, but he'd been unable to fill all the client requests until lately. The street kids had seemed like a great idea to fill the requests for older product, and with no payment to junkie mothers, his profit margin had increased. The kids would have wised up eventually and gotten too hard to capture, but if his clients hadn't gotten sloppy, he might have continued for another couple months—maybe long enough to fund a nice boat along with his oceanfront home in an extradition-free country. Now it looked like the boat was off the table.

It was time to close up shop. Clean house and nail the doors shut.

Starting with the skater kid.

CHAPTER SEVEN

Jackson knocked on the door to the bar. The building was no different from the many other run-down structures in the Tremé—bar on the ground level and probably storage or maybe an apartment on the second floor. Developers were slowly renovating all the neighborhoods around the French Quarter, buying the properties at a big discount and reselling for a huge profit once they'd spruced them up.

The sign in the window said Closed, but the tip Jackson had gotten was that a card game went on Sunday mornings before the bar opened. Thick shades covered the window, so he couldn't see inside. He knocked on the door again and heard some rustling inside. Finally, the door opened and a young black man with dreadlocks peered out.

"We're not open yet, man," the guy said.

Jackson flashed his badge. "I don't care anything about the card game you've got going on. I'm working a homicide and want to see if you can tell me anything about the victim."

The man narrowed his eyes. "Why would we know some dead guy?"

"I heard he played here sometimes."

The man stared at him a couple seconds longer and must have decided it was more trouble to keep him out than let him in, so he opened the door. Jackson followed him inside to a table with four other men, a deck of cards and poker chips in front of them.

Dreadlocks pointed to Jackson. "He's five-oh. Says he thinks some dude that got whacked used to play cards here."

A guy wearing a Bob Marley T-shirt nodded at Jackson. "What you got, five-oh?"

Jackson took out the picture of Joker and showed it to the men. They all looked at the picture, then one another. Finally, the one with dreadlocks nodded.

"He played with us a couple times," Dreadlocks said. "I think he rotates to different games around here, but we figured he was due to come around this week. Guess we know why he didn't."

"What happened to him?" Bob Marley T-shirt asked.

"He was shot and dumped into Lake Pontchartrain," Jackson said. "A fisherman pulled the body out on Friday."

Dreadlocks held up his hands. "Look, we don't play that kind of card games, you know? Dude played with us a couple times and he seemed all right."

"I heard he was a real shark at cards," Jackson said.

A couple of guys nodded, and Bob Marley T-shirt scowled. "Dude played me like a piano a couple weeks ago, but that's no reason to kill somebody. Not for what we're betting."

"He's right," Dreadlocks said. "No one ever walks away from the table with more than a hundred bucks. We play more for the fun of it—the money just makes it a little more interesting."

Jackson nodded. "Can you tell me anything about him? Other games he might have been in…ones with the kind of stakes that might motivate people in the wrong way?"

They all shook their head. "There's not any big money games in the Tremé," Dreadlocks said. "Only small stuff like this. We're street musicians, man. Not a lot of money in what we do."

Bob Marley T-shirt nodded. "You better head to the business district for the high-dollar games. I hear some of them suits play for ten thousand or better a game. Too rich for my blood."

Another of the men snorted. "Like they'd even let your raggedy ass in the front door."

"How did Joker get in here?" Jackson asked. On the surface, a scrawny white street kid didn't appear to have anything in common with the men in front of him. If Jackson knew how Joker had wrangled his way into their game, maybe he could find the other places Joker had played.

"Dude could seriously play the sax," Dreadlocks said. "He walked up on us on Bourbon Street one night, asked to borrow an instrument, and totally threw down. We got to talking, found out he liked cards, and invited him to drop in sometime."

Jackson nodded, his frustration building. Playing the

saxophone might get Joker a pass in the Tremé, but he doubted seriously it would register favorably with the high-stakes suits. "There's nothing else you can tell me about him—people he hung around with, where he stayed?"

They all shook their heads.

"If you don't ask a lot of questions of people," Dreadlocks said, "then you don't have answers. Cops aren't the only people who come around asking about things."

Jackson knew exactly what he was referring to. Loan sharks, bookies, and any number of other nefarious characters might come looking for someone. The less you knew the safer you and the person they were looking for were. It was the official motto of the streets—Don't Ask. Don't Offer.

Jackson pulled out his card and handed it to Dreadlocks. "If you think of anything or hear anything, let me know."

He stepped outside the bar and blew out a breath of frustration. That conversation had led absolutely nowhere. Unless they were the world's best actors, those guys didn't seem the type to shoot a kid and dump the body. He'd checked the money on the table, and it had amounted to about sixty dollars. Unless they'd cleared it off before he walked in, they weren't lying about the game being low stakes. A hundred bucks was a good payoff for Joker for what probably amounted to a couple hours work, but it wasn't worth killing over.

So where would a kid pick up a high-stakes poker game in the business district? And how would Jackson find where they were? He couldn't exactly walk into corporate offices and start asking about cards. The suits would lawyer up before he got the first sentence out of his mouth.

His cell phone rang and he checked it. Shaye.

"What's up?" he answered.

"I just finished talking to the priest."

"You get anything?"

"No. He admitted to recognizing Jinx, but said he didn't know anything else about her and hasn't seen her since last Tuesday when he gave her the Bible."

"That's what he said. What did you see?"

"I don't know. I got a mixed read on him. I don't think he was lying about his interaction with Jinx, but I got the impression he's worried about something, and I mean specifically worried, not I'm-a-priest-and-care worried. If that makes sense?"

"Definitely. I'll run a check on him—claim a couple of the kids saw the priest talking to Joker. No one can prove he didn't, so it shouldn't raise any red flags down at the department. Vincent won't be in until Monday anyway."

"God forbid he skip his weekend off to solve a homicide. How does he sleep at night?"

"I'm betting very well, all while dreaming about retirement and ways to make my life miserable."

"Probably. Did you find any card games Joker made?"

"One, but I didn't get anything. Joker played with the guys, but I don't like them for killing him. Not enough at stake in the game, and they didn't give me any indication to think they wanted him dead. Seemed surprised when I told them." Jackson paused for a moment, thinking about Shaye's connections.

"Hey," he said, "you wouldn't happen to know about any high-stakes card games in the business district, would you?"

"Ha. I can't even win at Go Fish. I'd be the last person who'd know about high-stakes card games. Are you thinking Joker got into something big and beat the wrong guys?"

"It would only take one wrong one, right?"

"True. I don't run in those circles, and it's usually a guy thing, but I bet Eleonore knows some of them. I hear she's hell at seven-card stud."

Jackson smiled. "That woman is full of surprises. Is there anything else I can check on for you?"

"Not that I can think of. I'm going to meet with Hustle and see if he found anything new."

"Sounds good. Let me know on the card game. Oh, and Shaye, you looked great last night."

He hung up before she could respond. And before he said too much.

Shaye stared at the phone for a moment still trying to formulate a response, but Jackson had already hung up. Which was just as well, she supposed. For the first time in a while, she was speechless.

Why does he do that to me?

Because you're attracted to him and apparently, even kids like Hustle can see the chemistry.

She sighed. What an unexpected and unwanted turn of events in her life. Jackson had everything she claimed all the men she'd turned down were missing. He was honorable and fierce, and cared about what was right and wrong, even to his own detriment. He wasn't cocky but he was confident. He was smart but not arrogant. And he was seriously hot.

She sighed again. Thank God Corrine had been distracted by the charity biddies and by Jackson's role in her last case. Otherwise, she might have noticed the attraction as well. Except Shaye doubted Corrine would have been pushing Jackson at Shaye the way she had some of those other awful choices. Corrine would take Jackson's job as a cop as the single worst thing in the world for Shaye to add to her life. More danger. More exposure. More risk. Corrine would probably be on board with a male stripper before she gave her seal of approval to a cop.

Shaye climbed into her SUV and called Hustle, pushing thoughts of Jackson and her mother from her mind. Both were distractions she didn't need, for completely different reasons.

Hustle answered right away, and she arranged a place to meet him in Bywater, close to the hot dog vendor where he'd picked up lunch. When she pulled up to the curb, she motioned to him and he jumped into the passenger seat, sliding his skateboard onto the floorboard. Shaye filled him in on her conversation with Father Michael.

"Jackson is going to run a background on him," Shaye said once she finished recounting her conversation with the priest. "Maybe we'll get lucky and something will pop. In the meantime, you keep an eye out for him engaging any of the street kids."

"Do you want me to ask around about him?"

Shaye hesitated. "I don't think so. If you start asking questions, people might assume the priest is the answer and take action."

"You think he might get jumped. Yeah, if people thought he was responsible for all this, they'd go after him."

"But if anyone mentions him, feel them out for information if you can."

Hustle nodded. "Two more kids are missing—Scratch and Spider. I don't know Spider. He hangs in the Tremé, but I think he might be fairly new. Scratch is an oldie, though. Been on the streets for at least three years. Ain't nobody got the jump on him without a serious plan."

"What did he do for money?"

"He had a gig with one of those construction companies. Demolition. He was hoping they'd keep him on when they started building. You know, learn something that might get him off the streets."

"How old is he?"

"Gotta be close to eighteen. I think that's why he was looking to fix up something permanent. When he didn't show to skate, one of the others checked at the demolition site. The boss said he didn't show up for work on Friday or yesterday."

"Did you see him Thursday?"

Hustle shook his head. "He was at the docks Wednesday after work. Wasn't there Thursday."

"But he normally would have been?"

"Yeah, he usually skated there after work."

"So we could assume someone must have grabbed him Thursday after work but before he got to the docks, unless he wasn't planning to skate."

Hustle's eyes widened. "Yeah, I guess so."

"Do you know where the demolition site is?"

"Yeah. I been by there and seen Scratch working a couple times."

Shaye started her SUV. "Tell me."

Hustle directed her to the Upper Ninth Ward and down a block where a lot of the buildings were beyond repair. He pointed to a corner where a bulldozer stood in the middle of a pile of rubbish. Dumpsters lined a side street, some of them already full of construction debris. A white truck was parked at the curb and a man stood in the middle of the mess, watching as she drove up.

"I think that's the boss," Hustle said.

"Lucky break we caught him here on a Sunday," Shaye said. "Let's go see if he can tell us anything. Let me do all the talking."

Hustle nodded.

She climbed out of her SUV and headed over to the man, sizing him up as she went. He was fairly tall and a good two hundred twenty pounds. He sported the common stomach pooch and thinning hair of many forty something-year-old men, but he had that hard edge to him that left Shaye with no doubt he could hold his own in a scuffle. No one would work this area of town if they couldn't. Thieves had no problem killing someone over power tools. The bulge under his hip at his waistline told Shaye he was packing.

He studied her and Hustle as they approached, frowning the entire time. Careful, but she didn't blame him. Thieves came in all forms, women and children alike, and all equally dangerous.

"Hi," Shaye said. "My name is Shaye Archer. I'm a private investigator." She held up her wallet, which she'd removed from her purse in the SUV, to show him her identification.

He glanced at the identification and looked back at her. "I'm John Clancy. I'm the foreman for this site. What's a PI doing out here?"

"I'm looking for information on an employee of yours who disappeared recently. Friends called him Scratch."

John nodded. "You're talking about the street kid." He looked over at Hustle. "That's where I've seen you before. You were talking to him last week."

Hustle nodded but didn't say anything.

"What can you tell me about Scratch?" Shaye asked.

"He's a good worker—strong, reliable. I was surprised when he didn't show up Friday and Saturday, but then, I guess you never know."

"What do you mean?" Shaye said.

He shrugged. "Lots of street people get caught up in

drugs, and that's usually the beginning of the end, if you know what I mean. Others get caught up in stuff that gets them capped or are simply in the wrong place at the wrong time and go down with the rest. Some get picked up by the cops and held for a bit. Those usually turn up in a couple days."

"So you're not really concerned that he didn't show?" Shaye asked.

"I'm more concerned that I was one worker short, and with the rain, we're already behind schedule. These kids usually surface one way or another. Either way, there's nothing I can do about it."

"Did you report him missing?"

"Because he skipped a couple days of work? The police wouldn't even take the time to write a report on that."

Shaye knew he was right, but his casual attitude frustrated her.

"Look," John said, obviously cluing in on her displeasure, "I hope nothing happened to the kid. I like him and the truth is, I think he has a future in construction if he wants it. But I don't know anything about him except what kind of worker he is."

"I assume you have paperwork on him, for payroll?" Shaye asked.

"I've got a copy of his identification and Social Security number. He's contract and I agreed to pay him cash, so nothing else was necessary."

"So no payroll taxes and no benefits required."

"Hey, the kid asked for cash like most of them do, but I don't put laborers on payroll anyway. The turnover would cost me a fortune in administration costs alone. What I'm doing is hardly uncommon. No developer puts unskilled labor on payroll."

Shaye nodded. "Would you mind showing me the copy of the license and Social?"

He looked from her to Hustle then back. "You mind telling me what this is about?"

"Some street kids have come up missing. One of them was found murdered. Scratch's friends haven't been able to locate him, so I'm looking into his disappearance as well as that of some others."

He frowned. "How come the police haven't been around?"

"To ask you about whom, exactly?" Shaye asked. "A person that already doesn't exist who no one has reported missing? Assuming the others worked for cash as well, my guess is their employers' take on them not turning up for work isn't much different from yours."

"No. Probably not."

"I'd also guess that whatever identification Scratch provided is falsified, so cops running through the motions wouldn't produce much."

"You think you can do better?"

"It's a good possibility. The police have limitations placed on them that a private investigator doesn't."

"Yeah, but cops don't bill you by the hour."

"I'm calling this job community service."

He looked at her for a couple seconds, then nodded. "Okay. If you think it would help." He pointed to a building across the street that had bars on the windows and a dead bolt on the front door. "My temporary office is across the street."

Shaye turned to follow him, Hustle trailing behind. The young man's expression had remained completely neutral during the entire conversation, and Shaye wondered what he was thinking. When they got to the building, John unlocked the dead bolt and let them inside. He pulled a folder from a desk drawer and handed it to Shaye. She looked at the image of the identification and Social Security card, then glanced around the office.

There wasn't a copy machine or scanner in the room. "Is it okay if I take a picture of these?" she asked.

"Sure," John said.

She placed the two photocopies on a desk and took a photo of each with her phone. Both were probably fake, but it was still something she needed to pursue. She slipped her phone back into her pocket and gave the file back to John. "The address on the identification," she asked, "is it good?"

"I have no idea," John said. "Don't have any reason to mail anything until tax time when we send out the 1099s, and if they're still around, we hand them out on the job."

"Okay. I really appreciate you taking the time to talk to me."

"No problem." He grabbed a business card off the desk and handed it to her. "If you find out something, would you mind letting me know? Like I said, I think he has a future in this, if he wants it."

She slipped the card into her pocket and pulled out one of her own. "Of course, and if you hear anything or if he turns up, please let me know."

He nodded, glancing once more at Hustle before they turned and left. As they pulled away, he lifted his hand to wave.

"What do you think?" Hustle asked.

"I think he's telling the truth, what little he had to say."

Hustle frowned. "Me too. We're not getting anywhere. Jinx is still out there, and when I think about…"

"I know. We're doing everything we can. You have to stay positive. I'm going to keep working until we find Jinx."

He looked over at her and nodded. "Thanks."

"Where do you want me to drop you off?"

"Close to the docks. Might as well skate. Maybe some of the others showed up and know something."

Shaye headed out of the Ninth Ward and back to Bywater. She let Hustle out a couple blocks away from the docks, where they wouldn't run the risk of the street kids seeing them together. She'd talked to Hustle at the docks during the Frederick case, and the kids might recognize her. If they found out Hustle was working with an outsider, they might stop talking to him.

And right now, he was the only likely source of a lead that they had.

Chapter Eight

Corrine sat at the kitchen counter and tapped at the keys on her laptop, her fingers striking harder with every move.

"You're going to break either a nail or a key," Eleonore commented.

Corrine looked across the counter at her friend, who was pouring two iced teas, and frowned. "If you're not going to be helpful, you're welcome to leave."

"Great. How can I help? I have duct tape and superglue. We can reinforce either your nails or the keyboard. Your choice."

Corrine leaned back on the stool and sighed. "I'm sorry. I'm frustrated with my father and Shaye and being cooped up in this house all the time, and I'm taking it out on you."

"Well, you finally got something right."

"Your empathy is making me all squishy."

"I'm a psychiatrist. I don't do empathy. I do reality."

"Fine, I'll play. Tell me how to deal with the fact that my father is on an overprotective bent from hell and every time I want to yell at him about it, I hear my own voice saying similar things to Shaye. Then I want to slap myself for being as neurotic and annoying as he is."

Eleonore pushed a glass of iced tea across the counter, sat down across from Corrine, and reached for a raspberry croissant. "Pierce isn't neurotic. Not about you, anyway. Business, probably. I'll give you annoying though, at least from your perspective."

"Your halfhearted agreement is neither comforting nor helpful."

Eleonore laughed. "I'm sorry. You didn't tell me I was supposed to be realistic *and* helpful. Let me try again. Pierce loves you and worries about you because you're his only child. You work a dangerous job and despite the fact that this last incident wasn't about your job, it highlighted how vulnerable you are when you're working."

"But we've both always known the risks. They're hardly new."

"No. But this is the first time you've come this close to death. Dealing with a concept is a completely different issue than having reality slammed right into your face."

"This is supposed to make me feel better?"

"I'm not trying to make you feel better. I'm trying to help you understand why Pierce is annoying and more importantly, why it's not likely to change."

Corrine sighed. "Have you ever been wrong? I mean, you have to have been, but I've never witnessed it."

"I could probably work it in if it would make you feel better."

"*Now* you're worried about my feelings?"

Eleonore grinned. “Don’t waste time agitating over Pierce. Sooner or later the next big takeover will occupy his mind or it will be reelection time and all of this will start to fade.”

“That’s great and all, but doesn’t solve my problem of annoying Shaye the same way my father is annoying me.”

“You could make big strides in fixing that problem if you stopped thrusting your horrible choices of men at her.”

“Derrick Oliver is a perfectly fine young man.”

Eleonore raised one eyebrow.

Corrine threw a napkin at her. “You two are just alike.”

“You know he’s awful,” Eleonore said. “You just don’t want to admit it.”

“Fine, he’s sorta awful. But he’s got a great future. Shaye wouldn’t have to work—”

“You mean like you don’t have to work? Who are you trying to fool? Shaye doesn’t have to work now. She could probably support a small country on her trust fund. You could probably single-handedly erase the national debt with yours. I don’t see you giving notice.”

“Is it wrong for me to want her to have someone?”

“Of course not. Mothers are supposed to want the best for their children, and you’re a good mother. You just have awful taste in men. Shaye, on the other hand, is much better at picking winners than you are.”

“What do you mean?”

“You didn’t meet the dashing Detective Lamotte last night?”

Corrine frowned. "The policeman? He was dashing?"

"You didn't notice?"

"You did?"

"It was hard not to. I'm not dead."

"I suppose he was nice-looking, but I don't see what—oh my God, you don't think…"

"That he's totally into Shaye? Hell yes, I do. And that's my professional opinion."

Corrine groaned. "Please tell me you're joking."

"Why would that be such a horrible thing? He seems like a nice guy."

"Because he's a cop, that's why. The last thing Shaye needs is to be hooked up with someone whose existence puts her at even more risk. What in the world does he have to offer but trouble?"

"Well, he's a damned good shot and looks mighty fine in a suit, so that's two things."

"I'll give you the good shot part, and maybe the suit part."

"Maybe? He was the best-looking guy in the room, and probably the only one I'd elect to spend time talking to. Shaye didn't seem bothered by his presence, and you should take that as a good thing. Her long-running stance on avoiding men makes that a really big deal, even if it's not the man you want to see her somewhat comfortable with."

"She looked comfortable?"

"She was smiling and chatting when I walked up. She joked with me and introduced us, explaining our usual mocking charity exchange. That's personal information.

This is a good thing, Corrine. She's putting herself out there more. I know that makes you nervous for her physical safety, but it's a step forward in her emotional state."

Corrine threw up her hands. "Fine. It's a good thing. I just wish it could have been some boring investment banker or maybe an accountant with a good sense of humor." She took a drink of her tea. "I asked Shaye if she was still having the nightmares."

Eleonore shook her head. "You know I can't talk about anything Shaye's told me in session."

"Oh good grief, for someone paid to listen, you interrupt a lot. I'm not asking you to give me information. I'm trying to give *you* information."

"Well, why didn't you say so?"

Corrine sighed. "She admitted she's still having nightmares. I think that's the tip of the iceberg, though. My guess is they're getting worse."

"Did she say that?"

"No. Mother's intuition. I also asked her if she was remembering. She said she didn't know. That the dreams seemed real but when she woke up, she couldn't latch onto anything."

Eleonore nodded. "And she may not ever be able to. You know that."

"Yes, but I made her promise to tell me if she did. She said it wasn't my responsibility to deal with it. I told her I'd been waiting to deal with it for nine years."

"How'd she take that?"

"Fine, I guess. At least I hope she'll tell me. I don't

want to keep pushing."

"I know. It's a fine line between making yourself available and wanting to help, and stepping over the line that has her keeping it all to herself."

Corrine bit her lip and stared down at her glass of tea. Finally she looked back up at Eleonore. "I know you can't tell me what she says in therapy, but you'd tell me if she was in danger, right? If things ever get to the point that I need to get her security? She'd hate it, but I wouldn't care."

Eleonore reached across the table and squeezed Corrine's hand. "If Shaye is ever in danger, he'll have to go through both of us to get to her. That's a promise."

Corrine felt her eyes begin to water. For almost as long as she could remember, Eleonore had been there for her. And then she'd been there for Shaye. So many times, Corrine wished she had the words to tell her friend how much she meant to her, but each time she tried, the words never seemed enough. She looked across the counter at her friend.

Eleonore smiled. "I know."

Corrine smiled back at her friend and then jumped when her laptop started beeping.

"What's that?" Eleonore asked.

Corrine pulled her laptop over in front of her. "I got a hit on that missing girl that Shaye is looking for."

Eleonore hurried around the counter and leaned over, reading the screen with Corrine.

"Mandy LeDoux. Baton Rouge. Fifteen years old." Eleonore shook her head. "Looks like your counterparts over in the capital city paid her mother a couple of visits."

"Apparently not enough of them." Corrine leaned back in her chair and blew out a breath. "It's times like this that I want to scream at the system. It fails so many times."

"And it works thousands of others."

"It failed this girl and she wound up on the streets in New Orleans. Now God only knows what's happened to her."

Eleonore pointed to the screen. "Looks like it was her maternal aunt who reported her missing. She lives here in Uptown."

Corrine reached for her cell phone. "I better let Shaye know. She's going to want to talk to the aunt."

Shaye clutched the steering wheel, trying to control her emotions, but it was hard. Jinx's aunt was a five-minute drive away, and Shaye was excited to meet the woman and see what she had to say. All sorts of questions ran through Shaye's mind. Did Jinx come to New Orleans because of her aunt? If so, why was she on the streets? The aunt had listed Jinx's last known address as the shack Jinx's mother lived in outside Baton Rouge when social services had paid her a visit. Maybe the woman didn't know Jinx was in New Orleans.

The aunt's house was tiny and narrow and needed a coat of paint, but it was in a decent neighborhood. Shaye parked at the curb and walked up the sidewalk, hoping

Cora LeDoux was at home. Corrine had given her Cora's phone number, but Shaye preferred face-to-face meetings for this sort of exchange, and she liked it when people had no warning…no time to prepare in case they were hiding something.

She knocked on the door and waited. A couple seconds later, she heard movement inside. Several seconds later, the door swung open and a thin middle-aged woman with short spiky black hair and pale skin stared out at her.

"Cora LeDoux?" Shaye asked.

"Yes."

Shaye pulled out her wallet and showed Cora her identification. "My name is Shaye Archer. I'm a private investigator."

Cora's eyes widened. "An investigator? What in the world do you want with me?"

"I'm looking for your niece, Mandy."

"So am I."

"I know. You filed a report with social services in Baton Rouge."

She frowned. "I don't understand. I thought you were *here* looking for my niece."

"Not exactly. Your niece has been living on the streets in New Orleans. She went missing a couple days ago. A friend of hers hired me to find her."

Her eyes widened and she clutched the door, leaning against it. Shaye could tell it wasn't out of emotion but out of physical exhaustion.

"Do you mind if I come inside and speak with you?"

Shaye asked.

"Yes, please," Cora said and opened the door wider to allow Shaye inside. "I need to sit."

Cora closed the door behind them, then sat in a recliner and waved her hand at the couch. Shaye took a seat on the couch closest to the recliner. As she sat, she noticed that Cora's chair was the kind that had an electric lift option to help one rise.

"Ms. LeDoux," Shaye said, "I hope you don't find this intrusive, but are you ill? I can come back another time when you're feeling better."

Cora waved a limp hand at Shaye. "Please call me Cora. Tomorrow might be better. Might not be. I had breast cancer. I'm in remission, but chemo took it right out of me. The doctors say it will take a bit to regain my strength."

Shaye's heart clenched a bit. She hadn't had cancer, but she'd worked her way back from a broken body and broken spirit. It was a hard, painful journey. "I'm sorry the chemo was so rough on you, but I'm glad you're in remission."

Cora gave her a weak smile. "That makes two of us. You said Mandy was living on the streets here in New Orleans?"

"Yes. You didn't know she was here?"

"No. I had seen an attorney about filing for custody but then I was diagnosed with breast cancer. The attorney said the courts wouldn't award Mandy to someone in my condition, especially given that it was going to become worse before better. They would declare that Mandy was better off with a healthy parent than a sick aunt."

A flash of anger crossed Cora's face as she delivered the last sentence.

"I love my sister," Cora continued, "but I hate what she's become. The drugs, the men—what Gina exposed Mandy to is criminal."

"Has she been using for long?"

"According to Mandy, it's been about five years, but that's the memory of a child talking. Gina could have been using before then and Mandy might not have recognized the signs yet."

Shaye frowned. "You didn't know?"

Cora shook her head. "We're from North Carolina. After high school, Gina took off. I found her in California a few years later, and she had Mandy, who was a toddler at the time. She wasn't setting the world on fire, but she was waiting tables at a restaurant in LA and had an apartment nearby. It was tiny but clean, and she seemed to be okay for a long time."

"What changed?"

"One day, about eight years after I first located her, I called and her cell phone number wasn't good anymore. I checked with the restaurant and the apartment manager and they both told me the same thing—that Gina had taken up with a bad crowd and had bugged out. No one came right out and said exactly what she was up to, but from their tone, I knew it was nothing good."

"When did you find her again?"

"About a year and a half ago. I hired a private

investigator. He tracked Gina for three years."

"Three years? Wow. That's a long time and a lot of billable hours."

"My fiancé was killed in a car accident and had taken out a good life insurance policy for me. And I'm a programmer, so I make decent money. If it hadn't been for Mandy, I wouldn't have kept at it, but I couldn't stop thinking about what might happen to her, you know?"

"My mother is a social worker here in New Orleans. I know better than most people."

Cora nodded. "The investigator would locate her in one place only to find she'd left months before. It was almost as if she knew he was closing in on her. Hell, maybe she did know. Maybe some of the scumbags she was hanging out with warned her. Finally, he found her in Baton Rouge, and I came down to pay her a visit."

Cora's eyes filled with tears. "It was even worse than I expected. Gina looked like a skeleton, skin over bones, with tracks running up and down her arms and legs. Mandy was basically raising herself but she was protective of her mother, even though I could tell she was scared."

"Gina was the only thing she knew."

"Exactly. She didn't remember me and wouldn't tell me much, but I saw enough to call social services. They took her out of the house for a while, but without Mandy, Gina's benefits were cut in half, so she got clean long enough to get her back. I'd spent time with Mandy while she was in the home, and we were in a comfortable place with each other. When social services gave her back to

Gina, I went back to North Carolina and hired the attorney."

"And then you were diagnosed." Shaye shook her head. "I can't imagine how disappointing that was, after all the time you spent looking for Gina and Mandy only to have everything yanked away."

"I didn't like what the attorney told me but I knew he was right, so I made plans for the future. My doctor in North Carolina recommended a physician in New Orleans he considered a leader in the field of breast cancer. It wasn't Baton Rouge, but it was closer, and I had a friend here that I could count on to help me when my health got too bad to go it alone. I figured as soon as I was healthy enough to start the battle, I'd fight for custody of Mandy."

"Did Mandy have a way to contact you?"

"I gave her my cell phone number before I left Baton Rouge. They didn't have a phone but Mandy promised to call me collect every day from a pay phone at the drugstore, but she never called. I got worried after a couple of days and I sent the investigator to Baton Rouge while I was packing to move here. It was just as I feared—Gina had taken off again. The investigator finally located her in a run-down motel, known for prostitution and drugs, but he saw no sign of Mandy. When he pressed, Gina just said she was gone."

"And you filed the report with social services."

"Yes." Cora shook her head. "I can't believe that Mandy was here in New Orleans. Why didn't she call me? She knew I was trying to help her. I thought she trusted me."

"Maybe she lost the phone number. If Gina made them move in a hurry, maybe it got misplaced. You didn't know about the cancer before you left Baton Rouge, so Mandy had no way of knowing you'd moved. If she tried to locate you, it would have been in North Carolina."

Cora sniffed and wiped tears from the corner of her eye. "I should have checked in sooner. Hell, I should have kidnapped her and left her with a friend back home."

"Please don't blame yourself. You were working with what you had in a system that doesn't always do what's best for the child."

Cora nodded. "Thank you. So what can you tell me about my niece?"

Shaye shared everything she'd learned about Mandy with Cora. When she was finished, Cora shook her head.

"Jinx. That poor girl," Cora said. "She chose a name that represented how she viewed herself. Life with her mother was so awful she chose to live on the streets, and now this. You don't have any idea what could have happened?"

Shaye shook her head, dreading what she had to tell Cora next. "Unfortunately, Mandy isn't the only street kid who's missing." She told Cora about Jackson's investigation and the other missing kids that Hustle had told her about.

Cora's eyes grew wider and she clutched the edges of her shirt, wrinkling the fabric. "I don't understand," she said when Shaye finished. "What's going on?"

"Nothing good. That's all I'm sure about."

"And this detective you're working with…he doesn't have any ideas?"

"I'm sure he has plenty of them, just like me. What we don't have is evidence. I want to be completely honest with you. We don't have much to go on. Street kids live a very isolated existence for their own protection. It's hard to pin down what happened when none of them know much about the others."

"But this Hustle knew my niece?"

"I think Hustle likes your niece, as more than a friend. When she told him she thought someone was watching her, he tried to look out for her."

Cora inclined her head and looked at Shaye. "Can I ask how Hustle came to hire you? And how he's paying? I have money—"

Shaye put her hand up in protest. "Hustle helped me on a case. My client was being stalked. Hustle came in contact with the stalker and gave me information."

"Did you catch the stalker?"

"Detective Lamotte killed the stalker to save my client."

"Oh! Well, I hate to say it but that's probably the best outcome for your client. No looking over her shoulder any longer."

"The stalker actually turned out to be a serial killer, so it wasn't just my client that benefited. Who knows how many people were saved."

Cora sat up straight in her chair. "Wait. You're talking about the Emma Frederick case. I saw it on the news. She was your client? Oh my God. I don't know how you can speak so calmly about it. You must have nerves of steel."

Shaye smiled. "Something like that."

"Well, I'm glad that boy trusted you enough to ask for help, and I'm doubly glad that you and your detective friend are looking for my niece. The two of you saved that Frederick woman. It gives me hope that you can do the same for Mandy."

"That's the plan."

Shaye struggled to keep her smile in place. More than anything, she wanted to find Jinx alive and get her to Cora, where she had a shot at a normal life. But every day that passed made her less optimistic. Statistics didn't lie.

Jinx's time was running out. If it hadn't already.

Hustle looked back as he crossed the street. The streetlights were just starting to come on, but their sparse spacing didn't produce much light on the empty road. He'd been at the docks since Shaye had dropped him off, talking to different skaters as they dropped in to skate. No one had seen Jinx, Scratch, or Spider, and everyone had seemed genuinely shocked to hear about Joker. No one mentioned Father Michael or felt as if they were being followed.

His right ankle throbbed a little, causing him to slightly favor it. He had skated like crap, which wasn't surprising. His concentration was crap. Not a second passed that he didn't think about Jinx and what might be happening to her. Every time his thoughts went that direction, he forced them to the back of his mind, not wanting to think about the really bad things. The really bad things were final. The only ending he was willing to accept was one where Jinx was alive and well, even if she ended up in foster care. Maybe it would be better for her than it was for him. Maybe she'd have a chance at a normal life.

If anyone deserved it, Jinx did.

As he crossed the street, the hair on the back of his neck lifted and his skin tingled. Someone was watching him. He was certain.

Whoever had grabbed Jinx had probably ambushed her on the way to her hiding place. No way were they getting him the same way. Instead of continuing straight, he turned left and picked up his pace. There were a couple of dive bars only two blocks away. If he could make it to where people were, he'd be safe, even if it meant sitting on the sidewalk outside the bars until he could think of a better option. Then he remembered the phone. Shaye would know what to do. He pulled out the cell phone and accessed the Favorites.

The man rushed out of the doorway of an abandoned building so fast that Hustle barely had time to react. He twisted toward the man and saw his raised hand. Hustle threw his arm up to defend himself, and the man's hand crashed down onto the cell phone. Hustle swung his skateboard around, nailing the man in the side of the head. The man staggered backward just long enough to give Hustle an opportunity to escape. He dropped his board and propelled himself down the street as fast as he could go, his sore ankle long forgotten.

When he reached the bars, he looked back, but the street was empty. He checked his phone and saw that the screen was broken but it was still on. Saying a silent prayer, he punched in Shaye's number. His breath came out in a whoosh when the call went through.

"Hustle?" Shaye answered. "What's up?"

His heart pounded in his temples so loud he could barely hear her. "Someone just attacked me," he managed in between ragged breaths.

"Where are you?"

He gave her the cross streets.

"Are there people around?" she asked.

"Yeah. There's a couple of bars here."

"Don't leave. Not even a step. Stand in the doorway if you can, just make sure you're in view of multiple people. I'll be there in ten minutes."

The call disconnected and Hustle moved closer to the doorway, leaning against the wall just outside the opening. A group of people stood on the sidewalk outside the bar, smoking cigarettes. They glanced over at him but no one paid much mind to a street kid with a skateboard. They were common enough. Regulars at these bars were more concerned cops might be around to catch them with something more potent than Marlboros.

His pulse slowed a tiny bit and his ankle started to throb again. He reached down and rubbed it. It was already swelling. He cursed, and the smokers glanced over at him again. The last thing he needed was an injury slowing him down. He'd barely gotten away. Whoever the guy was, he was fast. If Hustle hadn't been faster, God only knows what would have happened to him.

He felt tears well up in his eyes and he brushed them away, angry at himself for being weak. Jinx needed him to be strong. If Shaye could go through what she did and take on serial killers, then he didn't have an excuse.

But now, more than ever before, he missed his mom.

CHAPTER NINE

Shaye floored her SUV, weaving through the traffic in Bywater like a madwoman, praying that no cops were around. If one came after her, she wasn't stopping. Not until Hustle was safely within her sights. She could deal with the rest after the fact. Her grandfather had no shortage of attorneys on staff.

GPS signaled a turn and she cut the wheel to the right, squealing around the corner. A guy starting to cross against the light jumped back on the sidewalk and shot the finger at her as she pulled away. She slowed a tiny bit, watching the sidewalks for pedestrians. This area of town had bars scattered throughout. The people out and about were often drunk and rarely obeyed traffic signals. A speeding ticket she could handle, even a reckless driving, but vehicular manslaughter might cost her her PI license.

Her hands clenched the steering wheel as a million questions ran through her mind. Was he hurt? And why Hustle? Did someone know he was working with her? Was she at risk as well? How did Hustle get away when others hadn't? Did he see his assailant? Would he be able to draw the man's face?

She rounded the last corner and headed for the end of the street where Hustle had indicated he'd be. He spotted her SUV and hurried away from the bar. Before she'd even come to a complete stop, he yanked open the door and jumped inside. He'd been limping when he ran for her car.

"Are you hurt?" she asked as she took off again.

"No."

She looked over at him. His face was pale and his eyes were puffy and red, as if he'd been crying. "I saw you limping," she said.

"I twisted my ankle a little skating today. I guess I aggravated it getting away."

"Tell me what happened."

Hustle told her about walking to his hiding place and the feeling that someone was watching. How he'd changed directions and the man had rushed at him from an empty building.

"Did you see him?" she asked.

"Yeah."

"So you can draw him?" she asked, her excitement growing.

"It won't do any good. He was wearing a mask."

She struggled to control her disappointment. "What kind of mask?"

"One of those Mardi Gras ones—those breakable kind that cover the whole face."

"A Venetian mask?"

"I think that's what they're called."

"That's still something. If you can draw it for me, I

might be able to find the store that sells that particular mask." She said it to make him feel better, but she knew it was likely that a dozen shops in the French Quarter alone carried the same mask. "What about his size, height? Could you tell anything about his age from his hands or the way he moved?"

"He was pretty tall, over six feet. He was wearing a hoodie and sweatpants so I couldn't tell how he was built. He had on gloves, so I couldn't see his hands, but he didn't move like someone old."

He was silent a couple of seconds. "He was really fast, and he wasn't wearing shoes. I saw his feet. He was wearing slippers, but they were boots."

"So you couldn't hear his footsteps."

"That's what I figure." Hustle looked at her, his fear apparent. "He knew what he was doing—made all the right moves. This isn't some chance thing…wait, that's not right…I don't know the word."

"It's not opportunistic."

"Yeah! There wasn't any hesitation, and he had something in his hand. It broke the screen on the phone. I think maybe it was a needle."

"That would explain how he was able to contain the other kids. You're probably the first person that's gotten away. If someone else had, they'd be talking."

"He has Jinx. This guy with drugs. I can't stop thinking about what might be happening to her. I kept trying to force my mind to something different but it keeps coming back."

"I know. Not imagining the worst is the hardest part of my job. But if I start thinking negative, then it might affect how I do my job. I have to believe in a happy ending. It keeps me pushing instead of giving up. I need you to do that, too."

He looked over at her. "You're not going to make us hold hands and sing or anything, are you?"

"My singing ability is definitely a negative, so no."

"I'm not so good myself." He straightened up a bit in his seat and looked out the window. "Hey, where are we going?"

"My place."

"No way! I can't stay there. What if he saw me get into your car? What if he knows about you? He'll come after both of us."

Shaye pulled up to the curb in front of her apartment and parked. "I'd love to see him try. Come inside. If you still think it's a bad idea, then I'll take you to a hotel."

He looked at the apartment, then back at her, his indecision clear. "I'll look. But I'm not promising anything."

"Sounds fair." She climbed out of the SUV and headed for the front door. She unlocked it and stepped inside, Hustle right behind her, and disarmed the security system. "So check this out."

She locked the door, then pushed in place two dead bolts, one high on the door, one low. Then she armed the security system. She pointed to the windows. "All the windows have bars on them. They can be unlocked only from inside and only I and my mother have the code. This way." She waved him toward the kitchen.

"This is the door to the alley between the buildings. It's got a lock and two dead bolts, just like the front door. Both are made of metal, not wood. The door frames are also metal. They're just etched and painted to look like wood. Now, take a look at this."

She headed down the hall to her bedroom and pointed to the wall. It contained four flat screens, each showing a different area inside and outside the apartment, the images shifting every five seconds. "No one is getting in here without us knowing they're coming."

"Jeez," Hustle said, clearly impressed. "You've got more security than a bank."

"Probably, and I'll bet mine's better. The banks don't have my grandfather to deal with."

"Your gramps did all this?"

"He didn't do it, but he paid a high-tech firm to secure both my and my mother's homes."

Hustle nodded. "Because of what happened with the Frederick lady."

"Yep. If he could have gotten away with assigning me armed guards, he would have."

"Might not be such a bad idea. I mean, if you're going to keep doing this kind of work."

"You're as bad as my mom. How about I hire a guard for you until we find Jinx?"

His expression—a mixture of shock and horror—was almost comical.

"Doesn't sound so pleasant when it's about you, does it?" Shaye asked. "So what do you think? Can you stay here tonight? I promise I'll have another option for tomorrow."

"I guess it will work for one night. I'll take the couch."

"You don't have to do that. There's a spare room right down the hall from mine. There's a bathroom across the hall. She opened her drawer and pulled out sweatpants and a big T-shirt. "You can wash your clothes if you'd like. Laundry is in the kitchen behind the folding doors."

He took the clothes and stared down at them for a bit, and she could tell he was both appreciative and embarrassed. "Go ahead and take a shower," she said. "I'm going to fix us something to eat. I'm a horrible cook, so your choices are frozen pizza and grilled cheese sandwiches."

He perked up. "How about both?"

"Both it is." She headed for the kitchen, trying to give him some space. His discomfort was so obvious, but she knew a hot shower was a luxury street kids usually didn't have. She pulled a frozen pizza out of the freezer and put it in the oven. A couple seconds later, she heard the shower turn on and smiled.

One hurdle down.

Now she just had to figure out a place for Hustle to stay starting tomorrow and who had attacked him, and find Jinx.

Piece of cake.

The door to the barn flew open and fading sunlight entered, making the man walking toward her look like a shadow. Jinx pushed herself back into the corner and watched as he drew closer. This one wasn't wearing a mask, but as he stepped up to the cage to look at her, she almost wished he had been.

His face was leathery from being out in the sun so long. A long scar ran down his cheek, from the corner of his eye to his lip, causing his eye to droop. His head was completely shaved and he had a dragon tattoo running down the side of his face and neck. But none of that was what scared her. Rough-looking men with bad tattoos were the kind her mother always hooked up with. They'd feed her drugs and beat her until they got tired and then move on to something new. Jinx had learned how to stay out of the way a long time ago.

It was the way the man looked at her that terrified her.

Plenty of her mom's losers had spent time staring, mentally undressing her. It always disgusted her, and some of them were downright creepy, but none of them had ever studied her so dispassionately. As if she was a thing and not a person.

He bent down and shoved a paper bag through the bars. "It's food," he said as he rose back up and resumed staring. "You don't look all that strong. We wanted a female for the last round. Maybe have a little fun before the game was over, but you're skinnier than I like."

Her stomach churned and bile rose in her throat. The

thought of his hands on her was far worse than death.

"I guess we don't have time to fatten you up any," he continued. "'A course, that would make you slower, so I guess it wouldn't be smart. Don't want the last hunt of the game to be too easy."

He grinned, his crooked, broken teeth magnified in her vision, like a row of tombstones. He banged on the cage. "Eat that and get some rest. I want you ready to run. Two more days and you're up, sweetheart."

He turned around and shoved a bag of food through the bars of Spider's cage, then sauntered out of the barn, whistling as he went. As he pulled the door shut behind him, most of the light fled the room.

"Jinx?" Spider called out to her. "Jinx, are you all right?"

She didn't even bother to fight the tears that welled in her eyes. They spilled out and ran down her cheeks. "I won't ever be all right again."

"Maybe we'll beat them. We're smart, right? We know how to get away. We've been doing it on the streets."

"And we both ended up here. How well do you think we'll do out in a swamp that they know like the backs of their hands and we've never seen before? How well will we do against guns when we don't have weapons?"

"We gotta get out of here." Spider's voice went up several octaves. "That's the only way. We gotta get out of here before they take us out to hunt."

"We're in cages. How are we supposed to do that?"

"I don't know, but there's got to be a way. Maybe

there's a part that's loose. Something. There's got to be something we can do."

Spider's desperation made Jinx's heart clench, and her mind shifted to thoughts of Peter—a little boy, alone and scared and running out of time. Spider was right. Their best chance was breaking out and trying to find their way out of the swamp. Find someone who could help.

An idea started to form in her mind, and she rose from the corner and headed for the cage door. "Start looking for weak spots," she said. "I'm going to see if there's a way to get this lock off."

She studied the lock for a moment. A typical padlock. She reached behind her and felt the rhinestones on the pockets of her jeans. The thin backings that the stones were glued onto might be just enough metal to make a lock pick. She pulled off her shoes and jeans and started picking at the stones.

This had to work. There wasn't anything else.

Shaye grabbed her laptop from the counter and plopped down on the couch. Hustle had consumed three-quarters of the frozen pizza, two grilled cheese sandwiches, half a bag of potato chips, and two milkshakes before starting to nod off. He'd given her an awkward 'thanks for everything' and headed down the hall. She peeked into the room ten minutes later and he was collapsed on top of the bed, softly snoring.

She turned on the television and for a change, switched to the news. Usually, she didn't watch it, especially before bedtime, but this case had her wanting to know everything that was going on in the city. You never knew what might be relevant.

She opened her laptop and started a search on crimes using immobilizing drugs. Then the reporter started with the lead news story and she jerked her head up toward the television.

"Police are looking for a ten-year-old boy who went missing this past Friday from a holiday celebration in Woldenberg Park. Peter Carlin was last seen by his nanny on a bench in front of an ice cream vendor near Conti Street. Peter was out of the nanny's sight for only a minute as she went to retrieve napkins and he was gone when she looked back at the bench. She alerted everyone nearby, and several festival attendees and vendors helped her search the grounds and surrounding area, but no sign of the boy was found.

"If anyone has seen Peter, please contact the New Orleans police immediately. Police are also asking for anyone who saw Peter at Woldenberg Park to call and let them know the time and place of the sighting. If anyone was taking pictures near the food vendors between two and three p.m., please email them to the New Orleans police at findpeter at NOLA police dot com."

Shaye's gut clenched as she looked at the photo of the smiling little boy. Another missing child, but this one had parents and a nanny. He was also much younger than the street kids who were missing, and was taken in broad daylight. An opportunistic crime, perhaps? The exact opposite of the street kid abductions?

She blew out a breath. It was almost 11:00 p.m. and she'd intended to call Jackson the next morning to tell him about the attack on Hustle. She also needed to see if he'd gotten any hits on Father Michael, and she wanted to ask if he could do a search on the ID she had for Scratch. And even though it didn't help move the case forward, she wanted to let him know about Cora LeDoux.

Before she could change her mind, she grabbed her cell phone and dialed his number. It rang four times and she was about to hang up when he answered, sounding a little out of breath.

"Did I catch you at a bad time?"

"I was just getting out of the shower and had to make a dash for the phone. Now I'm dripping on my living room carpet. The worst part is, this is still the best time you could have caught me today."

"That good, huh?"

"Yeah. Give me a sec to grab a towel."

She reached for the remote to turn down the TV volume, trying to focus on the news running across the bottom of the screen, but the thought of Jackson naked in the middle of his living room kept intruding.

Get a grip.

"Hey. I'm back," Jackson said.

"Sorry for the timing," she said, feeling the urge to apologize for something since she'd been thinking about him naked.

"No worries. I was planning on leaving you a message, then the day got away from me, and I figured it would wait until tomorrow."

"I thought the same. Then I saw the news."

"You're talking about Peter Carlin. Yeah, that's a real heartbreaker."

"You don't think it has anything to do with Jinx or the others, do you?"

"I don't think so, and believe me, I checked all the facts with the detective assigned to the case. Peter is from an upper-income family—father is a banker, mother is a marketing executive. They have a nice house in Uptown, a nanny, and take an annual vacation to Disneyland."

"Basically, the opposite life from Jinx."

"Exactly."

"Well, that's good, I guess. Hell, who knows, right? A little boy is still missing and no one knows why." She clenched the phone. "I hate this, Jackson. Kids shouldn't have to go through this. They shouldn't have to worry about being taken right off the street…"

Her voice started to waver, and she stopped to take a breath.

This isn't about you.

"Shaye?" Jackson asked. "Are you all right?"

"Yeah, sorry. Someone attacked Hustle tonight," she said, changing the subject.

"What? Is he all right? Did he see who attacked him?"

"He's shaken up but all right." She filled Jackson in on

what had happened.

"A needle?" Jackson said when she finished. "That makes a lot of sense. And you said this guy tried to grab Hustle on his way to where he sleeps at night, right?"

"Yeah."

"I don't get it. How is this guy managing to follow these kids when they're hyperaware of their surroundings?"

"I don't know. He's good, I guess?"

"Following someone who is actively watching to make sure they're not followed is better than good. It requires a lot of skill. The guy wore a mask and gloves and covering on his feet that wouldn't make noise."

"You're thinking military."

"It wouldn't surprise me."

Shaye blew out a breath. "If we're up against someone trained to track and evade detection while doing so, it's going to make him so much harder to catch. If he's that good, he probably already knows we're involved."

"Agreed, which means both of us have to be very careful. Since he didn't succeed in grabbing Hustle, he might have moved on to another."

"Hustle found out two more kids are missing. One from the Tremé called Spider that he didn't know, and another from Bywater that he knew well. I mean, as well as they get to know each other." She filled Jackson in on Scratch and what she'd learned from the construction foreman.

There was a pause, and she heard some rustling on his end of the phone.

"Give me the name and Social you got," he said.

She checked the images on her phone and gave him the information. She heard clicking, and then there was another pause.

"The name and Social are legit," Jackson said, "but they belong to a man who died eight years ago. The kid probably bought the ID to get a job."

"I figured as much. Did you get anything on Father Michael?"

"That's why I was calling you first thing tomorrow."

Shaye straightened up on the couch. "What did you find?"

"No criminal record, but he's changed cities three times in the last five years, New Orleans being the third. I know the church moves younger priests around, so that in itself isn't necessarily a red flag, but I decided to make a couple of phone calls to his previous employers. No one will tell me why Father Michael was transferred."

"What do they say when you ask?"

"I talked to two secretaries and an office manager. They all say the same thing, and I mean, the exact same thing. 'I am not privy to the church's decisions regarding Father Michael's transfer.'"

"You think they've been coached."

"Absolutely. It wasn't just the words, it was the way their tone shifted from normal voice to robot voice as they delivered the supplied line."

Shaye grabbed her laptop. "What were the churches?"

Jackson gave her the names. "You going to do some

poking around?"

"I'm going to try. The church has clamped down on stuff so much. They don't want to keep the bad rep stirred up, but maybe someone will talk. Either way, it means Father Michael needs a closer look."

"I could pay him a visit and ask him about Joker, but I don't have evidence to support anything else."

"I wasn't thinking about you. I was thinking about me."

"Doing what?"

"Hunting the hunter."

CHAPTER TEN

Jinx held the scraps of metal in the hem of her shirt and attempted to press them into a single rod. It was hard to manage the narrow pieces through the material, but she'd already cut three fingers with the sharp edges. What she needed was more light, but none would be forthcoming until the morning when sunlight crept through cracks in the barn.

Spider had pulled and tugged on every bar and piece of wood in his cage, but nothing had given an inch. He'd used his shirt to snag a piece of wood and was using that to pry one of the boards from the wall. Jinx didn't really think it would work, but it gave him something to do instead of talking, which tended to disrupt her concentration. If she could get her lock undone, then she could do Spider's.

That was their best bet.

It had taken her a while to get the rhinestones off her jeans and even longer to get the stones off the metal backings. With no tools but her ragged fingernails and the fleeting slivers of sunlight, it made for tedious work. She'd taken a break once to eat the sandwich when she finally got them all off her jeans. With her stomach still churning, she hadn't wanted to eat, but she had to keep her strength up. They were only feeding them twice a day, so it was a good thing that she'd gotten used to living on far less than a normal girl her age would consume. A normal girl would probably have passed out already.

A normal girl wouldn't even be in here.

The thought flashed through her mind, and she felt tears well up again. She'd thought when her Aunt Cora found her that she might have a chance. If Cora took her away from her mother, the shack they lived in, the drugged-out men who made her stomach roll, she might have known what being normal felt like. But her mother had found Cora's number hidden under her mattress and burned it on the stove, laughing at Jinx as she did it.

Her mother said no one was taking away her free ride.

Jinx had tried to grab the paper from her mother, but it was too late. The number was already gone. She'd been so angry, she'd shoved her mother, something she'd never done before. Her mother had fallen back over a kitchen chair and hit the wall with a thud. She'd looked up at Jinx, the hate in her eyes so clear.

"The next time one of them asks," her mother said, "I'm taking the money."

Jinx knew exactly what her mother meant. She ran back to her room and slammed the door, then threw a change of clothes into her backpack. Her mother banged on the door, screaming at her to unlock it or she'd pay. Jinx pushed open the window and climbed out, then hurried down the street. At the corner, she took one final look at the dilapidated shack before whirling around and running as fast as she could.

The door to the barn opened, startling her out of her thoughts, and she scrambled to hide the metal under the straw in the corner. She heard someone walking, then at the far end of the barn, a light flickered on and she saw the man with the scar carrying a lantern in one hand and a burlap bag in the other.

Jinx's heart dropped into her stomach. Another kid!

The man walked to the center of the barn and pulled down a thick rope with a big hook on it from one of the overhead rafters, then turned the bag upside down, dumping a wild hog on the ground. Blood seeped from a bullet hole right between the hog's eyes.

A breath of relief rushed out of Jinx and the man looked over at her and grinned. "Thought I had another one of you in here, didn't you? Not this time. All I got this time is dinner."

He grabbed the pig by its hind legs, which were bound with rope, and lifted it off the ground, suspending it from the hook. He stuck a bucket underneath the hog, then pulled a huge knife from his back pocket and made a cut down the center of the hog's stomach. Entrails tumbled out of the hog's body and fell into the bucket below, making a sickening plopping sound as they hit.

Jinx turned her head away and heard the man chuckle.

"Ain't got the stomach for it, do you?" he asked. "Did you know that if you hung a live hog up in the forest and cut its stomach open, it would still be alive when other animals started to eat it? I'm guessing a human would be the same."

Jinx's stomach rolled and she clenched her eyes shut and covered her ears with her hands. She waited a long time before the light went off. She opened her eyes and stared into the darkness but she couldn't see anything.

"Is he gone?" she asked.

"Yes," Spider said.

"What about the…uh…"

"He took the hog and the bucket, too."

Thank God. Even though the dead hog couldn't do anything to her, the thought of it hanging there dripping was enough to make her nauseous. Which is exactly what the monster intended.

"Jinx?" Spider said. "You still working on the key?"

"Yeah. I'm still working on it."

"I think I have one nail loosened a little."

"That's good. If you can work it out, keep it. We can use it as a weapon."

Jinx concentrated on the metal again. When she was out of here, she'd find her aunt, even if she had to go to North Carolina to do it. They were going to get out of here. She was going to find her aunt.

She was going to know what normal was. So help her God.

Hustle took a bite out of a cinnamon bun and hopped

in Shaye's SUV. He'd awakened in decent spirits, especially given that he'd been attacked the night before, but still seemed nervous about being in her apartment. Their first stop had been a store to pick up Hustle a new cell phone, then Shaye had taken them to a café she liked for breakfast.

"Where are we going?" Hustle asked.

"We're going to get you fixed up. I promised you that I'd find you a new place to stay, right?"

He nodded, looking a little guilty. "I don't want you to think I'm being ungrateful or nothing. Your place is great. That's probably the best I've slept since my mom died. But I don't want to cause you no trouble, especially with that guy after me."

Shaye pulled away from the curb of the café. "I don't think you're being ungrateful at all. Neither one of us wants another run-in with the kidnapper, so we're both going to be extra careful. You've seen my place and know it's secure. Now we'll get you a safe place and you'll be sneaky about getting there tonight."

"Okay."

She smiled at him. "Besides, while we seem to get along fine, I get the feeling that both of us prefer our own space."

"Yeah. I never minded being alone. I used to draw a lot, before…and read."

"Make me a promise."

He frowned. "Tell me what it is first."

"Okay. Promise me that when all this is over, you'll consider some options I can give you. I'm not saying you have to take me up on them, but at least give them some thought."

He stared at her for a couple seconds, then nodded. "I guess it don't hurt to think about something."

"Good. Then let's get your place lined up and get to work."

She drove to the west edge of Bywater and pulled into a hotel parking lot. The building was old and needed a coat of paint, but it was structurally sound, and more importantly, wasn't being used for the daily operation of the criminal sort of enterprise. In short terms, they didn't rent by the hour.

"Wait here," Shaye said and headed inside.

A large balding man with a perpetually red face looked over from the front desk as she walked in and smiled. "Shaye," he said, and extended his hand as she stepped up to the desk. "I saw that news piece about that serial killer. I'm glad you're still walking among us."

"Me too. How are you doing, Saul?"

"Oh, I'm doing fine. I guess the work you did on that insurance scammer for me was like a good night's sleep in comparison."

Shaye nodded. "The work I did when I was with Breaux was definitely less, uh, invigorating, we'll call it."

He raised one eyebrow. "'Dangerous' was the word I was thinking of. So what can I do for you? I doubt you're down in Bywater for a social call."

"No. I came to ask a favor. The kind I pay for, of course."

He frowned. "If you mean information or something, I don't know of anything sketchy going on around here. I mean, not outside the norm, anyway. Besides, I'd never accept money from you for information."

"It's not that. I have a friend, a client, and he's in trouble."

"What kind of trouble?"

"Someone attacked him last night. I need a safe place for him to stay."

"Well, ain't no one coming through that door that me or Roscoe don't see, that's for sure. And I got a nine-millimeter that says they better draw fast and fire accurately. I guess that's safe enough."

"I have no doubt. There's something else you need to know. This client has been living on the streets, and he's underage."

Saul's eyes widened. "Are you sure it's a good idea, you getting mixed up with him?"

"He's a good kid who's gotten handed a raw deal. He helped me with the Frederick case."

"You say he's a client? What does he need you for?"

Shaye gave him a brief rundown of the missing street kids. He listened intently, then shook his head when she was done.

"That's horrible," he said. "I don't even like to think why someone would...you know."

"Yes, I do. Anyway, I wouldn't feel right having him stay here without you knowing the facts. I don't know his real name or age, but I'm certain he's not eighteen. He's been living on the streets but he cares about this girl so much he sacrificed pride to ask for help."

Saul nodded. "I trust you. If you vouch for him then I got a place he can stay. There's a vacant room right above the lobby. If anyone comes after him they'll have to get through the lobby first."

"That sounds great." She pulled out her wallet and handed him a credit card. "I don't know how long he'll be here. Just put any expense on the card."

He swiped her card and handed it back to her. "Let me know if there's anything else I can do."

"Just keep an eye out. If you see anyone hanging around who wasn't here before, let me know."

"You got it." He handed her two card keys. "I figure you should have one. In case."

"Thanks." She stuck the spare card in her back pocket, headed outside, and rapped on the passenger window of the SUV. "Come on."

Hustle climbed out and followed her inside. Shaye waved a hand at Saul. "This is Saul. He owns the hotel. Saul, this is my friend Hustle."

"Nice to meet you," Saul said, and held out his hand.

Hustle hesitated for a moment, then stepped forward and shook it. "You too," he said.

"If you need anything," Saul said, "let me know. There's someone up here 24-7."

"Thanks," Hustle said, his gaze dropped to the floor.

"Let's go check out your room," Shaye said and headed for the stairs. They went up one flight and she handed him the room card. "It's this one here," she said, indicating the room that was over the lobby.

Hustle opened the door and they stepped inside. The room was small but probably looked like a palace to Hustle. It had a kitchenette on the right side and a table with two chairs on the left. To the left was a living room with a couch, chair, and television mounted on the wall. Beyond that was a tiny bedroom with connected bath. The entire thing probably wasn't four hundred square feet, but it was clean and had everything Hustle needed.

Hustle walked through the room, looking around, then opened some of the cabinets in the kitchen, checking out the dishes, pots, and pans. "This is great," he said. "But this kind of place is expensive. You're already working for free. I can't let you pay for this too."

"It's a business expense," she said.

"But you ain't got no income. I know how business works. I ain't paying you nothing, so this would come out of your pocket."

Shaye thought for a moment, then before she could change her mind, blurted out what she'd been thinking. "I don't say this to sound crass, but I'm loaded. I mean the kind of rich that renting this place for a year wouldn't even make a tiny nick in. My grandfather set up a trust fund for me years ago. I don't do this job for the money."

Hustle stared at her for a bit, clearly uncertain what to say. "But you can't do it for free all the time. Everybody's money runs out sometime."

"I don't do it for free all the time. Lord knows, the IRS

wouldn't like that one bit, but you know how some attorneys and doctors take cases on without charging?"

Hustle shook his head. "That's charity. I don't want no handout."

"It's not charity. It's call pro bono work."

"What's that mean?"

"It's work that professionals take on for no pay because they consider the work to be for the larger public good. Someone out there is kidnapping people. Everyone benefits when he's behind bars."

"Maybe, but it seems like I'm benefiting more than most."

"You're a critical part of my investigation. I need you on the streets, but I can't in good conscience have you there if I don't think you're safe. So far that we know of, this guy has taken kids at night and probably on their way to their nighttime place. In order for me to concentrate on the job, I need to know that you're safe at night. I need you back here every night before dark. That means leaving the docks or wherever early because you need to circle around and double back to make sure no one is following you."

Hustle looked around the apartment, and Shaye could see the longing in his expression. He desperately wanted this, but his pride was still strong. Finally he nodded. "Okay, but only until we find Jinx."

"Until we find Jinx," Shaye agreed, but she already had plans for Hustle once everything was over. Assuming he took one of her options. "I picked this hotel because I did some work for Saul and know him. You can trust him. He knows a little about your situation and he's going to be keeping a watch, too. If you see anything you think looks suspicious, tell him. He'll know if it's normal for this area or not. If something's not normal, then you call me."

"You trust him?"

"I do. He kept this place going through the rebuilding and never let it get filled up with crime like others. He did twenty years in the Marine Corps and his son is a decorated fighter pilot. If someone comes after you, rest assured, he will protect you with lethal force. He doesn't like injustice."

"Marine, huh? That's cool."

"So you'll stay here at night, but get here before dark, right?"

"Yeah."

"I'll be talking to you during the day, but when you get back here, I want you to text and let me know you're in for the night." She pulled her wallet out of her purse and handed him two hundred dollars in twenties. "This is money for food or whatever. I need you to get enough to eat."

He thrust the money back at her. "It's too much. I could eat for a month off that."

Shaye pushed his hand back toward him. "I wasn't finished. There's a clinic on the corner. When you leave here, go have your ankle checked. I need you in top shape. If the man comes after you again, you won't get away if you're limping or weak from dehydration or hunger."

Hustle dropped his gaze to the floor and nodded. Then he looked back up at her. "I'm gonna find a way to pay you back. For everything."

"If that's what you need to do, then that's fine. But we've got plenty of time to figure it out. Let's go grab your skateboard out of my car and you can go get that ankle looked at."

"What are you going to do?"

"I have something I need to work on with Jackson," she said, feeling guilty about lying, even though it wasn't completely untrue. Jackson had told her about Father Michael, and he did know about her plan to follow him. He just didn't like it. "Are you going to the docks after the clinic?"

He nodded. "I keep hoping I'll find out something."

"And you might. You might also see someone hanging around and make a connection."

"I need to warn them all about the guy, too."

"You do. Tell them he was waiting for you and that wherever they're staying at night might not be safe anymore. If they all change locations, it would slow him down at least."

She pulled her keys out of her pocket. "I'm going to get out of here. Call me if you find out anything. I've, uh, got a meeting today, so if it goes to voice mail, leave a message and I'll call you as soon as I can."

"Okay." He grabbed her arm as she started to leave. "Be careful. He might know about you, too."

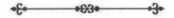

Hustle exited the clinic, trying to walk normally. Walking with a limp would be automatically perceived as a weakness, and a good hunter would exploit it. The doctor said it was only a sprain and had wrapped it and given him some aspirin to take for pain. The wrap was tight and limited movement, making walking normally a challenge. The pain was slight compared to the night before, so he pocketed the aspirin. He didn't need it now, but after a day of using his ankle, he might tonight.

Instead of skating to the docks, he chose to walk, thinking how lucky he was that Shaye knew someone with a hotel in Bywater. It was a good location for him—far enough from the docks that he could easily evade someone trying to follow him when he left, but close enough to walk there every day.

He almost wished he were with Shaye instead of going to the docks. She'd been evasive this morning when he'd asked about her plans. There was something she wasn't telling him, but then, he didn't have the right to know everything she did. For all he knew she had other clients she had to do work for as well. People who were actually paying her.

He shook his head. The money bothered him. Sure, Shaye had said she was loaded and he didn't think she was lying. According to the Internet, her grandfather was one of the richest and most powerful people in the state. But that didn't mean she should work for free. She wasn't Batman. No one was. Although the thought of a masked hero bringing justice to New Orleans was a cool one.

When this was over, he'd figure out a way to pay her back, even if it meant a couple of dollars a week for the rest of his life. It would be worth it. Shaye was a good person who put herself at risk to help people. He'd never met anyone like her before. Until he did, he'd started to think most everyone only cared about themselves and getting ahead.

Several kids were skating at the dock when he arrived. He'd wondered if anyone would show, given that they'd agreed to change up their routines, but change was hard, especially when skating was usually the only positive interaction they had with other people. He headed for the bank, waving them over as he went. They all picked up their boards and formed a circle.

"What's up?" Boots asked. "You heard something?"

"No," Hustle said. "Someone tried to grab me last night."

"What?"

"Fuck, man!"

"No shit?"

"Where?"

They all spoke at once, and Hustle could feel the heightened anxiety in the group surrounding him.

"I was headed to my spot last night and some dude came at me from an abandoned building."

"You didn't hear him?" Reaper asked.

Hustle shook his head. "Not until he was almost on me. He was wearing some sort of slippers made like boots. They didn't make any sound. I turned at the last minute and held my hand up to block him. He had a needle in his hand."

The kids started grumbling again and looked at one another, their fear apparent.

"I swung my board around," Hustle continued, "and clocked him hard enough to get away, but I was lucky."

"How are we supposed to be safe," Shadow said, "when this guy can follow someone like Hustle and Jinx and Scratch, and they don't even know they're being followed?"

"He wasn't following me," Hustle said. "He was waiting for me. He already knew where I was going. My guess is it was the same for Jinx and Scratch."

"That means he's been watching us for a while," Boots said. "Collecting data a little at a time so we wouldn't notice, then putting it all together for an attack. That's beyond fucked up. It's like he's…"

"Hunting us," Hustle said. "That's exactly what he's doing."

"Then he already knows everything about us?" Shadow's voice rose several octaves. "What are we supposed to do? There's nowhere safe."

"Don't panic," Hustle said, although he didn't blame the kid one bit. "We just need to do what Boots said yesterday—change everything up. That means even where we sleep."

"What about our stuff?" Reaper asked. "I mean, ain't no one got much but we all got a little something we don't want to lose."

"Get your stuff and find somewhere new," Hustle said. "But do it during the day. I know it's risky, but night is riskier. At night, there's fewer people around and not enough light on the streets."

"He's right," Boots said. "If this guy's been watching us for a while then he probably knows where all of us stay. Hell, we're screwing up now. We were supposed to change our routine and meet at the drugstore, but here we all are, skating at the docks like nothing's changed."

Hustle looked around at the construction crews working on a commercial building at the far end of the parking lot. "During the week, when the crew is working, we're probably okay here. But after you change sleeping places, if you come here, you should switch up your route every day."

"I thought he only took people at night?" Shadow asked.

"He tried to take me at night," Hustle said, "and I think that's when he got Jinx, but we don't know for sure. Doesn't matter anyway. I'll bet he's watching during the day, so no doing the same thing twice. Got it?"

They looked around at one another and nodded.

"We should all leave now and get our stuff…find new places to stay at night," Boots said. "He can't follow all of us, right?"

"That's a good idea," Reaper said.

Boots dropped his board. "Anyone that's not coming to the docks for a while, meet tomorrow at the drugstore at noon. If anyone sees the others, fill them in."

"I think Bugs is doing dishes at that café today," Shadow said. "I usually meet up with him in the afternoon for lunch. They let him have the leftovers from the buffet."

Boots nodded. "Tomorrow then. I don't have to tell you all to watch your backs. We're not going to let this guy win, okay?"

Boots stepped on his board and kicked away, the others following suit, except Reaper, who hung back with Hustle.

"Listen, man," Reaper said, "I didn't want to say anything in front of the others, in case I was wrong, but I saw a board that looked like Jinx's in the window of that pawnshop in Arabi."

"The one on Saint Claude?"

"Yeah, that's the one."

"You get a good look at it?"

Reaper nodded. "Black. A dragon with green eyes on the bottom. Red wheels."

Hustle ran a hand over his head. "That sounds like hers. Why would it be in a pawnshop?"

"I don't know, but I was thinking…maybe that dude didn't get Jinx. Maybe she sold her board and cut out."

A flicker of anger passed through Hustle. "She wouldn't have left without telling me."

Reaper raised one eyebrow. "Wouldn't she? C'mon man, none of us really knows each other. We ran out on our families. I mean, I'm sure we all had good reasons, but still. We're not what regular people consider stable."

"To hell with regular people! I know Jinx, and she

wouldn't have cut out without saying good-bye."

Reaper shrugged. "Maybe. Sure. I guess I was just thinking that it was better for her to have taken off and be safe than that guy to have gotten her, you know?" He clapped Hustle on the back. "I didn't mean to piss you off, man."

"You didn't. Not really. And you're right. It would be better if she left on her own. It's just that something tells me she didn't."

"I hear you. I guess I'm gonna go collect my stuff. You risking it?"

"No. I don't have anything but a couple blankets. It's not worth it. I can get more before winter."

Reaper nodded and held up his fist. "Stay safe."

Hustle bumped Reaper's fist with his own. "You too."

Reaper dropped his board and skated away. Hustle dropped his board and set out, ignoring the twinge in his ankle. The pawnshop was a good distance from the docks. He wanted to get there as fast as possible. When he stopped for a break, he'd send Shaye a text and let her know what he was doing.

CHAPTER ELEVEN

Jackson watched as Shaye pulled her SUV up to the curb two blocks away from Father Michael's church. She pulled out binoculars and trained them on the front entrance. He shook his head and got out of his car, then headed down the sidewalk. Stubborn as they come, he thought. He'd tried to talk her out of this crazy plan the night before, but she refused to let the idea go. Shaye was smart and had the makings of a fine investigator, but following people committing insurance fraud and those who were cheating on their spouse was nothing like surveillance on a violent criminal.

When he got to her car, he leaned over and rapped on the window, causing her to jump. She looked out and lowered the window. "Damn it, Jackson. Are you trying to get yourself shot?"

"Are you?"

"I'm doing my job, just like we discussed last night."

"Uh-huh." He pulled open the door. "Out of the car."

"No!"

"Seriously. Come with me. I have something you need to see."

She glared at him for a couple seconds, then climbed out of her car and followed him down the street to an older model Corolla. He waved at the passenger door and she got in.

"I figured you for more of a V-8 sort of guy," she said as he slid into the driver's seat.

"I am. I have one of those loud trucks with big wheels back at my apartment. But this is the car I use when I'm working."

"Why?"

"Because if you're going to follow someone, you need to be in a vehicle that no one pays attention to, especially if you're combing the less affluent areas of the city. Your SUV is too new, too shiny, and too expensive to go unnoticed by some people, but an older white economy car is practically invisible."

She gave him a grudging nod. "Why aren't you at work?"

"I called in sick. I figured I'd get more work done that way."

"That makes sense. How sad is that?"

He reached into the backseat and grabbed a duffel bag. "Here's something else that makes sense." He reached inside and pulled out a blond wig. "Father Michael has seen you. Put it on."

She looked at the wig and sighed, but lowered the sun visor and slid on the wig. She frowned at the mirror, then flipped the sun visor back up and looked over at him. "No disguise for you?"

"Father Michael's never met me, but if it makes you feel better, I can wear the wig next time."

"If we're working Bourbon Street no one will notice."

He laughed. "Yeah, probably not."

"So, Mr. Expert at Surveillance, what's the plan?"

"Wait for Father Michael to leave and follow him."

She shook her head. "Genius."

He started the car and pulled down the street to get a clear view of the church. "Notice the tinted windows?" he said. "That's why I picked this one. No one can see in."

"I have tinted windows."

"Which makes you look like the Secret Service or one of those rap stars."

"Fine, you've made your point. I am going to consider purchasing a car strictly for following people."

"I know a place that sells late-model white Corollas."

"I bet you do." She pointed at the church. "Front door's opening."

They both lifted binoculars.

"It's Father Michael," she said.

"He's headed for his car. The blue Escort. I checked registration last night."

They watched as Father Michael got into his car and pulled away. Jackson handed Shaye his binoculars and set off after the priest, careful not to get too close. Father Michael drove safely and within the speed limit and presented no trouble as far as following went.

When he turned onto Saint Roch Avenue, Shaye touched his arm. "Slow down. I think I know where he's going."

"Where?"

"To the cemetery."

He nodded. Saint Roch cemetery was two blocks away. He slowed some, allowing a truck to pull out in front of him, but he could still see the blue Escort. It pulled to the curb in front of the entrance to the cemetery and stopped. Jackson moved to the curb a block away and parked, watching as Father Michael exited his car and went into the cemetery.

"Let's go," he said as soon as the priest was out of sight. He grabbed a camera from the back of the car and slung it over his neck as they headed down the sidewalk.

"You gonna ask him to pose?" Shaye asked.

"It's the tourist look. Plus, you never know when you might need to get a shot of something. I'm surprised you don't carry a camera."

She sighed. "It's in the backseat of my rap-mobile. You distracted me."

"Sorry," he said, trying not to smile. It was nice to know he flustered her. It meant he'd gotten beyond the steel wall she had erected for everyone. That was important to him. He liked and respected Shaye and wanted to be a true friend to her.

And maybe more.

He chased those thoughts away. They had no place here and definitely not now. Shaye might have let him past one layer of defense, but that was hardly an open door. She was far more guarded than that.

"Do you want to split up?" she asked as they walked into the cemetery.

"Yeah, that's the quickest way. The goal is to locate him before he sees us. Take out your phone. You can become absorbed in taking pictures if he spots you. Text with a location if you see him."

Shaye nodded and headed off to the right. Jackson set off down a row to the left. At the end of the row, he peered around the corner down the north wall of vaults but saw no sign of Father Michael. He worked his way down the back wall of the cemetery, checking each row for the priest. When he got to the end of the row, he peered around the corner and spotted the priest kneeling in front of one of the wall vaults.

He pulled out his phone and sent Shaye a text.

Back wall. North side. Wall vaults.

A couple seconds later, she texted back.

At chapel. Will check from this angle.

Jackson lifted his camera and stepped around the corner, focusing on the display in the back corner. He glanced sideways at Father Michael as the priest made the sign of the cross and rose from the ground. He touched a wall vault in front of him and Jackson could see his lips moving, then he turned around without even looking Jackson's direction and left. Jackson lowered the camera and pulled out his phone.

Coming your way.

He pressed Send.

On it.

Jackson hurried down the row and located the wall vault that Father Michael had prayed for.

Bradley Thompson
Born August 3, 2001
Died June 2, 2015

He took a picture of the vault, then set out after the priest. When he reached the main aisle that ran down the center of the cemetery, he spotted the priest halfway to the entrance. He waited until the priest was at the entrance, then half jogged down the center aisle. When he got to the front of the cemetery, Shaye was standing off to the side, next to a crypt. He slipped beside her and they watched as the blue Escort drove by. They headed out of the cemetery as the priest's car turned the corner a block away.

"Hurry!" Jackson took off for his car, Shaye sprinting beside him.

They jumped in and he squealed away from the curb.

"There!" Shaye grabbed his arm and pointed down the street as they approached the intersection. "He's going around the block."

Jackson turned and headed toward the street where the Escort had crossed, turned again and caught sight of the priest as he stopped at an intersection. They followed him several more blocks without stopping and finally Shaye sighed.

"He's going back to the church," she said. "We didn't get anything."

"We might have." Jackson drove around the corner to where Shaye's SUV was and parked behind her. "Look at this."

He pulled up the photo he'd taken of the wall vault and showed it to her.

Shaye's eyes widened. "He was only thirteen"

"Died a month ago. It might be nothing, but it's worth checking out."

Shaye started to respond, and her cell phone signaled a text message. She looked at the display and yanked off the wig. "It's Hustle. I've got to run."

"Is everything all right? Do you want me to go with you?"

"He says he has information and we need to meet. He's in enough trouble if people see him with me. He can't afford to be seen with a cop, and the other kids would probably make you as quickly as Hustle did."

He didn't like it but he couldn't argue with the reasoning. "If you need help, let me know. I'm going to stick around here for a bit. See if our friend Father Michael makes any more moves."

"Thanks for the disguise and the car," Shaye said.

"Any time."

She jumped out of the car and hurried to her SUV. Jackson frowned as she pulled away. He hoped Hustle had found out something useful, but at the same time, he wished Shaye didn't have to go down to the docks, which is where he assumed Hustle was. The likelihood of the kidnapper lurking somewhere in the vicinity was high, especially if he was itching for another shot at Hustle. He supposed if pressed, Shaye would pass off talking to Hustle as an extension of her mother's social work, but she was right about Jackson. The street kids would disappear like vapor if they spotted him anywhere near them, and Hustle had already proven that they could easily spot a cop.

He brought up the picture again and pulled out his phone. At least while he was sitting here, he could do some Internet research. Anything deeper would have to wait until he was back at his computer. He typed in the boy's name and hit Search.

A list of hits filled the tiny screen. School events mostly, and an obituary.

He clicked on the obit and read the facts. Two parents, one sister, much loved. Funeral service presided over by Father Michael. He frowned. No cause of death.

He dialed the police department, and the desk sergeant answered. "Hey, this is Lamotte. I need you to do me a favor."

"I thought you were out sick."

"I am, but I was doing some research at home and my Internet's crappy. There's a boy that died last month. I want you to see if we have anything on him."

"Give me the name?"

Jackson gave him the name and heard the sergeant typing.

"You still working the kid case?" the sergeant asked.

"Yeah, but it's going nowhere fast. I'm starting to grasp at straws."

"Sometimes that's all we have. Hold on, something's coming up. Well, what do you know…maybe this is one of those straws that has meaning."

"You got something?"

"Says here the kid committed suicide."

Shaye pulled up to the curb on a less-than-reputable-looking street in the Holy Cross section of the Lower Ninth Ward and Hustle jumped inside. "Your ankle hurting?" she asked, as she'd observed him limping as he made his way over to her car.

"A little," he said. "I probably overdid it, but I wanted to get there fast, you know, and I didn't know if you'd be available. When it started hurting too much, I stopped and called you. It's feeling better now."

Shaye nodded. She understood the often irrational desire to take immediate action, even when it wasn't in your best interest physically or mentally. With help from Eleonore, she'd learn to recognize and control those urges…most of the time. Although she supposed given her excursion this morning, Jackson would have claimed differently.

"What did the clinic say about your ankle?" she asked.

"It's a sprain. Not even a bad one. Should be all right in a week or so."

"If you rest it."

"Yeah, they might have said that too."

He almost managed to sound contrite, and she groaned internally. "God, I'm starting to sound like my mother. Okay, enough about your ankle. Tell me about the skateboard."

Hustle filled her in on what Reaper saw in the pawnshop window. Shaye punched the address into the GPS.

"He didn't know for sure if it was Jinx's board?" she asked as she pulled away.

"No, but the description sounded like hers, and I ain't seen one like it before Jinx." He stared out the window and frowned. "Reaper said maybe that guy didn't get Jinx. That maybe she sold the board and cut out."

"What do you think?"

"I don't think Jinx would have left without saying something. But maybe I'm fooling myself."

"I don't think you are. Look, I found out some things about Jinx last night. I didn't tell you because you already had enough going on and this morning, I had that, uh, meeting to get to."

"What things?"

"My mom found Jinx's aunt. She's here in New Orleans, and I went to see her yesterday." Shaye told Hustle about Cora's search for her sister and niece and how she lost track of Jinx, but left out the worst details of Jinx's life with her mother. That was for Jinx to tell.

"Cancer." Hustle shook his head. "That sucks. She's going to be all right, though?"

"She's really weak from the chemo, but she's in

remission. And she's determined to give Jinx a stable home."

Hustle nodded and was silent for several seconds. "What did you think of her?" he finally asked.

"I liked her. She's smart and strong and she cares about Jinx. She has the money and the time to give Jinx a good life."

"That's cool. Jinx deserves it. She's a good person. I just hope we find her."

"We're not going to stop looking until we do."

He gave her a grateful look. "Yeah."

"Here's the place," Shaye said as she parked.

The street the pawnshop was located on looked like a war zone. Hardly any of the buildings were fit for occupancy, and the ones that still had four walls standing were so damaged the repairs would cost more than they were worth. A scattered few still had signs for businesses, but there were no pedestrians around. It was the sort of place Shaye would normally avoid in the daylight and the dark, but if there was a chance the pawnshop held a clue that could lead to finding Jinx, then it was worth the risk.

As they got out of the SUV, Shaye thought about Jackson's comments on her vehicle, and although she'd been slightly annoyed at the time, what he'd said made good sense. Right now, she could have used a nondescript, lower-end automobile, and as soon as she had a chance, she was going to purchase one. They walked over to the storefront and Hustle pointed to the skateboard in the window.

"It's Jinx's board," Hustle said, his voice registering his excitement. "It's got a deep scratch on the back where she slid across some glass one time. What the hell is it doing here?"

Shaye shook her head. "I don't know. Let's go find out."

She pushed open the door to the pawnshop and headed for the counter. A stocky guy, about thirty years old and maybe six feet tall, gave them the once-over as they approached.

"You looking to buy or sell?" he asked as she stepped up to a glass counter filled with jewelry.

"I'm interested in the skateboard in the window," Shaye said.

"Fifty bucks," the guy said.

"Where did you get it?" Shaye asked.

The guy narrowed his eyes at her. "I bought it. Same as everything else in here."

Shaye pulled out her PI license and showed it to the man. "That board belongs to a missing girl. I'd like to know who sold it. You keep records for the IRS, right?" She doubted most of the purchases ever hit any sort of accounting record, but sometimes even a mention of the IRS had people offering information just so she'd go away.

"This ain't a business selling information. Our customers want privacy, and that's what I give them."

"I can appreciate that. The New Orleans police are looking for the girl, too. I probably ought to let them handle it."

The guy shuffled around a bit. "Hey, how about I give you the seller's name and you take the board…on the house."

Shaye held in a smile. "That's very generous of you."

The guy smirked and went to retrieve the skateboard. He handed it to Shaye.

"Are you going to check your records?" she asked.

"Don't need to," he said. "The seller was Rick Rivette."

Hustle stiffened, and Shaye knew he recognized the name. "Did he tell you where he got it?" Shaye asked.

"No. And I didn't ask."

"Part of your policy?"

He smiled. "Seems like a good one."

Shaye nodded. "Thanks for the board and the info."

He turned around and walked into an office behind the counter, not bothering to respond. Shaye headed outside, Hustle right on her heels. Before he even shut the door to her SUV, Hustle was already ranting.

"That piece of shit, Rick Rivette!" Hustle clenched his hands. "If he hurt Jinx, I swear to God…"

"Slow down. We don't know how he came to have the board. Tell me who he is."

"Johnny Rivette's nephew. He's sixteen or seventeen and nothing but a thug."

Shaye frowned. The name sounded familiar but she couldn't place why. Then suddenly it hit her. "Johnny Rivette was arrested for racketeering, but the prosecutor couldn't make the case."

"That's the one. New Orleans's own godfather, 'cept he's not big enough to run the French Quarter. He just lords over this side—Bywater, the Ninth Ward."

Shaye looked down the street and bit her lower lip. The situation was far less than optimal. One didn't just accost a gangster's nephew and start demanding information. On the other hand, Rick was the only lead they had. She considered her options and finally settled on the play she thought would work best.

"Do you know where to find Johnny Rivette?" she asked.

His eyes widened. "Are you shitting me?"

"I wish I were."

He shook his head. "You can't just walk up on Johnny Rivette and get information out of him like you did that pawnshop guy. Rivette ain't afraid of no police or the IRS. The devil himself probably couldn't even get Rivette to flinch."

"I don't plan on threatening him. I'm hoping he'll give me the answers I want out of the goodness of his heart."

He stared at her in disbelief. "Man, I don't know what you been smoking but if you think he'll tell you something, then I ain't gonna stop you. He has a place in Bywater in one of the old warehouses. I think he lives there. I'm sure he does business there."

"You know where it is?"

"Yeah, I can show you."

"Then let's get going. We're burning daylight."

CHAPTER TWELVE

Corrine pushed open the door to the police department and rushed inside, Eleonore right behind her.

"Ms. Archer." The desk sergeant jumped up to greet her. "They're waiting for you in the conference room. Let me take you back."

Corrine glanced over at Eleonore as they walked down the hallway and into a conference room that already contained Police Chief Bernard and a man and woman Corrine didn't recognize. They went silent when Corrine and Eleonore entered the room.

"Has something happened to Shaye?" Corrine asked. "Someone tell me something?"

It couldn't be about Pierce. Corrine had talked to her father just fifteen minutes before she'd gotten the call from the police, asking her to come down to the station.

The chief shot a dirty look at the other man, then looked back at Corrine. "I'm so sorry, Ms. Archer. Nothing has happened to Shaye. That should have been conveyed to you when you were requested to come here."

"I don't understand," Corrine said. "Whoever I talked to said it was important that I get here right away."

"And it is," Chief Bernard said. "Please, won't you sit down and let us explain. This is Detective Grayson, who didn't do a very good job when he spoke to you, and this is Dr. Melissa Wells, our medical examiner."

Corrine shot at look at Eleonore as they took seats at the conference table. She didn't need to spell things out for her friend. When the chief of police calls you in for a meeting with him, a detective, and the medical examiner, something was seriously wrong. Chief Bernard took a seat across the table from Corrine and Eleonore, and Grayson and Wells followed suit. All of them kept glancing at one another. Corrine felt her back tighten. Whatever was going on, she wished they'd just spit it out.

Chief Bernard opened a folder and looked across the table at Corrine. "Ms. Archer, do you know a woman by the name of Lydia Johnson?"

Corrine slowly shook her head. "It doesn't sound familiar, but over the years, I've seen hundreds of people, if not more."

"I understand," Chief Bernard said. "I don't think she was a client of yours, but I wanted to verify whether or not you knew her before I explained the situation."

"Please," Corrine said. "I can tell something is wrong. Just tell me. As long as my family is safe, I can deal with anything else."

Chief Bernard nodded. "Two days ago, paramedics responded to a 911 in the Lower Ninth Ward. A woman's body was found in an alleyway, a needle in her arm. She was already dead when the paramedics arrived, and no ID was on the body. The body went to the morgue and police canvassed the area with photos to see if they could get an ID on her. When her body was processed by the medical examiner, her DNA was entered into our database."

"You use it to match missing persons," Corrine said.

"Yes, ma'am," Chief Bernard said. "Detective Grayson located a bartender who identified the woman as Lydia Johnson. In a kitchen drawer where she lived, officers found an expired driver's license that provided a physical match."

"I don't understand what all this has to do with me," Corrine said.

Chief Bernard glanced over at the medical examiner. "We also got a hit on her DNA. It wasn't a hundred percent match, but it indicated a strong familial relationship. I'm sorry to tell you this, but Lydia Johnson was Shaye's mother."

Corrine gasped and her left hand flew over her mouth. Eleonore grabbed her other hand and squeezed. "Oh my God," Corrine said as she looked back and forth between the medical examiner and Chief Bernard. "You're sure?"

Chief Bernard looked at the medical examiner, who cleared her throat.

"Given the circumstances, I ran the tests three times to be certain," Dr. Wells said. "I'm positive the tests are correct, and given the strength of the match, I have no doubt that Ms. Johnson is Shaye's mother."

"When Dr. Wells called me with her findings," Chief Bernard continued, "I sent my detectives back to Ms.

Johnson's house to do a more thorough search." He pulled an old piece of wrinkled paper out of the folder and pushed it across the table to Corrine. "They found this."

Corrine pulled the paper over in front of her and stared down at it. "It's a hospital record."

She ran her fingers over the worn document.

Baby Johnson
Mother Lydia Rose Johnson
Father Unknown
Born August 5, 1991

Corrine choked back a cry. "She didn't even name her."

"I've already checked birth records," Chief Bernard said. "There's no record of Lydia Johnson giving birth. The detectives also found this." He pushed a yellowed photograph over to Corrine.

The girl in the picture was probably two years old, but there was no doubt in Corrine's mind that it was Shaye. The eyes, chin, and nose were the same even today. Tears welled up in her eyes and she felt Eleonore's arm slip around her shoulders as they started to fall.

"But Shaye was educated," Corrine said. "She knew how to read. Knew basic math."

"Schools in the Lower Ninth probably would have let her in without any records," Chief Bernard said. "There are lots of home births in the ward. Not a lot of recordkeeping. We'll attempt to locate school records, but I wouldn't expect much with the damage from Katrina."

"I appreciate anything you can find," Corrine said.

"You can keep those documents," Chief Barnard said. "I've made copies for our records."

"Thank you."

Chief Barnard glanced at Detective Grayson. "There's something else that is likely to arise. I've issued a gag order on my department and Dr. Wells has done the same, but the likelihood of this remaining a secret is probably slim."

Corrine's stomach turned and resentment coursed through her. "And everyone will be dissecting Shaye's life all over again."

"I'm so sorry," Chief Barnard said. "What you've accomplished with Shaye is extraordinary. She's a remarkable young woman and I wish she didn't have to deal with what's coming. I know processing through this will be hard, but if you need anything at all, please let me know."

"Thank you for giving this your personal attention and for attempting to keep it confidential," Corrine said. "If that's all, could I please have a moment alone with Eleonore?"

"Of course." Chief Barnard rose from his chair and ushered the detective and medical examiner out of the room.

Corrine managed to hold it together until the door closed behind them, then she collapsed onto the table, sobbing so hard she could barely breathe.

"You've faced worse than this," Eleonore said, her arm

draped across Corrine's shoulders. "We always knew this day might come."

"What if she remembers?" Corrine cried. "What if her mother is the one that did all those things to her? Or allowed them to happen? Same thing."

"Shaye can handle it."

Corrine choked back a cry and rose up to look at Eleonore. "You can promise that?"

"Yes, I can, and you know I would never lie to you. Shaye is so much stronger than I think either of us knows. We'll handle this, the three of us. Just like we have everything else. One day at a time, Corrine. We'll get through it one day at a time."

Corrine leaned over to hug her friend. "I don't know what I would do without you."

"That makes two of us."

Jackson entered the police station, and the desk sergeant gave him a once-over.

"I thought you were sick," the desk sergeant said.

"I started feeling better," Jackson said as he scanned the room, praying that for once Vincent had found something to do outside of the station. The room was oddly empty, only a couple of officers at their desks. "Where is everyone?"

"Vincent's out to lunch and to 'look into' some leads on your case, which in my estimation means he's hitting the casino after he eats his way through enough food for three people. Everyone else is probably holed up in closets and break rooms discussing the latest news."

"What happened?"

The desk sergeant glanced around and leaned toward Jackson. "We're on gag order, so no repeating this."

"Yeah, sure." Probably another illegal indiscretion by a local politician. He looked up as the hallway door opened and gave a start when Corrine Archer rushed by him, closely guarded by Eleonore Blanchet.

Shit. It must be something involving Pierce Archer.

As soon as the door closed behind them, Jackson motioned to the desk sergeant to continue.

"Cops brought a junkie to the morgue couple days ago. Turns out it was Shaye Archer's mother."

Jackson straightened as if he'd been slapped. "They're sure?"

"The medical examiner has been in the chief's office all morning. Grayson and his men searched her apartment and brought some stuff back with them. Chief Bernard wouldn't have called Corrine Archer to the station unless he was sure."

A million thoughts ran through Jackson's mind, and all of them concerned Shaye and how she was going to take the news. "This is going to get out," he said.

"Only a matter of time," the desk sergeant agreed. "It's too big a story. Someone's bound to tell." He shook his head. "That poor girl. She's been through so much already and it's a damned miracle the kind of person she turned out to be. I hate that she's got more to deal with."

"Me too."

The desk sergeant narrowed his eyes at Jackson. "You've gotten friendly with her, haven't you?"

"I guess so. As friendly as she allows people to be, anyway."

"She's cautious. Can't hardly blame her for that."

"No. You can't. Thanks for telling me. I won't say a word."

Jackson headed to his desk and plopped into his chair. What a bomb drop. He had no doubt that Shaye was a strong person. He'd witnessed it himself, but this kind of news was going to be rough.

What if she remembers?

The thought flashed through his mind and he clutched at the armrests of his chair. This could be the thing that brought it all back, and if her mother was responsible for what Shaye had been through… He ran his hand through his hair. The sergeant had said the woman was a junkie. That spelled all kinds of bad things.

You're getting ahead of yourself.

He sat up straight and rolled himself up to his desk. No use panicking before it was required. If Shaye started remembering, then he'd be there for her and help in any way possible, assuming she let him of course. If she didn't want his help, then she had her mother and Eleonore, and both of them knew more about handling the emotional stress that Shaye would experience far more than he did. She had two of the most qualified people in the state supporting her and enough money to insulate herself from the media storm if it got to that point. She'd be fine.

He was going to keep telling himself that.

CHAPTER THIRTEEN

Shaye parked in front of the warehouse Hustle indicated but didn't get out of the SUV. She had thought about this confrontation the entire drive over and still had no idea if what she was doing was a smart move.

"It's not too late to change your mind," Hustle said.

"This is the only lead we have."

"I know, and I want to find out where Rick got the board, but if Johnny Rivette is behind all this, we're volunteering for death by going in there and asking questions."

"I'm volunteering." She handed him the keys. "You're not. Do you know how to drive?"

Hustle's eyes widened and he nodded. "Yeah, sort of."

"Good. Take the truck around the block and park at the far end."

He shook his head. "I ain't letting you go in there by yourself."

"Yes, you are. The best way to help me is to stay here and wait. If I don't come out in fifteen minutes, call Jackson. I put his number in your phone."

"Fifteen minutes is about fourteen more than he needs

to cap you."

She opened the door and hopped out. "I'll take my chances."

"Shaye—wait! What are you going to say?"

"The truth."

Hustle stared at her as if she'd lost her mind. He probably wasn't far off base. She shut the door before he could launch another argument and headed for the door to the warehouse. She waited until Hustle had driven down the block and around the corner, then rang the doorbell. Only seconds later, the door flew open and a big guy with a shaved head covered in tattoos stared at her. Clearly he filled the bodyguard position.

"What do you want?" he asked.

"I need to speak to Rick Rivette."

He narrowed his eyes at her. "What about?"

"About a skateboard he pawned."

"You the skateboard police?"

"No. I'm not the police at all. I'm a private investigator."

"Well, Rick don't live here and Mr. Rivette don't talk to cops or anything like 'em. That includes skinny bitch private investigators."

He started to close the door and she put a hand out. "The girl who owned that skateboard is missing. Rick can talk to me or I can turn everything I have over to the cops. Your choice."

He smirked. "You think I'm scared of the cops? You got it all wrong, sweetheart."

"Who's there?" A man's voice sounded from behind the door.

"Just some broad asking about Rick and some skateboard. Nothing you need to bother with."

"Let me be the judge of that," the man said.

The bodyguard stepped out of the way and a man in his forties wearing a black suit stepped into the doorway. "You have questions about my nephew?"

"Yes. Mr. Rivette? I'm not here to cause any trouble."

The bodyguard snorted. "Like you could."

Rivette shot him a disapproving look and gestured at her to come inside. Shaye hesitated for a second, then stepped through the doorway.

The interior of the building was in stark contrast to the grungy outside. The foyer of the warehouse had a marble floor and ornate wood walls. Double doors to the right were open, exposing an office. A staircase at the back of the foyer led upstairs. Rivette walked into the office and took a seat behind the desk, waving at the chair across from him. Shaye took a seat in one of the chairs. The bodyguard moved to the side of Rivette, his arms crossed.

Rivette looked up at the bodyguard. "There were some problems in the back. I need you to check on them."

The bodyguard shot Shaye a dirty look and headed out of the office.

"Please excuse my associate's manners," Rivette said. "My business doesn't usually attract ladies, especially in this area of town."

"What business is that?" Shaye asked.

"Oh, a little of this and a little of that. Real estate, import/export...all of it tedious and nothing particularly interesting."

He delivered the reply with a confident smile that basically said "I'm humoring you."

"You said you needed to talk to my nephew?" Rivette asked.

"Yes. He sold a skateboard to a pawnshop. I'd like to find out where he got it."

"What makes you think it wasn't his to begin with?"

"Because it belonged to a missing girl I was hired to find."

Rivette leaned back in his chair. "I see. And you think my nephew attacked this girl?"

"Right now, I don't think anything at all, except that the sooner I find the girl the better. That's why I need information."

"Fair enough." Rivette picked up his cell phone and made a call. "Send Rick to my office." He placed the phone back on his desk. "He'll be here in a moment. Then you can see for yourself and make your own judgment."

"You don't think he did it," Shaye said.

"I think my nephew is weak, stupid, and lazy. Attacking someone requires action, and making a body disappear so that even a private investigator can't easily locate it requires a certain level of intelligence. Selling the victim's personal items to a pawnshop requires a huge lack of intelligence."

He shook his head. "I can't imagine my nephew having

the intelligence or putting forth enough effort to pull off something like what you're suggesting. I'm sure it won't take more than a minute of conversation for you to form the same conclusion."

A couple seconds later, a teen boy entered the office. He was about five feet ten and maybe a hundred forty pounds soaking wet. He definitely wasn't the man who attacked Hustle. As much as Shaye hated to admit it, Johnny Rivette appeared to be right about his nephew. The teen was hardly imposing

Rivette waved a hand at Shaye. "This lady would like to ask you some questions, and you'll be happy to answer her."

Shaye looked up at Rick. "You sold a skateboard to a pawnshop. Black with a dragon on the bottom."

He shuffled a bit and nodded.

"Where did you get it?"

"Found it."

"Can you tell me where?"

He shrugged. "I don't remember."

"The hell you don't," Rivette said. "Answer the question."

The teen glanced at his uncle and Shaye could tell he didn't want to answer.

"Off Rampart somewhere," he said finally. "I don't remember the exact street."

"What district?" Shaye asked. Rampart was a long street and ran through several districts.

"Lower Ninth," he grumbled.

Rivette shook his head. "You've been hanging around those potheads again, haven't you? How many times are we going to have this conversation?"

"I guess at least once more," Rick said.

Rivette stood up and slapped him on the back of the head. "Don't disrespect me in front of guests." He looked at Shaye as he took his seat again. "Do you have any more questions?"

"You found the skateboard on the street?" Shaye asked.

"In an alley between buildings. It was sorta under some cardboard. Probably why no one saw it."

"What day was this?"

"Last Friday."

"Did you find anything else or see anything that looked odd?"

Rick looked confused. "I don't guess so. I mean, it's the Lower Ninth so shit's not normal or nothing."

Shaye pulled up a picture of Jinx on her cell phone and showed it to Rick. "Have you ever seen this girl?"

Rick stared at the screen, then shook his head. "I don't know her."

He's lying.

Shaye was as certain about that as she was that the sun had risen that morning. "You sure?" She held the phone up higher.

He didn't even look at it again. "I said I don't know her. Can I leave now? I'm hungry."

Rivette looked at Shaye and she nodded. She wasn't

going to get anything else out of him. Once he'd left the room, Shaye pushed her phone across the desk to Rivette. "Have you seen her before?"

Rivette picked up the phone and studied it. "Pretty. I assume this is your missing girl?"

"Yes."

He pushed the phone back across the desk. "I've never seen her before."

Rivette appeared to be telling the truth, but then, he'd had decades of experience lying and was pretty much an expert. Shaye knew she wasn't going to get anything else out of him and antagonizing him seemed like a bad idea, so she rose from her chair.

"Thank you for your help, Mr. Rivette," she said.

"Of course," he said as he rose. "I hope you find your missing girl."

"Me too."

She headed outside and looked down the street. Hustle was parked one block over, and she heard the engine fire up as soon as she stepped out of the building. She started up the sidewalk toward the corner and waved Hustle onto the side street. He made the turn and pulled to a stop. She jumped in the passenger's side.

"Go down a couple blocks and then I can take over," she said.

Shaye was certain Rick wasn't the person who attacked Hustle, but she wasn't taking any chances. She didn't want anyone in Rivette's building to see Hustle with her. Her cell phone vibrated and she saw her mother's name come up on the display. She tucked it back in her pocket. If it was important, Corrine would leave a message. If it wasn't important, it could wait.

Hustle gripped the steering wheel and increased speed slightly, his brow creased in concentration. It was obvious to Shaye that he understood the mechanics of driving a car but wasn't comfortable with it, especially given that he hadn't asked a single question about Rick Rivette yet. It was hard to get experience driving when your main means of transportation was a skateboard and you had no adults around teaching you. He continued down two more blocks, then pulled over and changed places with her.

"Did you find out anything?" he asked as he shut the passenger door.

"Not much." She told him what Rick said.

"You think he's telling the truth?"

"The location fits with my idea that the kidnapper took her when she was on her way to her sleeping space. Assuming he used the same tactic he tried on you—rushing her from an abandoned building—she could have either dropped the board or been knocked off of it and it slid under the cardboard where Rick found it."

"That's true."

"The one thing I know for sure, Rick definitely isn't the kidnapper."

"No," Hustle agreed. "He's scrawny."

"I showed him a picture of Jinx and asked if he'd ever seen her. He said he hadn't, but I could tell he was lying. Have you ever seen Rick hanging around Jinx or at the docks?"

"No. He's usually with a bunch of potheads in the Lower Ninth. He's definitely not a skater."

"If he's usually in the Lower Ninth, he could have seen Jinx there before, maybe followed her. Do you think there could have been a second person around when you were attacked?"

Hustle frowned. "I didn't see or hear anyone else. I looked back once I got away, but there's not much light so I couldn't see anything. If there was a second guy, why wouldn't he come out and help while I was fighting?"

"I don't know. Maybe because you got away too quickly. Maybe he's not the muscle. You said Rick was a thug, but he definitely doesn't have the mass to go around starting fights."

Hustle nodded. "He just throws around his uncle's name and people leave him alone."

"I can see that. His uncle is a rather interesting character."

Hustle's eyes widened. "You met Johnny?"

Shaye nodded. "I can see why his name makes people nervous. His public persona is all polish and manners, which is either arrogance or confidence. I tend to favor the second given his ability to avoid prosecution."

"He's bad news."

"Do you think Jinx could have seen something she shouldn't have? Maybe something Rick did?"

"Anything's possible, but what about the other missing kids?"

"True. The likelihood of them all witnessing the same thing at the same time is slight, right, and besides which, someone would have talked." She took in a deep breath and blew it out. There was a pattern here somewhere and she couldn't figure it out. It's like the answers were just beyond her reach. "I asked Johnny about his business and he mentioned real estate. Do you have any idea what he owns?"

"A couple bars and I think some of those scary motels, you know the kind."

"What about the construction around Bywater? Is he involved in any of that?"

Hustle straightened in his seat. "I saw his Mercedes at the site where Scratch works."

"When?"

"Couple weeks ago."

Shaye made a left turn on the next street. "Maybe we'll go talk to that foreman again."

CHAPTER FOURTEEN

Jackson pulled up in front of Bradley Thompson's house and killed the engine, still uncertain of his next move. His plan was to talk to Bradley's parents and see if they could provide any information on their son's suicide, particularly what might have led up to it. But he had no idea how to broach the subject, and there was no legitimate reason for the police to be interested at this point.

Finally, he climbed out of his car and headed to the front door, hoping he'd figure out something once he was sitting in front of them. A middle-aged woman with brown hair and a sad expression answered the door. When he showed her his credentials, she seemed a bit surprised but invited him inside, explaining that her husband was at work but he could talk with her.

Jackson took a seat in a chair in the living room and looked up at a picture on the fireplace mantel. It was a photo of Bradley taken at a Mardi Gras parade. He was smiling and looked like any other teen having fun. Mrs. Thompson sat on the couch across from him, her hands crossed over each other in her lap.

"What can I do for you, Detective Lamotte?" she

asked.

"I wanted to ask you about Bradley, but if you'd rather not speak to me, I respect that."

Mrs. Thompson frowned. "I don't understand. I thought the police were done with their investigation."

"We have closed the investigation into his death, but I'm working on another case and Bradley's name came up. I'm afraid I can't give you more information as it's an open investigation, but I wondered if you would answer some questions for me."

"If you think it will help."

"I read in the file that Bradley didn't leave a note. Do you have any idea why he did what he did?"

Mrs. Thompson shook her head. "I've thought about little else ever since it happened. What could have been so bad that he wouldn't talk to me? We'd always been close."

Jackson clued in on her phrasing. "You'd always *been* close? At the time of his death, was that not the case?"

"Something was bothering him. I knew it but I couldn't get him to talk. He was distant, almost sullen. Sometimes he'd be staring out the window and when I'd speak to him, he wouldn't even hear me. He was lost in his own thoughts."

"Did you ask his friends?"

"Yes. He'd been good friends with two boys since elementary school, but both of them said the same thing—that he was different but wouldn't tell them what was wrong. One of his friends was so distraught he had to be hospitalized right after…they're both in therapy. The whole thing is such a waste and so maddening. How can you prevent something bad from happening if you don't know what's triggering it to begin with?"

"I wish I knew."

Mrs. Thompson nodded. "I'm sure you wish it more than most given your line of work. Do you think my son's death has something to do with another case?"

"I'm not sure. Given the facts, I can't see a connection, but since your son's name came up, I thought it wouldn't hurt to talk to you. I saw a Father Michael did the service. I've been considering a return to my childhood roots. How do you like him?"

"He's been such a comfort. Visits me at least once a week to pray with me. He's done wonders with the teen groups at the church. It's hard to get teens excited about anything, especially religion, but he has a way of talking to them that they respond to. Bradley really liked him."

"Did Bradley spend a lot of time at church activities?"

"He did for a while, but when everything started to change, he slowly dropped out of all the groups and hobbies he'd participated in. Father Michael visited him several times, trying to convince him to return to the teen group, but he wouldn't even consider it."

The woman's grief was so apparent that Jackson could almost feel it. "I'm so sorry, Mrs. Thompson," he said, and rose from his chair. "I won't take any more of your time."

"I hope you solve your case," Mrs. Thompson said. "This world needs less horror."

"Yes, ma'am. It does."

He headed out of the house and climbed back into his car. Bradley Thompson's fade out of life sounded typical of every teen suicide story he'd heard. So was Father Michael an empathetic priest, worried about the emotional health of his parishioners?

Or was it guilt prompting him to visit Bradley's grave and pray?

He pulled away from the curb and turned on his radio. The evening news was on, giving the latest update on the Peter Carlin disappearance, or lack of update as the case was. As far as Jackson knew, no one had come forward with information on the boy's whereabouts. Given the amount of time that had elapsed, Jackson knew the chances of finding Peter unharmed, just as he knew the chances of finding Jinx unharmed.

As he pulled up to the curb, he realized he was only a block away from Peter's home. He tapped his fingers on the steering wheel. The cases didn't appear to have anything in common, and he had absolutely no reason to think they were related. But still…maybe it wouldn't hurt to talk to Peter's parents, assuming they were open to it. After all, he wasn't working on their case.

Vincent will have a stroke if he finds out you butted into another detective's investigation.

Jackson parked in front of Peter's house and jumped out of the car. To hell with Vincent. The so-called senior detective hadn't done squat to solve this case. Aside from informing the parents of the boy's death and taking an entire afternoon for lunch, he hadn't even bothered to leave his desk. It was just as well for Jackson as it left him free to do what he wanted, but it still rankled that the man was being paid to solve crimes and he did nothing to justify his continued salary.

Jackson headed up the sidewalk and knocked on the door. A woman with puffy eyes and who looked as if she hadn't brushed her hair in days opened the door. "Can I help you?" she asked in a robotic way.

He pulled out his badge. "My name is Detective Lamotte. I'd like to ask you some questions about Peter, if that's all right."

Her eyes widened a bit and she opened the door for him to come inside. "My husband isn't here."

"That's all right."

She sat on the couch and he took a seat in a chair beside her.

"I thought that Detective Grayson was working on Peter's case," she said.

"He is. I'm working on another case that involves a missing teen. I will be honest with you, Mrs. Carlin. I don't have a good reason to assume my case has anything to do with Peter's abduction, but I'm out of ideas and at the point where I'll work even the biggest long shot to try to solve it."

Mrs. Carlin nodded. "I can appreciate that. It's worse for the parent, of course, but what you do is hard and has to take a toll. If you think there's a chance, however slim, that I can help, I'm willing to try."

"Thanks. I know the story the nanny told about that

day. Has she remembered anything else?"

"No. The poor girl had to be sedated. She feels responsible. She's been on suicide watch since it happened. I don't blame her for what happened, mind you. She's nineteen and Peter probably intentionally slipped out of her sight. He's done it to me."

"I imagine most little boys have. I know I did."

"It's just that most of them don't disappear permanently."

"No. They don't. Before that day, did you notice anyone hanging around your house?"

She frowned. "No. I didn't."

She wasn't lying, but he could tell there was something she wasn't saying.

"Whatever it is," Jackson said, "please tell me. Even if it's just a feeling. I am the last person who would discount something simply because it wasn't seen."

She looked down at the floor, then back up at him. "It wasn't me. It was Peter. Early last week, he said a scary man was watching him in the park. I looked in the bushes where Peter said he saw the man, but no one was there."

"Did he recognize the man?"

"No. He said he was big and tall but he couldn't see his face. He was wearing a hat and standing in the shadows."

"But Peter thought the man was watching him? Did he see the man again?"

"He said he saw him outside his bedroom window, but that time, he was wearing a mask."

Jackson's pulse ticked up a notch. "A mask?"

"Based on his description, I'd say a Venetian Mardi Gras mask. He said it was a purple and white face with gold on it. Peter's cousin let him watch some horrible horror movie the last time he went to visit. It gave him nightmares for a week."

She looked up at Jackson and stopped talking, then her eyes widened. "Oh my God. You think he *was* being watched. Peter told me and I didn't believe him. What do you know?"

"A homeless teen was attacked last night by a man wearing a Venetian mask. He's the friend of another missing teen, also homeless."

"I don't understand. Why would the man who took Peter also take homeless teens? They don't have anything in common."

Jackson shook his head. "I wish I knew. I have a feeling that when we know the answer to that question, we'll know who took Peter and the missing teen."

He rose from his chair, anxious to talk to the lead detective on Peter's case and call Shaye and get a description of the mask. It had been the thinnest thread of investigation he had and damned if he didn't believe they were connected.

"Thank you so much, Mrs. Carlin. I promise you if I find out anything, you will be the first to know."

"I should have listened," she said, tears streaming down her face.

Jackson put his hand on her shoulder. "There's no way

you could have known. And if this man has been watching Peter for a while, it was only a matter of time until opportunity presented itself and he made his move. Short of locking Peter in Fort Knox, you couldn't have prevented this. Not if the man was settled on Peter as his target."

She sniffed and wiped the tears from her cheeks with her fingers. "I know what you're saying is true. I've read up on the subject. But it doesn't make me feel any less guilty."

Jackson felt the weight of her burden and knew there was nothing he could say that would lighten it. If he were in her position, he'd feel the same way. The only thing that would alleviate some of her guilt was finding Peter alive. If they didn't…suffice it to say that things didn't always turn out well for those left behind.

Jackson started to leave, then a thought came to him. "Mrs. Carlin, may I ask if you are a religious person?"

She shrugged. "I suppose I'm a typical Catholic in that I don't attend as often as I should, but I do believe, if that's what you're asking."

"No. It's not that. I just thought if you were religious, there might be someone you could call to talk with you and pray."

"Oh, I see. Father Michael came to pray with us as soon as he found out. He said to call any time I needed to talk. I suppose it wouldn't hurt to do so."

"Father Michael with Sacred Heart?"

She looked up at him. "Yes. Do you know him?"

"We've never met, but I've heard about some of his ministry work."

"He's really good with the kids. We attend Saint Louis, but Father Michael taught some Bible classes there for the younger kids. Peter likes him a lot."

Jackson nodded. "I'm sure he does."

John Clancy was at the site, directing a man driving a bulldozer. He looked over as Shaye and Hustle got out of the SUV and held up a single finger. Shaye nodded and they waited on the sidewalk until Clancy finished with the driver, who drove the dozer toward the front of the lot.

"Did you find Scratch?" Clancy asked as he walked up to them, practically shouting to be heard over the loud machinery.

"Unfortunately, no," Shaye said, "but I wanted to ask you a couple of questions, if you don't mind."

"Sure. Let's go into my office. Easier to talk there."

They headed across the street and into Clancy's office. Shaye took a seat in a chair on the opposite side of Clancy's desk and Hustle hopped up on the window ledge. Clancy sat behind the desk and looked across at her.

"What can I help you with?" he asked.

"This site you're working here, are you the developer?" Shaye asked.

"I wish I were. That's where all the construction money really is, but you have to have a ton of it to get in the business to start. I haven't been able to afford anything on this scale. The developers I work for inherited either their companies or the money to start them."

"So you contract with them?"

"Exactly. All the hurricane damage created a lot of work. I managed to get some more equipment and have two crews running now. I'm not getting rich, but more people have jobs and I'm doing all right."

"Do you know Johnny Rivette?" Shaye asked.

Clancy's scowl left no doubt of his upcoming response. "I know him," Clancy said. "Mobster piece of shit. Sorry for the language, but there's no polite words for him."

"Is he the developer for this site?"

"No way. Not that it matters."

"What do you mean?"

Clancy looked out the window and back at Shaye, tapping his finger on the desk the entire time. "Look, I'll tell you, but if the cops come around here asking, I'm going to say you lied about this entire conversation."

"Okay," Shaye said. She already had a good idea where the conversation with Clancy was headed.

"Rivette owns some dive properties around the city," Clancy said, "but he's not the developer on any of the big construction projects that I know of, including this one."

"But he's involved somehow?"

"If you consider extorting money out of subcontractors 'involved' then yeah, he's involved up to his neck."

"And these payoffs buy you what exactly?"

"Rivette's goons don't scare my workers off the job.

Equipment doesn't disappear. I tried not paying him at first. Couldn't keep a man on the job more than a day. As soon as Rivette's guys got to them, they took off. I started paying after that and been paying ever since."

"I don't blame you," Hustle grumbled.

Clancy nodded. "He's a nasty piece of work. I heard plenty of stories—things I don't want happening to me or anyone that works for me. You think Rivette had something to do with Scratch disappearing? I've been paying. I swear."

"I believe you," Shaye said. "And to answer your question, I don't know. Rivette's nephew pawned a skateboard that belonged to another missing kid. When I asked him about it, I could tell he was hiding something, but I have no idea if it's relevant or not. It could be he was just keeping something from his uncle."

"I know the kid you're talking about," Clancy said. "I've seen him lurking around sometimes."

"Lurking around the site?" Shaye asked.

"Yeah. At first, I thought he was some punk casing the place to steal stuff. I started to run him off but Scratch stopped me…told me who he was."

"When did he start hanging around?" Shaye asked.

Clancy rubbed his chin and shook his head. "Two weeks ago, maybe. Can't remember exactly, but that sounds about right."

"Maybe he's spying for his uncle," Shaye suggested.

Hustle snorted. "Johnny Rivette don't need no spies. More likely, Rick was trying to skim off the workers, same as his uncle is skimming off Mr. Clancy."

Clancy's eyes widened. "You think he was getting money from my contractors?"

Shaye nodded. "That would make sense. He sees his uncle making money doing nothing but threatening people and figures the contractors are easy pickings. They already see their boss paying Rivette. They probably figure Rick is their payment collector."

"Piece of shit," Clancy grumbled. "I wish the whole damned lot of them had to work an honest day's work."

"They probably aren't capable," Shaye said. "At least not with the honest part." Shaye rose from her chair. "I appreciate you taking your time to talk to us, Mr. Clancy, and being candid. If you see Rick around the site again, will you let me know?"

"Sure. Nothing would please me more than to get rid of the Rivettes altogether. I don't mind starting with the nephew."

Shaye and Hustle headed back to her SUV and climbed inside, but instead of starting the vehicle, she sat and stared down the street, the conversation with Clancy replaying in her mind.

"What are you thinking?" Hustle said.

"I'm not sure. There's a lot of moving parts. I guess I'm thinking about the Rivettes' presence at construction sites. Scratch was working at one of them. There's another right next to the docks, and we have to assume Rivette's collecting from every contractor down here. Have you ever seen his men around the docks?"

"No. But the street's on the other side of the building. That construction trailer blocks the view of it."

"That's right."

"So what now?"

Shaye's phone vibrated and she pulled it out. It was Corrine again. She hadn't left a message earlier, which was strange. Usually she left something, even if it was just to say she was calling to say hi.

"It's my mother again. One second," she told Hustle and answered the call.

"Shaye?" Corrine said, her voice several octaves higher than normal. "Are you busy?"

Shaye clenched the phone. "What's wrong?"

"There's something I need to talk to you about. It's serious and, uh, has a time limit on it. Can you come see me?"

"Now?"

"That would be best. If possible."

Shaye felt her back tighten. Her mother was always direct. Always deliberate. This uncertainty in her voice and her directives were so far from the norm that Shaye knew something was seriously wrong.

"I'll be there in twenty minutes," Shaye said.

"Is something wrong?" Hustle asked.

"Yeah, but she's not saying what. I need to go now. Where do you want me to drop you off?"

"Here's fine. I'm going to grab a sandwich at a shop around the street, then see what the word is."

"Okay. If I don't call you beforehand, remember to let

me know when you get back to the hotel."

He climbed out of the SUV. "I will. I hope everything's all right."

"Me too."

But as she drove away, she knew it wasn't.

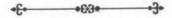

He stared down at the unconscious boy and scowled. That idiot had dosed him up so much that the boy might never regain consciousness. And even if he did, there would be no more sales to the customer he was supposed to supply the boy to. There had been a heated argument with them earlier, but he didn't care. They could threaten all they wanted, but the bottom line was they didn't know who he was. They dealt only with his associate, and that person was expendable. It served him right for screwing up with this kid and the little boy. What the hell had he been thinking, taking a kid with parents who would raise the roof to find him?

He turned around and punched a wall, putting a hole in the Sheetrock. Last night, he'd planned on cleaning up part of the mess his associate had made, but the skater kid had gotten the best of him. If that cell phone hadn't gotten in the way, he would have been able to make it work, but blocking the needle had given the kid time to swing the skateboard around.

The kid was quick. He'd give him that. And he was smart. The way he checked his surroundings, he knew he was being watched. And now he knew someone was after him, which meant he wouldn't return to the place he usually went at night. The woman had found somewhere for him to hide at night, but he doubted it was with her.

Shaye Archer. Daughter of heiress Corrine Archer and granddaughter of State Senator Pierce Archer. And a huge fucking problem.

He'd thought she looked familiar when he first saw her, and then it had finally clicked—the news story about the stalker that she'd run down a couple weeks ago. Ms. Archer was young and brave, and had all the money in the world to put behind her investigative efforts. Unfortunately, killing her would only bring more problems. Shaye Archer's murder would put the limelight on her current case, and he had no doubt Pierce Archer would turn the state upside down looking for an answer.

If the skater kid was gone, though, she wouldn't have anyone to help her any longer, and the whole thing would die out. All he needed was a month or so to wrap up everything here. Sell off his business interests, buy that property he'd been looking at overseas, and wave good-bye to Louisiana for good.

He'd have his associate get rid of the unconscious boy tonight. Even if he was going to wake up, he was no longer useful since the client had been cut off. The longer he was in the house, the bigger the risk that he'd be discovered. As for the skater kid, he needed to find his new nighttime hiding place. Last night, the kid had been prepared to be followed, but if he thought he was safe, then his guard wouldn't be up the way it was before.

Which gave him the opening he needed to finish the job.

CHAPTER FIFTEEN

Shaye parked in front of her mother's house, noting that the police security was still in place. Eleonore's car was there as well. Whatever was coming, Corrine had decided either she or Shaye was going to need support. This kept looking worse. Shaye climbed out of her car, waved at the officers, and headed up the walkway. Eleonore must have been watching, because she opened the door before Shaye even had a chance to use her key.

"She's in the kitchen," Eleonore said, both her tone and expression grim.

Maybe something happened to Pierce. He'd left this morning for China. What if his plane went down? Or maybe something was wrong with Corrine. What if the injuries she got when she was attacked were worse than they thought? What if it was cancer, like Cora LeDoux?

She took a deep breath and shoved all those thoughts from her mind as she entered the kitchen. There was no point in going through the options. She'd know what was wrong soon enough.

Corrine jumped up from her seat at the kitchen counter as soon as she entered the room. Her distress was apparent, and it was obvious she'd been crying. Shaye rushed to her mother and gave her a hug. "What's wrong?" Shaye asked. "Has something happened to Grandfather?"

"No," Corrine said as she released Shaye. "Your grandfather is fine. I'm fine. It's nothing like that."

Shaye looked back and forth between her mother and Eleonore. "Then what?"

"I think you better sit down," Corrine said and waved at the breakfast table.

Shaye sat at the end of the table and Corrine pulled a chair around so that she was right in front of her. Eleonore took a seat on the other side of Corrine. They looked at each other, then at Shaye, then at each other again. Finally, Corrine took her hand.

"Police Chief Bernard called me down to the station today," Corrine said. "They found a body a couple of days ago in the Lower Ninth. A woman."

Shaye sucked in a breath, then processed what her mother had said.

Woman, not girl. It's not Jinx.

Shaye struggled to get control of her emotions before they raced unnecessarily out of control. It wasn't Jinx or her mother or Eleonore, but it could still be any number of clients or someone she'd met during her recovery or school.

"Who is it?" Shaye asked.

Corrine squeezed her hand so hard it hurt. "I don't know how else to say this. Shaye, it was your mother."

Shaye sucked in a breath and clutched the table with

her free hand as the room began to spin. Her mother and Eleonore waved in front of her like the current in the ocean. Their faces were blurred and distorted. Their mouths were open, but she couldn't hear anything except the incredibly loud ringing in her ears. Her stomach rolled and she swallowed, trying to fight off the nausea.

"Shaye?" Corrine's face swam in front of her, closer and closer. "Can you hear me?"

Corrine looked at Eleonore. "She's not responding."

Eleonore rose and took Shaye's face between her hands. "Breathe, Shaye. One deep, long breath, then let it out slowly. We've done this a million times." Her voice sounded like an echo in Shaye's mind, as if she were speaking from inside a deep well, but her words still clicked.

Shaye drew in a huge breath and focused on slowly releasing it. The room stopped moving, and her vision began to clear. Her racing pulse remained. She blinked and looked at Corrine as Eleonore removed her hands from Shaye's face.

"Thank God," Corrine said. "I thought we'd lost you there for a minute."

Shaye nodded, still unable to speak.

"I can't even imagine what a shock this is for you," Corrine said.

"And you."

"Yes, it's horrible," Corrine agreed, "but I'll be fine. I'm worried about you."

Shaye took another deep breath. "I'll be fine," she said, trying to reassure her distressed mother as well as herself.

So many questions raced through her mind that she didn't even know where to begin.

"Who was she?" Shaye asked.

Corrine looked at Eleonore, who nodded. "Her name was Lydia Johnson," Corrine said. "Do you recognize that name?"

"Lydia Johnson," Shaye repeated. She rolled it around silently several times, then shook her head. "How did she die?"

"She overdosed. The medical examiner said she'd been using a long time."

A junkie.

Shaye had never harbored any childish dreams that she was a princess who had been abducted from her kingdom. She knew better than most what kind of people didn't report a missing child. She'd never held out an expectation that if her parents were found they'd be upstanding citizens still desperately searching for their missing daughter. But to have her worst fear confirmed was still a blow.

"You're sure she gave birth to me?" Shaye asked. She didn't want to use the word "mother," because that designation was reserved for Corrine.

"The medical examiner said the DNA match was conclusive. When the medical examiner realized everything the match implied, detectives were sent to search her house." Corrine rose from the table and retrieved something from the table. She handed a picture to Shaye. "This is one of the things they found."

Shaye looked at the smiling girl in pigtails. Her hair

needed a good brushing and her shirt was threadbare, but she knew it was her. It was the face from her dreams.

"They also found this," Corrine said, and handed her a piece of paper.

Shaye looked down at the document. "There's no name."

"I know," Corrine said. "The police chief checked the birth records, but they didn't find anything."

"So that's it," Shaye said. "My entire childhood with this…this junkie was reduced to a single photo and a piece of paper from the hospital."

Corrine bit her lower lip and glanced over at Eleonore. "We always suspected that the past wasn't going to be pretty. I'm so sorry."

Shaye looked at her one true mother. "Don't ever apologize for her choices. And they *were* choices."

"She was an addict," Eleonore said. "You know what her limitations were."

Shaye looked over at Eleonore. "And you know that she could have gotten clean. You make the choice every day not to drink, even when it's completely legal and offered directly to you on a platter at every social event in New Orleans."

"Not everyone is strong enough to do it," Eleonore said.

Shaye shook her head. "Not everyone gives a shit about something other than themselves. Look, I appreciate what both of you are trying to do, but the most important thing that bonds us is the truth. I don't want either of you to feel like you can't tell me things."

"You know we'd never lie to you," Corrine said.

"I'm talking about saying what we really think," Shaye said. "I'll start. My birth mother was a junkie who clearly had no interest in her child and because of that, something horrible happened to me. That's the bottom line. There's nothing anyone can say that can dispute that."

"Oh, Shaye!" Tears formed in Corrine's eyes and spilled out over her cheeks. "Everything was her loss. Her loss and my gain."

"Mine, too," Eleonore said.

Corrine leaned over and hugged Shaye, clutching her as though she'd never let go. "I hate her for what happened to you. That's my truth."

Shaye wrapped her arms around her mother and held her tight. She knew how hard it was for Corrine to say what she did, and she'd always feel guilty for her harsh feelings. She simply wasn't made to carry around hate, much less admit it out loud.

Shaye pulled back so that she could look Corrine directly in the eyes. "I was lucky. I got you out of the deal."

Corrine began to weep and kissed Shaye's cheek. "You will always be the best thing that ever happened to me."

Shaye's heart swelled with both love and pain. Her relationship with Corrine was so special, so unique. The life Shaye had now would never have existed if her childhood had been different. But what had it been? When had her biological mother become a junkie? Shaye showed no medical signs of being born addicted, but it was a possibility. If Shaye could find out more about her life with Lydia, would she remember when that life came to an end and why?

Shaye looked over at Eleonore. "I need answers."

Eleonore nodded. "And we'll do everything we can to help you get them."

Corrine squeezed her hand. "I'll hire the best private investigators."

Shaye gave her a small smile. "I thought *I* was the best private investigator."

"You can't do this. You're too close to the situation."

"Which is exactly why I *should* do it," Shaye said. "Someone else walking through my childhood home or the park I played in isn't going to remember for me. This is mine. It has to be me."

Corrine glanced over at Eleonore and frowned. "There's something else to consider."

"There's a lot of something elses to consider," Shaye said.

"This is a biggie," Corrine said. "The police chief put a gag order on the department, as did the medical examiner, but…"

"It's going to get out," Shaye finished, then cursed. It would be hard enough to dig up good information from her childhood given that the type of people her biological mother likely associated with were either the kind that didn't remember anything or the kind that simply claimed they didn't remember anything. But if a bunch of reporters started poking at people before she had a chance, they might ruin any ability she had to get information.

"So I'll move fast," Shaye said. "I'm working the Lower Ninth right now anyway. It won't be hard to combine the two. Do you have an address for where she lived? Can I get access?"

Eleonore rose from her chair and grabbed a file folder from the counter. She handed it to Shaye. "I got everything I could from the police and made some calls myself. Lydia lived in Section 8 housing, and had been at the same address for twelve years. I spoke with the landlord and explained the situation. He is happy to meet with you any time over the next two days and let you into the apartment."

"Why only two days?" Shaye asked.

"Because a new tenant is moving in there next week. His crew is scheduled to take everything out of the apartment in three days, so if you want anything, you have to get it now."

Shaye blew out a breath. Two days.

Forty-eight hours to try to remember fifteen years.

Scratch stirred, his head aching so much it felt as if it would explode. A man's voice sounded somewhere in the building. He'd heard the voice before, but he'd thought he was dreaming. Now he'd awakened in a strange room, chained to a bed, and knew that it wasn't a nightmare. It was reality.

The voice grew louder and he realized the man was coming toward him. He could hear two distinct male voices now, one angry, the other defensive. He tugged on the handcuffs, but knew it was a waste of time. He'd never get loose that way. The footsteps stopped outside the door and he stopped moving altogether.

"Get rid of him tonight," the angry man said.

"I think he's going to come around," the defensive man said. "He moved a little earlier."

"It doesn't matter. The client broke the agreement, so the boss told them we're done. Conscious or unconscious, he's a liability as long as he's in this house. The boss's orders are clear. He has to go now."

"How am I supposed to get him out of here now? It's still daylight."

"The van is around back. I pulled it right up to the back door. The tarp and weights are in the back. Wrap him up, haul him out, and drive him deep into the swamp before you dump him."

"Why's it got to be now?"

"Because when we locate that kid, you gotta take care of him tonight."

"Yeah, all right."

The door rattled and Scratch went limp, figuring his best chance of escape was pretending to be unconscious, then overtaking his captor when it was just the two of them. He heard a dead bolt sliding back, then the door creaked open and he heard the man walking toward the bed.

The man poked him hard in the ribs and it was all he could do not to respond. He concentrated on keeping his body limp as the man poked him again. Apparently satisfied that he was still unconscious, the man unlocked the handcuffs from the metal headboard. Scratch let his arms drop as the cuffs came loose.

The man then cuffed his hands together across his body, grabbed his feet, and pulled him off the bed. Scratch's body slammed into the floor and he clenched his jaw so hard it ached, forcing himself to remain silent. He could hear the man breathing above him and figured he was waiting to see if Scratch woke up. Finally, the man grabbed him by the feet and started dragging him down the hall.

After he'd gone on for what seemed like forever, he dropped Scratch's feet and Scratch heard a door opening. He barely opened his eyes, trying to get a look at the man, but his back was turned and he was hunched over in a van. It was the opportunity Scratch had been waiting for.

He gathered all his strength and tried to roll over, planning to spring up from the ground, but when he tried to spin, his body barely moved. Pain shot through his limbs and he felt his legs, arms, and back start to tingle. The man whirled around and Scratch went limp again, clamping his eyes shut.

Shit!

Between the drugs and the amount of time he'd been restrained, his muscles were weak and had protested at the quick movement he'd tried to force upon them. He had to get some blood flow back into them or he'd never be able to overpower his kidnapper. Even from behind, he could tell the guy was big.

The man tossed something next to him and when Scratch heard the rustling of plastic, he began to panic. The man was going to wrap him up before he left. He didn't have the strength to fight back now, so he had to come up with another plan. The man grabbed his shoulder and rolled his body onto a tarp, wrapping it around him. It was all Scratch could do to keep from ripping the tarp from his face. He forced himself to breathe naturally, trying not to let in the claustrophobia that threatened to take over.

Refusing to give up hope, he scrambled to come up with another plan. If he could work off the cuffs, then he might be able to break out of the tarp once the man dumped him in the swamp. That was assuming he could get his limbs to cooperate, and assuming he could get free of the handcuffs, and assuming a bunch of other things that he couldn't process all at once.

One thing at a time.

That was the key. He needed to concentrate on one thing at a time. That would allow him to control the rising panic he felt. He had only one shot at getting out of this, and he was going to make it count.

The man tied the ends with rope and then Scratch's legs went up and he was being dragged again, he assumed into the van. He heard the doors close and immediately went to work on trying to free one of his hands from the cuffs. When he heard the driver's door open, he paused, waiting for the man to start the van. Once they were in motion, he worked on the cuffs again, while slowly flexing his feet and legs, careful not to make too much noise. A little bit of rustling was normal given the movement of the van, but too much would alert the man that he was awake.

The cuffs weren't police issue. Scratch had a recent enough experience with those to know the difference. These were standard cuffs with links between them. If he had a paper clip, he could probably pick them, but he was going to have to settle for breaking them instead. If he got the cuffs twisted in just the right way, he was pretty sure he could exert enough pressure on them to break one of the links.

He moved his hands around, twisting the links in the position he wanted, and then waited. The van wasn't the quietest vehicle on the road, but Scratch was afraid the engine noise wouldn't be enough to hide the *pop* of the link when breaking. Sweat formed on his forehead and ran down the side of his face. The air grew warmer as he breathed, and he fought back the feeling that he was smothering.

Suddenly, the driver cursed and laid on his horn while slamming on the brakes. Scratch pulled as hard as he could, and the link broke. The man was still cursing as Scratch felt the links for the broken one. He slowly worked it off the chain and clutched in it his right hand. He had to be ready when the man dumped him into the swamp. He might be able to hold his breath for a minute, but that was pushing it, especially given movement. He probably needed to plan on thirty seconds. And all this was assuming the man didn't shoot him before dumping the body.

The man drove probably forty-five minutes before stopping, but Scratch had no clue what that meant as he didn't know where he'd been. The angry man had ordered this man to go deep into the swamp, so Scratch had to assume they were far from civilization. That meant no possibility of help nearby.

The back of the van opened and Scratch felt the man pulling him out of the van. He braced himself for the inevitable pain when his body dropped out of the van and hit the ground, but it was even worse than he imagined. Pain shot down his back and legs and his head slammed into the turf so hard, it felt as if his eyeballs would pop out of their sockets. He closed his eyes and drew in a deep breath as he felt the desire to drop off into unconsciousness pass over him.

He opened his eyes and concentrated on his breathing, forcing himself to stay alert. If he lost consciousness now, it was all over. The man grabbed the tarp and began dragging him again, but this time, it was rougher going than on the tile in the building. Rocks and sticks dug into his back through the tarp, and he clamped his hand over his mouth to keep any sound from escaping.

The man stopped and Scratch stiffened, his panic increasing with every passing second of silence. Was he loading a gun?

"To hell with both of 'em," the man said out loud. "I ain't weighing this down. It ain't going anywhere but the bottom."

Weights! Scratch had completely forgotten the other man had mentioned weights. Lucky for him this guy wasn't interested in following instructions. His body weight alone was enough to sink him straight to the bottom of any water source, and probably another several inches into the muddy bottom. Additional weight would be one more thing to worry about.

The man grabbed his shoulder again and rolled him over. They must be at an overhang on the bank of the swamp. The man was going to roll him off of it and into the water. Scratch said a prayer and waited for the inevitable drop. The man rolled him over once more and suddenly, he felt the ground disappear beneath him.

It took only a couple of seconds before he hit the water, but it felt like forever…almost as if he were suspended in midair. As soon as he hit the water, he took in a deep breath, reached up with the broken link, and dug into the tarp. He had to get an opening big enough to put his hands into. Then, if he was strong enough, he could tear the tarp.

You're strong enough.

He repeated the words over and over again as he tore at the tarp with the tiny piece of metal. Water seeped through the tarp and he felt his body falling and falling. He stopped thinking about how far he was sinking and focused on the tarp. He felt it rip and jabbed the link into the hole, pulling as hard as he could. It opened a couple of inches and he put the link between his lips and stuck his fingers in both sides, yanking them to make the hole larger.

It gave another couple of inches, but it wasn't enough. He felt something jab into his back and realized he'd hit bottom. His lungs started to burn, and he let out a bit of the air he'd been holding to relieve the pressure. He grabbed the tarp with both hands and pulled again, this time gaining a gap of about a foot, but the exertion also forced the remaining air out of his body in a giant whoosh.

Panicking, he grabbed the tarp once more and pulled so hard he felt his shoulder pop. The tarp split and he forced his body through the hole, then pushed off the bottom and swam for the surface, praying that the man had left as soon as the deed was done and wasn't standing at the overhang waiting.

He looked up, trying to see light in the murky water, but all he saw was brown. His chest started to convulse, and he clamped his mouth shut, trying to control his body's natural attempt to draw in oxygen. He kicked harder and flapped his arms as fast as he could, ignoring the burning in his right shoulder.

Just when he thought he didn't have one second more of air left, he broke the surface of the water and dragged in a huge breath, choking on it as he did. He twisted his head up to look at the overhang and relief coursed through him when he saw it was empty. He began paddling toward the bank downstream, just in case the man hadn't left yet. Twenty feet away was a thick growth of trees and brush. He should be able to exit the water there without being seen.

When he reached the bank, he grabbed a set of roots and tried to pull himself up, but his shoulder gave out and he let out an involuntary yelp. He ducked low in the water, hiding behind the roots and peering back at the overhang, but the man never appeared. He eased out from under the roots and paddled a little farther downstream where the bank was shallow enough to crawl up.

Using his legs and one arm, he managed to get up the bank, then collapsed in the marsh grass, gasping for air. He reached over with his left hand and felt his shoulder. The protrusion was obvious and he yelped again as his fingers ran over it. Using his one good arm, he struggled to his feet and staggered up the bank. As he neared the overhang, he slowed, making sure the van was gone before he walked out into the clearing.

A dirt trail led away from the clearing so he set out on it, clutching his shoulder. He stumbled every other step on the uneven ground. Everything in front of him grew blurry and he felt his body start to give out. He forced his eyes open as wide as he could get them and started singing, trying to keep his mind awake.

Twinkle, twinkle little star

How I wonder what you are.

He couldn't remember the rest of the lyrics, so he sang those two lines over and over and over again as he forced one foot in front of the other. When he couldn't go another step, he fell onto his knees and crawled until he reached a fork in the trail. He looked up and down the stretch of dirt but he could have been in a thousand different places in the backwoods of Louisiana. Nothing stood out.

He tried to stand up again but his ravaged body

couldn't handle anything more. He collapsed on the trail, his captors' conversation back in the house replaying in his mind. The last thought he had before he lost consciousness was that the angry man who gave the orders had a familiar voice. It was someone he'd met before. He just couldn't quite grasp who.

CHAPTER SIXTEEN

Shaye clutched the steering wheel as she pulled up in front of her apartment. It was almost eight o'clock, and the sun was starting to drift down behind the buildings. Corrine had begged her to stay at her house for the night, but Shaye had needed to get out, away from Corrine and Eleonore. Alone where she could process everything she'd learned. But now she didn't want to go into her apartment and sit there alone.

You're a mess.

It had been a long time since she'd felt so disjointed. So spacey. She killed the engine and let go of the steering wheel. What the hell was she supposed to do now? First thing tomorrow, she'd call the apartment manager and get access to the unit, but that left a long night stretching before her. Somehow, she didn't think Netflix and a root beer float were going to make it go any faster.

She glanced at her watch. Eight o'clock. A whole two minutes had passed while she was sitting here and it had felt like an hour. No way could she go inside. All the showers and beers in the world weren't going to make her relax. She needed something to do. She pulled out her phone and brought up her Favorites. Her finger hovered over Jackson's number as she wavered with indecision.

He needed to know about the angle she'd drummed up with Johnny Rivette, but was she calling him for business or because she wanted to talk to someone other than her mother and Eleonore? Given the juicy nature of the situation, she had little doubt that Jackson had already heard about the latest revelation into her mysterious past. The precinct was probably buzzing with the news. Which meant she wouldn't have to explain it to Jackson.

Shaye believed that Jackson would be concerned for her, but he didn't have the investment in her life that Corrine and Eleonore did. The entire time she was at her mother's house, she could feel them watching her, as if they were waiting for something to happen. Maybe a breakdown? Shaye had known she had to get out of there before being under a microscope was what triggered it.

Before she could change her mind, she touched the phone, dialing Jackson. He answered on the first ring.

"Shaye? Is everything all right?"

The uncertainty in his voice left no doubt that he'd already heard about her birth mother. "I have some information for you about the case, but first, I need a favor."

"Okay."

She smiled. "Just like that? You're not even going to ask what the favor is?"

"I didn't think I needed to."

"You might change your mind after I tell you. I'm sure

you heard that I got some news today."

"Someone mentioned it."

"I've got the number for the apartment manager. I want to go see that apartment."

"Right now?"

"Yes. If I wait until tomorrow, my mother and Eleonore will insist on going with me, and I won't be able to…feel if they're there. I know that sounds crazy and weird—"

"No. It doesn't. Are you at home? I'll pick you up."

"I can drive us."

"I need more responsibility than being a passenger," he said. "I'm in the neighborhood. I'll be there in five minutes."

Her next call was to the apartment manager. He took a little coaxing, but finally agreed to meet her at the apartment in twenty minutes and provide her with a key. She slipped her phone into her pocket and climbed out of her SUV. She paced the sidewalk down to the end of the block, then back to the corner three times before Jackson pulled around the corner in his undercover car. Shaye pulled open the door and hopped in before he even came to a complete stop.

He checked the address in GPS, and as he pulled away, he looked over at her.

"How are you holding up?" he asked.

"Good. I guess. My mind is sorta all over the place between this and the case."

"I bet. Tell you what, on the way to the apartment, let's

talk about the case. Then by the time we get there, we'll both be up to date and you can concentrate on that without your attention being split. You go first."

"I like that idea," Shaye said, and filled him in on the trip to the pawnshop, her visit with Johnny and Rick Rivette, and the follow-up with John Clancy.

When she finished, Jackson shook his head. "Johnny Rivette. He's bad news. You think he knows something?"

"Honestly, I have no idea. Rick is hiding something, but I have no way of knowing if it's something he didn't want me to know or something he didn't want his uncle to know. Johnny is a professional liar. I'm not sure a polygraph would trip him up."

"You might be right about that. I'll do some checking…see what the cops got on him before. Maybe it's something. Maybe not."

Shaye nodded. "What about you? Did you get anything else on Father Michael?"

"Oh yeah. I had a very busy day chasing after information on our priest." Jackson told her about his visit with Bradley Thompson's mother and then his diversion into the Peter Carlin case.

"Holy crap," she said when he was done. "I never would have thought the cases were related."

"I wanted to call you right after I spoke with Mrs. Carlin and ask about the mask, but given the other situation, I figured I'd wait until I heard from you."

"It sounds like what Hustle described. He said he was going to check some of the shops in the French Quarter and see if he could find one like it. If not, he promised to pick up some colored pencils and sketch it. I know it doesn't do anything to forward the case, but he needs to feel like he's doing something."

Jackson nodded. "And if you give him assignments, you have some level of control over what he's doing."

"Exactly. I don't want a repeat of last night. If something happens to that kid on my watch…"

Jackson looked over at her. "Nothing's going to happen to him. You've got him set up in the best possible situation. He's smart. He knows how to avoid trouble, and last night was a big wake-up call. He'll be even more careful now."

"I hope so, but he's still a teen. A teen with pride, a big heart, and a good dose of tough guy. I just hope the smart side wins out."

"Me too."

"So what next?" Shaye asked.

"I'll get what I can on Rivette, but I think we need to take a harder look at Father Michael." He pulled to a stop in front of a run-down apartment building. "This is the place. I'm glad you asked me to come with you."

Shaye nodded. Neither the building nor the street was an area she would feel completely comfortable in alone, especially getting toward dark. She climbed out of the car and they headed for the entrance. An older man with silver hair and a dirty shirt stood by the front door.

"You Shaye Archer?" he asked.

"Yes. Are you the manager?"

The man nodded and handed her a key. "Unit 114. You want anything in there, it's yours. Just get it out before Thursday."

"Wait!" Shaye said as he started to walk away. "Is there anything you can tell me about Lydia?"

"She lived here twelve years on the taxpayers' dime. I don't know anything beyond that. The less I know about these people the better." He turned around and headed down the sidewalk.

Shaye watched as he walked away. "He was pleasant."

Jackson shrugged. "Typical. If he doesn't know what goes on with his tenants, he can't be compelled to talk to the police about it and be blamed for allowing it to happen."

Shaye turned to face the apartment entrance but didn't make a move to open the door. Jackson stood calmly beside her, not saying a word. She knew he had to be anxious, but he wasn't showing any sign of it. It was both comforting and irritating. She drew in a breath and blew it out.

"Let's get this over with," she said, and entered the apartment building.

She headed down the hallway to the unit the manager had indicated. The door had flaking baby-blue paint and was missing the molding over the top. Shaye slipped the key into the lock and pushed the door open. The apartment was pitch black, so she felt inside the door for a light switch. When she clicked it on, she got her first look at the place she might have lived.

It wasn't much to look at. In fact, it looked a lot like the condemned building Jinx had been sleeping in. One room formed kitchen and living room, a tiny stove and refrigerator against the far wall, sink on the wall around the corner. The cabinets and walls were once white but had yellowed with age and cigarette smoke. The smell of stale cigarettes permeated the room.

The windows were all covered with blankets, blocking any chance of sunlight entering the depressing space. Torn linoleum with faded blue diamonds on it covered the tiny kitchen area. Gold shag carpet covered the living room floor and continued into a bedroom. Shaye stepped inside and walked to the center of the living room. She looked around, studying every square inch, waiting for some glimmer of recognition.

But none was forthcoming.

Finally, she moved from the living room and into the bedroom. The same yellowed walls carried into the bedroom and adjoining bathroom. A box spring and mattress sat in the corner of the room against the wall, a battered nightstand sitting beside it. Shaye walked over to the nightstand and opened the drawer, but all it contained was a hairband and a pair of socks.

She opened the closet and riffled through the tiny collection of threadbare clothing. A shoe box on the shelf contained undergarments, worn through in places. She left the closet and moved into the bathroom. The counter contained a brush and some barrettes. She pulled open the vanity drawer and stared in disgust at the needles and rubber band contained inside.

She slammed the drawer and walked back into the living room. She turned slowly around in a circle, growing more desperate by the second. Jackson, who'd silently stood to the side of her the entire time, frowned and reached out to touch her shoulder.

"Shaye?" he said.

That one word opened the floodgates.

"I don't know this!" she said. "I don't know any of this."

"You might not have lived here. She might have moved here after…"

"After she lost track of me? Lost me like someone might lose their car keys? The difference being that people actually go looking for their car keys when they're missing."

Jackson stared at her, his dismay apparent. "I don't know what to say."

"There's nothing to say. There's nothing here for me. There never was."

She walked out of the apartment without even a single glance back.

Hustle left the convenience store clutching the bag of art supplies. He'd checked at least twenty retailers in the French Quarter but hadn't spotted a mask like the one the man who attacked him had been wearing. He'd started to purchase a similar one, but had decided he could do a better job drawing it than explaining the differences. It was almost dark by the time he left the store, and it would be dark before he got back to the hotel.

He considered getting a cab—he had plenty left from the money Shaye had given him, and she didn't want him walking the streets after dark. But the thought of coughing up so much money for something as simple as a ride in a car was too much of a stretch for someone like Hustle, who usually only had enough money for his next meal, if that. If he hurried, he could make it back to Bywater in probably twenty minutes. His ankle wouldn't be happy about it, but he could ice it and prop it up the rest of the night.

Mind made up, he dropped his skateboard onto the street and took off, weaving around the potholes, manhole covers, and cars, and ignoring the honking horns as he slipped through narrow spaces in between vehicles. He managed to make it halfway before he had to stop to catch his breath. The sun was already sinking over the tops of the buildings. There wasn't much daylight left.

He dropped his board and kicked off again, not wanting to admit, even to himself, that he was scared to be on the streets at night. Scared that whoever had attacked him the night before would return, and this time with help. The pain in his ankle ticked up a notch with every kick but he didn't slow. When he reached the street the hotel was on, he stumbled off the board and bent over, trying to catch his breath.

The sunlight was almost completely gone and the sparsely placed streetlights were starting to flicker on. He picked up his board and headed for the hotel, limping heavily. He was thirty yards from the entrance to the hotel when he felt it—someone was watching him.

He took off for the hotel as fast as his ankle would allow, glancing back as he ran. A man burst out of the shadows and raced toward him. Hustle tried to pick up the pace, but his injured ankle wouldn't support any increase in speed. He wasn't going to make it.

The light in the lobby was on and Hustle yelled as loud as he could for the manager. He heard the *swish* of fabric moving behind him and knew the man was almost upon him. As the door to the hotel lobby flew open, the man grabbed Hustle's shoulder and yanked him to the ground. Hustle held his skateboard up to block the man's hand, which was descending on him with a needle.

When the gunshot rang out, Hustle clenched his eyes, certain it was over. He'd been mistaken. The man hadn't been holding a needle. He'd been holding a gun. A second later, the man dropped on top of him and Hustle opened his eyes and shoved the body, panicking as he tried to escape the weight.

"Take my hand," Saul said, and reached down.

Hustle clasped the hotel manager's hand and struggled to his feet, then looked down at the man and saw blood seeping through the bullet hole in his chest. He looked over at Saul, who was still clutching the nine-millimeter in his hand.

"Thank you," Hustle managed.

Saul nodded. "You all right?"

"Yeah. Is he dead?"

"I'm pretty sure." Saul looked over at Hustle. "We've got a problem here. I have to call the police and they're gonna want to talk to you, seeing as how you were the one he was attacking."

"You're not going to get into trouble, are you? I mean, you was just protecting me."

"I'll be fine," Saul said, and pointed to a security camera behind him. "If they don't want to take my word, I've got proof. But you're underage and got no family. The police will take you into custody, for your own protection."

"No! They'll put me in one of those homes again, and I won't be able to help find Jinx."

"I figured you wouldn't like that too much, so this is what we're gonna do. I'm gonna tell the cops you're my buddy's kid, visiting for a week while my buddy and his wife are on a camping trip. The kind where cell phones don't work, if you catch my drift."

Hustle stared at him. "You'd do that for me?"

"That man took a big risk trying to kill you right in front of my hotel. That tells me you know something that very bad people don't want anyone else to know. I don't like bad people in my neighborhood. I'm trying to help turn this area around. And even if I didn't know shit from Shinola about you, what I do know is that Shaye Archer wants you protected. If Shaye is invested in you, then it's not by mistake."

"What do I say? I mean, they're gonna ask a lot of questions."

"Say very little. You're in shock, after all. I'll probably need to take you to the hospital for them to check you out. I'm sure you know how to feed someone a line of bullshit. Get ready to do it." He pulled out his cell phone and dialed. "This is Saul Bordelon at the Bayou Hotel. I just shot someone attacking a visitor. Send the police."

Saul slipped the phone back in his pocket. "Call Shaye and let her know what happened. Tell her it's probably best if she steers clear until the police are gone. She can meet us at the hospital."

Hustle nodded and pulled out his phone, but before he made the call, he leaned over and took a picture of the man in the mask. He reached down to remove the mask, and Saul grabbed his arm.

"Don't touch anything," Saul said.

"I have to see him…before the police get here."

"Shit. If you know him, you might react and how could you know someone if you don't live here." He ran one hand through his thinning hair. "Okay, but let me do it. I can claim I was checking his vitals."

Saul bent over and pulled off the mask. Hustle leaned over and stared at the man, searching his face for some sign of recognition, but whoever he was, Hustle had never seen him before.

"Do you know him?" Saul asked.

"No." He took a picture and dialed Shaye's number, already dreading the upcoming conversation.

Chapter Seventeen

Shaye burst into the emergency room, Jackson right behind her. Saul jumped up from a chair and hurried over. "He's all right," he said, clearly anxious to calm her down. "He's limping pretty bad, but that's it."

"What happened?" Shaye asked, her voice low. She glanced around the room. "I didn't see any police cars."

"They didn't come with us," Saul said, and directed them outside.

"How did you manage that?" Shaye asked. "I figured they'd take him into custody as soon as they found out he was living on the streets."

"I told them he was my buddy's son who was visiting while his parents were camping in some cell phone–free zone."

Shaye stared. "Holy crap, Saul. Promise me you won't ever move to the dark side. That was some fast thinking, especially given that you'd just shot a man."

Saul scowled. "That piece-of-shit excuse for a human being wasn't a man." He gave her a sheepish look. "Sorry."

"It's okay," Shaye said. "I share your opinion. I don't know whether to hug you or chastise you. You're going to be in trouble once the police find out you lied."

"Trouble for what? Lying about the boys' living situation because I don't want him going into one of those homes? The cops can get over it or arrest me."

"They won't do anything," Jackson said. "Some might find it annoying, but it's not a surprising opinion. Plenty of people, including cops, don't think much of the homes these kids are put into."

Jackson's words relieved a bit of Shaye's worry, but there was still the entire situation to take into account. "So what happened with the police at the hotel?"

"We answered questions," Saul said, "and Hustle played off being in shock so he didn't have to say much. Then I insisted on coming to the hospital, not because he's hurt, but to get Hustle away from the cops before they dug too deep."

"That will only work for so long," Shaye said. "You killed the man attacking him, right? Even though it's a justifiable shooting, they'll still have to dot the *i*'s and cross the *t*'s."

Saul nodded, and Shaye looked over at Jackson.

"Do you know the cops' names?" Jackson asked.

"The one I spoke to was a Detective Elliot. I didn't catch the other one's name."

"Elliot's good," Jackson said. "He won't make something out of it that it's not."

"Meaning?" Shaye asked.

"The prosecutor won't even read the file," Jackson said. "You got a man attacking a child with a hypodermic needle. Given the current tension in the department for crimes against children, you're more likely to receive a thank-you than a reprimand. But they're going to be back to talk to Hustle."

"We'll figure something out," Shaye said. "Right now, there are more important issues at stake. What can you tell me about the man you shot?"

"He was wearing a mask. Hustle said it was like the one he'd seen before. He was a big guy, white, probably midthirties."

"Did Hustle recognize him?" Jackson asked.

Saul shook his head. "He took a picture, though, before the police got there. Maybe he'll recall something later."

"I doubt it," Shaye said, remembering Hustle's recount of the stalker in her previous case and his drawing of Jinx. "I think Hustle might have eidetic memory. When he sees something, his ability to describe it or re-create it in a drawing is far beyond that of a normal person. If he'd seen the man before, he would have remembered."

"Can you tell us what happened?" Jackson asked.

"I was at the front desk and heard the boy yelling for me," Saul said. "I could tell by the sound of his voice that he was in trouble, so I grabbed my gun and ran outside. The piece of sh—crap had Hustle on the ground and was about to stab him with a needle so I fired. Hit him right in the chest."

"Did Hustle say anything else?" Shaye asked.

"Just said he knew someone was watching him when

he got to the street the hotel was on and he took off running. The guy came after him and he yelled for me when he knew he wasn't going to make it. I turned the security video over to the cops to cover my butt; otherwise, I'd show you."

Shaye put her hand on Saul's arm. "Thank you. If you hadn't been there…"

"And a damned good shot to boot," Saul said, and smiled.

"And a damned good shot," Shaye agreed.

A nurse walked outside and gestured to Saul. "Mr. Bordelon, the young man is ready to leave now."

"To keep up appearances, cover the bill," Shaye said. "I'll reimburse you."

Saul nodded and headed inside to handle the charges. Shaye hung back with Jackson, not wanting anyone to overhear what she had to say.

"I need you to talk to Detective Elliot and find out who the man was," Shaye said. "This 'visiting friend's son' story isn't going to hold for long. The cops will be back and they'll want Hustle's name, address, the works. How much trouble is Saul going to be in when they find out he lied? The truth?"

Jackson blew out a breath. "The video will back up his defense story for the shooting, so I don't think he'll have any issues at all with that part of things. If he claims he didn't want to see the kid go into the system, he probably won't get more than some stern words. It's not like the police aren't aware of kids living on the streets."

"Good. If you hear they're going to try to make more of it, let me know. I'll get Saul a good lawyer."

"And that would probably be the end of it. There's nothing worthwhile to pursue, especially if he lawyers up."

"So that potential problem is covered, but we have a bigger one now," Shaye said. "That man was our connection to Jinx, and without a legit case, you can't butt into Elliot's investigation."

"No, but he was also our connection to Peter Carlin, assuming the mask was the same. I need to call Detective Grayson and fill him in. He's handling the Carlin case. I don't think Elliot will have any problem turning it over to Grayson. He doesn't have the ego some of the others do, and finding Peter Carlin is a top priority right now."

"Good. Then you get a hold of Grayson and work on Elliot, and I'll figure out something to do with Hustle. I can't send him back to the hotel. I guess I'll have him stay at my place again."

"No way. There's a really good chance this guy wasn't working alone. If that's the case, then there's someone else out there who knows about Hustle and probably about you. If you've poked the hornet's nest with your investigation, your place could be under observation."

"My place is as safe as they come," Shaye argued.

"Inside. But all someone has to do is wait for Hustle to step out the door and then put a bullet in him."

"They could do the same to me. I don't have a choice. I don't have anyone else I trust to protect him."

"Sure you do." Jackson stared at her.

"Oh no. I'm not moving us in with my mother."

"Why not? It's away from Bywater and the Quarter. You've got armed policemen parked outside, and the house is probably secured better than Fort Knox."

"The thought of me moving back home right now isn't one I can entertain. I can't go running back to Mommy every time I'm in danger. I took this job knowing the risks."

Jackson didn't look happy, but he also knew when it was a losing battle. "Then at least get Hustle to stay with her."

Shaye shook her head. "I can try, but my mom is a social worker. Getting Hustle under the same roof as her won't be easy."

"It will if the choice is her house or the police station."

"That's just mean."

"That's probably the way he'll see it. But until we know for sure this man was working alone, we can't assume the threat to Hustle has been eliminated."

Shaye nodded, trying to formulate a good argument for her upcoming talk with Hustle, when Saul came hurrying outside.

"You better get in here," Saul said. "Hustle's pitching a fit."

Shaye ran inside after Saul and past the startled nurse at the front desk. Hustle was standing outside a doorway and arguing with a paramedic.

"You gotta let me in," he yelled.

"Sir," the paramedic said, clutching Hustle's shoulders. "If you don't calm down, I'm going to have to call the police."

"What's going on?" Shaye asked as she ran up.

"That's Scratch!" Hustle said. "They just brought him in on a bed and they won't tell me nothing."

Before Shaye could say a word, Jackson stepped forward and presented his badge. "The police have been looking for the young man you brought in. We suspected he was the victim of foul play. What can you tell me?"

The paramedic released Hustle, who backed up and leaned against the wall, slightly lifting his right leg.

"We got a call from a park ranger over at Lake Maurepas. They found the boy on a trail."

"What was his condition when you found him?" Jackson asked.

"Not good," the paramedic said. "He was unconscious and hasn't regained. His vital signs are weak."

"Did he have any injuries?"

"A bunch of scrapes and bruises and a good knot on the back of his head." The paramedic glanced at the others before looking back at Jackson. "He was wearing handcuffs. The chain in the middle was broken, but the cuffs are still around his wrists."

"Anything else?" Jackson asked.

"He was wet. All over. And had a bunch of swamp mud on him."

Jackson pulled out his phone. "I'd like the name of the park ranger."

As the paramedic gave him the name, his pager went off. "I have to go," he said.

Jackson handed him a business card. “If you think of anything else, give me a call.”

The paramedic took the card and ran down the hallway and out the back door.

“Can’t somebody tell us something about Scratch?” Hustle asked.

As if on cue, the door to the room opened and a doctor stepped out. He looked a bit surprised to find them all standing there.

“You can’t be here,” the doctor said. “You have to wait in the lobby.”

Jackson flashed his badge again. “Can you tell me anything about the boy you just saw? What his condition is?”

“He’s nonresponsive and weak. We’ll know more after we run tests.”

“But he’s going to live, right?” Hustle asked.

The doctor frowned. “I’m afraid I can’t say until I know the extent of his injuries. If you’ll excuse me, I need to prepare the techs.”

“Let’s go,” Jackson said. “He can’t give us anything yet.”

“I’m not going anywhere,” Hustle said. “I’ll sit in the lobby all night if I have to.”

“It wouldn’t matter,” Shaye said. “The doctors won’t give information to anyone but family or the police.”

Hustle looked expectantly at Jackson, who shook his head.

“I have to pursue information on your attacker and try

to contact this park ranger. It would be a waste of valuable time for me to sit here doing nothing. I'll leave my contact information with the front desk and they'll let me know when they have something concrete."

"Is he safe here?" Hustle asked.

"I don't know, but I'll have someone stationed outside of his room."

Hustle didn't look happy, but he knew it was as good as he could get. "Fine, then I guess I'll go back to the hotel with Saul."

Shaye held in a sigh. "About that…we need to talk."

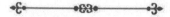

Jinx checked her watch for the hundredth time in the last hour. Ten more minutes. Six hundred seconds and it would be exactly three hours since the crazy man had brought them dinner and almost two hours since the sun had gone down, extinguishing all light in the barn.

"Is it time yet?" Spider asked.

What the hell. Ten minutes wasn't going to make a difference. It was dark outside. Time to get the hell out of here.

"Yeah," she said and pulled the lock pick she'd made from her pocket. She stuck her hands through the bars and grasped the padlock, feeling the bottom for the keyhole. She stuck the pick into the hole and leaned up against the bars, listening as she felt her way around the inside of the lock. It took about ten minutes of delicate twisting, but finally, she heard a *click* and the lock dropped.

"I got it," she said. She let herself out of the cage and walked across to Spider's cell, her arms in front of her as she went.

"Oh my God!" Spider said as she grabbed the lock on the door to his cage. "You're serious. You really did it."

"Of course. Did you think I was lying?"

"I'm so scared, I don't know what to think anymore."

"Just give me some time, and keep quiet so I can listen."

She made quicker work of the second lock and opened the door to let Spider out. "Do you remember where everything is?" she asked.

"Yeah. I've been reciting the steps all day."

"Okay, then go collect your items, and move slowly. We can't afford to make any noise or we'll alert the dogs."

Jinx moved to the right until she felt the door to her cage, then walked at a deliberate pace ten steps ahead, then turned and walked five steps to the right. She waved her arms in front of her but felt only air. Leaning forward, she reached out again and her fingers brushed the edges of the workbench she'd been trying to reach. She took two more steps forward and inched her hands over the surface of the bench until she felt the hard cylindrical object she'd been seeking.

"I got the flashlight," she said.

"I got the rope."

"Good. Start for the door. Be careful not to hit that engine. There's all sorts of things balanced on the top of it that would make noise. I'll meet you at the door as soon as I get the crowbar."

They'd been scouting the barn all day as the sunlight moved through the cracks, exposing one inch at a time. The flashlight was critical, and Jinx prayed it worked. The rope might be needed given the terrain, and the crowbar was the lightest-weight object that made a good weapon. She worked her way down the bench, using her fingers to keep her straight until she reached the end where the bench turned. She stopped and slid her hand across the surface until she felt the cold, hard iron rod.

She lifted the crowbar and turned to the left, then walked fifteen more steps. "Spider?"

"Right here," he said, his voice sounding only inches from her.

She moved closer until her shoulder brushed against his, then reached out and ran her hands down the door, looking for the knob. She unlocked the door and twisted the knob, easing the door open only a crack. She peered through the crack, but couldn't see anything. She pushed the door open another inch and saw a patch of light coming from the porch of an old farmhouse.

The dogs she often heard barking were nowhere in sight, but that didn't mean they weren't outside and on the job. Slowly, she pushed the door open a bit at a time, hoping the old wood didn't creak too loudly. When there was enough room to slip through, she eased out and held the door while Spider did the same.

Spider tugged on her sleeve and pointed toward the

house, but she shook her head. She knew there was a road there—the crazy men had to have a way to get to their property but no way could they risk going that close to the house. Not with the dogs. And the road would be the easiest place for the men to find them. The swamp was a risk, but it offered far more places to hide.

Storm clouds rolled through the night sky, and the moonlight faded in and out, making it harder to see. She could hear thunder booming in the distance and prayed it held out long enough for them to get away. Silently, they headed around the side of the barn and out of view of the house. They'd gone over the plan so many times in order to avoid speaking until they were far enough away from the house to be unheard. When they reached the point where the barn completely blocked them from the house, they headed for the swamp. Jinx waited until they entered the trees before pulling the flashlight out of her pocket.

She felt her back tighten as she pushed the button and let out a breath of relief when the light came on. It was weak, but it worked. Hopefully, it would work long enough to get them out of the swamp and somewhere they could find help. She shone the light in different directions, trying to find the easiest way to pass, and saw a trail to the right.

She tapped Spider on the shoulder and pointed to the trail, then set off down it. The cypress trees formed a canopy around them, thick moss hanging down, sometimes brushing across her face and shoulders. She used her hands to push brush out of the way and found that the swamp was thick with spiderwebs as well. The thin, sticky strands seemed to wrap themselves around her hands, and she struggled to maintain her cool every time she had to pull the sticky webs from her skin. Jinx had never liked spiders.

At a fork in the trail, she stopped and listened, certain she heard water running off to the right. It was a sound she'd been hoping to hear. If there was a bayou, it might lead into a town. There might even be a boat.

"This way," she whispered.

She stepped onto the trail to the right and onto a hard dry stick. The *snap* echoed through the swamp like a gunshot. She froze, not even drawing in a breath, but it was too late.

The dogs started barking, and she heard the door to the farmhouse bang open. "What the hell are they barking at?" a man yelled.

"Probably coyotes again. Grab my gun. I'll get those shotgun shells we was loading from the barn."

"Run," Jinx said and took off down the trail.

Branches and thorns tore at her clothes and her bare arms and face, but she barely felt them. All that mattered was getting away, and the water was their only hope in putting the dogs off their scent. As soon as the man entered the barn, the hunt would be on, and she and Spider were at a huge disadvantage. They didn't have guns and they didn't know the terrain.

The brush thinned a little and she ticked up her speed a notch. She heard more yelling and dogs barking behind her, but couldn't make out the words. It didn't matter. She knew the score.

"I think they're coming," Spider said, his voice breaking in panic.

She was on top of the water before she knew it. She dug her heels in, trying to keep from sliding over the bank, but Spider crashed into her, knocking her over the ledge. It wasn't a big drop—probably only two feet—but the noise it made was deafening in the still of the swamp. She bolted upright, then squatted again, realizing she'd dropped the flashlight when she fell. Her hand clasped around it and she yanked it out of the water, but it was too late. It no longer worked.

The clouds parted a bit, and she saw a small flat-bottom boat just a few feet away. "There's a boat," she said.

Spider hurried down the bank and they hopped in the boat. Spider pushed it off the bank as he jumped inside and headed for the motor in the back. Jinx didn't have any experience with boats other than being an occasional passenger, but Spider had told her he'd fished with his uncle before he'd died. He fiddled with something, then grabbed the pull cord and yanked it. The motor turned over a bit but didn't start.

The barking was getting closer and sometimes Jinx caught a flash of lights bouncing through the swamp. The men were headed straight for them. "Hurry," she said.

He pulled again and this time the engine fired up. "Hold on," he said.

Jinx grabbed the edges of the metal bench and planted her feet on the bottom. The engine roared and the boat practically leaped out of the water. She leaned forward to keep from falling backward off the bench. When the boat leveled out, she raised back up just as the moon slipped behind the dark clouds again. The running lights on the front of the small craft barely illuminated a foot in front of the boat, and didn't reach nearly far enough for the speed at which they were traveling. Spider cut the speed and she looked up at the night sky, praying for the clouds to clear.

The first gunshot hit the front of the boat, shattering one of the lights, then a second one came right after, pinging on metal. She dropped onto the bottom of the boat, barely managing to control the scream that threatened to break through. Spider ducked as low as possible and twisted the throttle again, even though Jinx was certain he couldn't see well enough to navigate the bayou.

A third shot rang out and Spider screamed. "I'm hit!"

The front of the boat crashed to a stop on top of the water and Jinx crawled over the bench and to the back, where Spider lay in a heap in front of the motor. "Spider." She shook him. "Can you hear me?"

"It went through my shoulder," he said, weeping. "It hurts so bad."

Jinx heard the men yelling behind her and she reached up for the throttle that she'd seen Spider use. She moved onto the back bench, staying below the top of the motor, and twisted the throttle. The boat jumped and she let off, then tried it again, but twisting more evenly. The boat took off and she tried desperately to focus on the tiny patch of illumination that the remaining light provided.

"Jinx," Spider said and tugged on her jeans. "We're sinking."

Only then did she realize water had covered her feet and was creeping up her ankles. One of the shots must have pierced the hull of the boat, and they were taking on water.

"Is there a bucket?" she asked. "Can you bail it?"

"It's too much. Coming in too fast."

"What if I slow down?"

"Then we'd just sink slower and wouldn't be as far away. Keep going until we can't anymore."

Jinx clenched her jaw, holding in the curse words she wanted to yell at the swamp, her mother, the universe, and God for putting them in this situation. She twisted the throttle a bit more in an effort to put as much distance between them and the men as possible, but she worried that it wouldn't be enough. Sooner or later, they'd have to make a go of it on foot, and with Spider losing blood, she didn't know how quickly or how far he'd make it before he passed out.

Or before the men caught up.

She's seen a glint of metal when Spider had launched the boat from the shore. It could be another boat. If that was the case, then the men would be close behind.

CHAPTER EIGHTEEN

Corrine tossed a loaf of French bread into the oven and slammed the door shut. "She's lost her mind. I don't have to be an expert to know it. Tell me I'm wrong."

Eleonore took a sip of coffee. "You're wrong."

"Damn it, Eleonore. Stop taking me so literally."

"I wasn't. I actually think you're wrong."

"How do you figure? That poor boy has been attacked twice, and if it wasn't for that hotel owner, he'd probably be dead or worse, and Shaye is right back out on the street, looking for clues like it's an Agatha Christie novel. Her life is not fiction."

"No. But parts of it are even worse than a horror novel. Look, I get it. I don't want her out there tonight or tomorrow or even the next day, but I respect what she's doing. Who else is going to look out for these kids? Detective Lamotte is doing everything he can, but his hands are as tied by the bureaucracy as yours are."

"Detective Lamotte." Corrine wiped her hands on a dish towel and threw it on the counter. "Don't even get me started. He could have told her to stay put and let him do his job. Instead he agrees to let her tag along while he chases down murderers."

"So if he hadn't agreed to take her with him," Eleonore said, "do you think she would have stayed here?"

Corrine pursed her lips, not wanting to answer the question. "No," she said finally. "What's your point?"

"That maybe Detective Lamotte knows her well enough to have figured that out and thinks she's better off with him than being out there alone."

"I guess," Corrine said, not yet ready to concede.

Eleonore cleared her throat and rolled her eyes toward the entrance to the kitchen.

Corrine glanced over as the hesitant teen hovered in the doorway. She forced a smile, hoping it looked even remotely genuine. Whatever her problems with Shaye, this boy was not part of them. As far as Corrine was concerned, bringing him here was the first thing Shaye had gotten right since she'd taken on this case.

"Come have a seat," she said and waved a hand at the counter. "I'm warming up pot roast and crisping some bread. You must be hungry. Do you drink soda? I'm happy to pour you one."

He nodded and shuffled over to the counter, then took a seat two stools over from Eleonore, casting a suspicious glance in her direction.

"This is my friend Eleonore," Corrine said. "She took care of me when my mother died when I was just a young girl. Now that I'm an injured old woman, she's taking care of me again."

He gave Corrine a small smile. "You're not old. It's

nice to have someone who'll take care of you, though." He looked over at Eleonore. "Shaye said you was a shrink."

"That's right," Eleonore said, "but I promise not to talk to you in a professional capacity. We just want you to be comfortable and safe."

"You got police on the road outside," Hustle said, "two armed guards walking around the lawn, and a badass security system. I'm definitely safe, but I don't know that I'd ever be comfortable. This place is like a palace. It's fancier than the Ritz."

"You've been in the Ritz?" Eleonore asked.

Hustle nodded. "I made it as far as the front desk before they kicked me out, but it was beautiful. Still, this place is even prettier."

"Thank you," Corrine said as she slid a glass of soda across the counter to him. "I think so too."

"How are you feeling?" Eleonore asked.

Hustle narrowed his eyes at her.

"Your ankle," Eleonore hastily threw in. "Not your mental state."

"It's all right, I guess. Stiff from all the skating and running, but it ain't nothing bad." He took a drink of the soda, then looked over at Eleonore. "I don't mind sharing my mental state if you want to know."

Eleonore glanced over at Corrine, then nodded. "Please."

"I'm pissed is what I am," he said, his face flushing as he spoke. "I'm pissed that someone killed Joker, and pissed that Scratch is laying there in the hospital and I don't know if he'll live. I'm pissed off that someone is taking street kids and even though Saul shot that man, we don't know that it's over. More than anything, I'm pissed that we got a raw deal and have to live the way we do. Jinx and Scratch are good people. Sure, there's bad people on the streets, but not them."

He looked down at the counter, seemingly embarrassed from his outburst.

"I'm pissed too," Corrine said. "Shaye told me she's shared some of her story with you, and you know what I do for a living, so I'm sure you have a good idea how Eleonore and I feel about people who hurt kids."

Hustle looked up at her and nodded. "Shaye's a good person. She didn't deserve what happened to her either."

"I think being pissed is a good thing," Eleonore said. "If you're just a little angry, then you let things go, but if you're really pissed, you make sure that things change. I've made a lot of positive changes in my life because of being pissed."

Hustle stared at her, then shook his head. "You're a strange person, you know it?"

Eleonore snorted. "You're not telling me something I don't already know."

"But I think you're right," he said. "I'm gonna stay pissed until we know everyone who was behind all this. And if there's more than just that dude that Saul shot, I'm gonna help Shaye and Detective Lamotte take them down."

Corrine placed a plate of pot roast with potatoes and carrots in front of him and a big hunk of French bread.

"You're gonna need your strength."

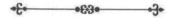

The man threw his glass against the fireplace and it shattered on the bricks. Things had gone from bad to irretrievable. Now they were on the verge of spiraling out of control. Instead of taking care of the skater kid as he was supposed to, the idiot had managed to get himself killed. He should have known not to trust him. All these years he'd been carrying the idiot's weight, cleaning up the messes he made. Sure, the idiot was loyal to a fault, but had it been worth it?

Granted, he'd had no intention of leaving his associate behind with the ability to talk, but getting shot in the middle of the street while attacking the skater kid was a bit more fanfare than he'd planned for the man's death. His preference would have been a quick bullet to the head and a drop into the bayou with a block of cement. Now he had to worry about what his associate might have kept at his apartment that connected them.

His first inclination when he got the news was to hurry over to the apartment and scrub it clean of anything that might track back to him, but the idiot had a criminal record. As soon as the police ran his prints, they'd have his address and would go straight there. Bad enough he may already be at risk, but he wasn't stupid enough to be caught red-handed.

He'd known the skater kid and the woman would be a

problem, but they'd proven to be a bigger issue than he ever imagined. They'd single-handedly destroyed his business and forced him to move his escape timeline from one month to a matter of days. He'd be leaving money on the table by bowing out so quickly, but he'd have to make do with what he had.

All he had left to do was destroy the records and take care of the boy. He'd make the delivery himself and collect the rest of his money. Then he would leave on the next private plane he could charter out of New Orleans. His new identity had been in place for months now. He even had credit established and a bank account. A nice fat bank account waiting for him in Indonesia—extradition-free paradise.

Shaye stared across the street at the police station as the waitress poured her another cup of coffee. Jackson had been in there for thirty minutes already, and she was going stir-crazy waiting on answers.

"You sure you don't want something to eat, hon?" the waitress asked.

She couldn't remember the last time she'd eaten or what she'd eaten, so despite not feeling the least bit hungry, late dinner probably wasn't the worst idea. "You know what, I think I will," she said. "Let me have an egg and cheese sandwich and some hash browns."

"You got it." The waitress headed back to the kitchen,

and Shaye stared out the window and across the street once more and sighed.

She should have stayed at Corrine's. If Detective Grayson let Jackson in on his investigation, he couldn't exactly request that Shaye tag along. And who knew how long it would take to identify the assailant, much less run down information on him. More than likely, she was wasting her time sitting here and would end up taking a cab home.

Her mother had been on the verge of having kittens when Shaye announced her intention to leave with Jackson and continue the investigation into the night, and Hustle hadn't been any happier about the situation. The looming threat of CPS kept Hustle interred in his mother's house, but Corrine didn't have anything to hold over Shaye's head. Not that she would have anyway. Her mother was a pleader, not a blackmailer. Pierce would be far more likely to play the blackmail card.

Still, if Shaye had remained behind, she might have been tempted to tell her mother and Eleonore that she'd gone to Lydia's apartment. If she let that cat out of the bag, there would be no end to the questions and glances and worry. It was something she knew she'd have to share with both of them, and sooner rather than later, but she wanted more time to process it before she had to talk about it.

Her outburst at the apartment in front of Jackson had been uncustomary and a bit embarrassing. She liked Jackson and trusted him as much as she did anyone, but she didn't really know him well enough to dump her emotional baggage on him. He had seemed momentarily taken aback, but not really surprised. She had to give him points for the calm demeanor. He hadn't even brought up the subject after they left the apartment. He'd simply driven away in absolute silence. The first words he'd spoken had been when she'd gotten the phone call from Hustle.

The bells on the door jangled and she looked up, surprised to see Jackson walking in. She jumped up from the table. "Did you find out something?"

He motioned for her to sit, and he slid into the chair across from her. "Yeah, we got something."

The waitress stepped up to the table and placed Shaye's food in front of her. "You want something, hon?" she asked Jackson.

"That looks good," he said, pointing to Shaye's plate. "I'll have the same with coffee, please."

"I guess we don't need to rush out of here, then?" Shaye asked, more than a little disappointed. "You couldn't identify the attacker?"

"We got an ID. He was in the system. Elliot and his team are tossing the apartment right now."

"What about Detective Grayson?"

"He was out of town today for a funeral and is on his way back right now. He should be here within an hour, but he gave Elliot and me the go-ahead to pursue whatever leads we came up with."

"So who was the man who attacked Hustle?"

"Bobby Fuller. He's done time for theft, assault, and extortion, small-time stuff mostly. Do you recognize the name?"

She shook her head. "What about employment?"

"The last record of employment we had was over ten years ago when he was a truck driver. Lost his license over drunk driving convictions. My guess is that didn't stop him from driving, but it would have prevented him from driving the big rigs. Too many regulations to get around for that to happen. Companies aren't taking those kind of risks."

"Extortion," Shaye repeated. "Does that sound like anyone we know?"

"We have no way to connect him to Johnny Rivette."

"We're just getting started."

The waitress slid a plate of food in front of Jackson, and he tackled the sandwich like it owed him money. "No time for lunch today," he said after he swallowed. "I didn't even realize how hungry I was until I saw your sandwich."

Shaye nodded. "There's something else that's been bothering me."

"Just one thing?"

"In this respect, yes."

"What is it?"

"How did this Bobby Fuller find Hustle so quickly? I just arranged for Hustle to stay at the hotel this morning. That's not even a full twenty-four hours."

"Maybe he's one of those guys who grew up hunting everything. Maybe he's good at tracking."

"So good that he followed a boy all over the French Quarter, then managed to keep up with him skateboarding at top speed, through traffic, all the way from the French

Quarter to Bywater?"

"Maybe he followed you this morning from your apartment."

"I was careful. I doubled back and turned off time after time before finally approaching the hotel. I promise you, if someone was following me, I would have noticed."

"But you wouldn't have noticed multiple people following you. What if one was in a taxi and another in a truck with the cable company logo on it and yet another in a white economy car. When we put surveillance on someone on the move, it's never a single vehicle."

Shaye frowned. "Maybe. But still. That's taking things to a whole other level."

"But if someone like Johnny Rivette *is* pulling the strings, then given his track record, you need to adjust your expectations in regard to competence."

Shaye started to reply, then Jackson's cell phone rang. He answered it, listened, then hung up.

"That was the hospital," he said. "Scratch is stabilized but still hasn't regained consciousness. They're optimistic that he will, because they didn't find any damage other than the things the doctor already mentioned, but they have no way of knowing how long it will take for him to wake up."

"You have a guard on him, right?"

"Yeah, and I talked to that park ranger. Unfortunately, he couldn't tell me anything more than what the paramedic did, but I asked him to keep it quiet for the time being. If the media get wind of another teen being pulled out of the bayou, they'll start a storm that will make investigating much harder."

"Not to mention putting a spotlight on Scratch. Right now, we have to assume that whoever did that to him isn't aware that he survived."

"Or the man who did it to him was Bobby Fuller."

Shaye poked at the remainder of her sandwich, then sighed. "What are we doing here? I feel like we should be moving, but there's nothing to move on."

"The worst part of the job is waiting on information."

"Maybe Grayson will find something that links Fuller to Johnny Rivette."

"Anything is possible. But it would have to be something big to connect Johnny to the attack on Hustle. Rivette's slick and smart and has a team of sleazy lawyers at his disposal. He's skated on more charges than most criminals are brought up on in a lifetime."

Shaye knew he was right, and it was possible that Fuller was acting alone—that he was a disturbed person who had been abducting street kids and killing them. Or perhaps simply an evil person. She had no problem believing in evil. She was living proof it existed.

Jackson's phone rang again and Shaye pulled out her own. "I'm going to call Hustle and tell him about Scratch," she said, and headed outside the diner in search of some fresh air. With any luck, when she returned inside, Jackson would have something for them to do.

The call to Hustle didn't take long. The teen still didn't sound overly happy with his quarters for the night, but he wasn't as sullen-sounding as he'd been when she'd left with

Jackson earlier. She had no doubt Corrine had been trying to spoil him with food. Perhaps it had put him in a better mood. He was definitely encouraged to hear about Scratch's condition and relieved that a policeman would remain outside Scratch's room until everything could be sorted out.

She slipped her phone into her pocket and was about to head back inside when Jackson came rushing out. "I took care of the bill," he said. "We need to roll."

"Where? What's happened?"

They crossed the street and hurried to Jackson's car. "That was Grayson," Jackson said as he pulled out of the parking lot. "Fuller's been working as a mason—at Sacred Heart Church."

"Father Michael!" Shaye said. "That's the connection. Not Rivette. Where are we going now?"

"To pay the good priest a visit."

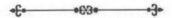

Hustle wandered across the bedroom and into the connecting bath. He hadn't been lying earlier. The house was unlike anything he'd ever seen before. Even this room—reserved only for guests—had ornate furniture and crystal bowls and vases. The bathroom was the size of his old bedroom, the one he'd lived in when his mom was still alive. He ran his hand across the marble counter and fingered the towels, so soft that they felt like tissue.

He couldn't imagine living like this. How hard had it

been for Shaye, with everything that had happened, to accept that this was her life now as long as she wanted it? But then, when Shaye had come to live with Corrine, she'd had far bigger things to dwell on than the opulence of the guest room towels.

He walked back into the bedroom and flopped backward onto the bed. As much as he appreciated Shaye's trying to protect him and Corrine's making sure he was fed and comfortable—and he definitely appreciated the dinner—he couldn't control his impatience. It was great news that Scratch was stable and the doctors thought he'd wake up. But Jinx was still out there and he was sitting inside this palace doing nothing.

He pulled out his phone and looked at the picture of the man who'd attacked him again. Shaye had sent him a text with the name, Bobby Fuller, but that didn't mean any more to him than the man's face did. He had never seen him before and he'd never heard that name before. He sighed and tossed the phone onto the bed beside him. He'd been thinking about both attacks since he'd come upstairs, physically unable to stop them from rolling through his mind over and over again.

Something bothered him about them, and not for the obvious reasons. Something subtle that he couldn't quite put his finger on, but that he knew was there. But what? He went through the attacks again—the dimly lit streets, the abandoned buildings, the feeling that he was being watched but only right at the end, the man who burst quietly out of nowhere, and whom he'd barely managed to overpower the first time and wouldn't have the second time.

And then it hit him.

He jumped up from the bed and stood stock still, focusing his mind on his attacker's arm. That was it. The arm. It was all wrong.

The man who had attacked him the first time held the needle in his left hand, but the man who'd been killed tonight had been holding it in his right. And their positioning when they'd tried to stab him was different, one held high and the other lower and at an angle.

It was two different guys!

That meant the first guy was still out there, maybe making his move on another street kid. And then he remembered something…something that might mean nothing, but might mean everything.

He grabbed his phone and stuffed it back into his pocket, then headed downstairs. Corrine and Eleonore were still in the kitchen, and they stopped talking the moment he entered the room.

"I was thinking I could use some air," he said. "Is it all right if I go out back?"

Corrine didn't look happy with the idea, but she apparently knew a caged animal when she saw one. "Sure," she said. "There's a nice place to sit on the right side of the pool. Comfortable chairs, and that area usually has a breeze, although it's not really the time of year that you can hope to get one."

"That's fine."

Corrine disarmed the alarm system and let him outside.

"Knock when you want back in. I'm going to rearm it so that no one can enter another way."

"Cool." He headed outside, closing the patio door behind him, and walked off to the right, hoping Corrine thought he was taking her advice about the chairs. He found the area and while he agreed that it looked like a nice place to sit, that wasn't what he had in mind. He scanned the well-lit yard, first to make sure that the armed guards weren't patrolling back here, then to find the perfect place for his plan. He spotted it just beyond the sitting area, then grabbed one of the comfortable chairs and headed for the brick wall.

One short run and a good jump, and he was scrambling up the top of the wall. He lowered himself as far as possible on the other side, then dropped. His ankle smarted a little from the drop but it was good enough to get him where he was going. He half walked, half jogged a couple blocks away, to make sure the cops guarding the house wouldn't see him, then called for a cab. It wasn't what Shaye had in mind when she'd given him the money, but it was definitely going to come in handy.

CHAPTER NINETEEN

Jinx felt the water creeping up her shin, and the boat's speed grew slower and slower. They had made it maybe another fifty yards down the bayou, but hadn't seen any other sign of life except for the glowing eyes of the swamp creatures. Soon, they were going to have to abandon the boat and keep going on foot. Spider had moved onto the bench and held a piece of a torn life jacket against the bullet hole in his shoulder.

"We don't have much longer," Jinx said.

"I know. You better head toward the bank or we'll be swimming. It's filling up fast."

Jinx directed the boat toward the opposite bank from where the men lived. At least that left water separating them. She pulled up close to a low spot and stopped. "Get out," she told Spider.

He stepped out onto the bank, then turned around, waiting for her to follow. But Jinx had other plans. She started the engine again and directed the boat toward the center of the bayou. The water was over halfway and the boat barely inched forward a tiny bit at a time.

"What are you doing?" Spider's panicked voice

sounded from the bank. "Come back. It's going to sink."

"That's exactly what I want. If we let it sink on the bank, they'll know where we went ashore."

Jinx grabbed a tattered life jacket from under the bench, cut the engine, then bailed into the bayou and set off for the shore. The moonlight faded in and out, barely leaving her enough light to see the bank, then as if someone had blown it out, the sky went completely black.

"Say something," Jinx said. "I can swim toward your voice."

"Uh, okay. The Lord is my shepherd. I shall not want."

Jinx turned slightly to the left and started kicking again, reciting the prayer along with Spider. His voice grew louder with every thrust of her feet. She had to be close.

A huge splash nearby made her stop kicking. "What was that?" she asked. Had Spider gotten too close to the bank and fallen in? She couldn't hear his voice any longer.

"Jinx?" Spider called, and she could hear the terror in his voice. "It's an alligator. Swim. Swim fast!"

All the air in Jinx's lungs came out in a whoosh as panic shot through every inch of her body. She started swimming again, kicking as hard and as fast as she could, clutching the life jacket with one arm and using the other to paddle.

"This way," Spider said. "I can see you. You're only fifteen feet from me."

"Alligator?" Jinx asked and sucked in a huge mouthful of nasty swamp water. She choked, spitting it out, but never slowed.

"I can't see it. It must have gone under."

Jinx had heard the myth that alligators didn't attack underwater, but she knew it wasn't true. The creatures were just as capable of killing below the surface as above, and her kicking would draw it right to her.

Something solid brushed against her leg and she choked back a scream. It was large and moving. It had to be the gator. She heard the water splash behind her and spun around. At that moment, the clouds parted and the moonlight illuminated the open mouth of the gator, just inches from her face.

She yelled and shoved the life jacket right into the creature's open mouth, then spun around again and swam as fast as she could for the bank. Her limbs burned and her heart pounded so hard she thought her chest would break. She heard the gator thrashing around behind her and prayed that the life jacket would keep him occupied.

Or that he didn't have a friend nearby.

"Hurry!" Spider said. "He's moving again."

Jinx looked up and saw the bank about five feet away. She pushed her body as hard as she could and the moment she felt the bottom, she shoved her feet down and propelled herself out of the bayou and onto the bank. As soon as she hit the bank, she jumped up and ran to the tree right in front of her, where Spider sat on a low limb. She scrambled up behind him and turned around to see the alligator launch up the bank, still shaking the life jacket in its powerful jaws.

"Holy shit!" Spider said. "Look at the size of that

sucker. He's got to be ten feet at least."

"Twelve," Jinx said, still choking on swamp water.

Spider whacked her on the back, then cried out and clutched his shoulder again.

"Don't move your arm any more than you have to," Jinx said. "I just need to catch my breath."

The alligator stopped shaking the life jacket and tossed it to one side. He remained in place for a while and Jinx could swear he was looking straight at them. Then he finally turned and slid back into the bayou, his long tail disappearing beneath the surface of the murky water.

"Let's go," she said, and jumped off the branch.

She grabbed what was left of the life jacket and hid it in the brush. Between the swim and the panic, her body was almost spent, but that didn't matter. What mattered was that they were still in the swamp and their captors were hunting them. They hadn't gotten far enough away in the boat, and she had no idea how long it would take to reach help. The one thing she did know was that their only chance was to keep moving.

Jackson rapped on the door to Father Michael's apartment. It was part of one of the older church buildings, and Shaye could see the brickwork being done on the outside walls. Brickwork that Bobby Fuller was doing. It was close to midnight and all the lights in the apartment were out. Jackson waited about ten seconds, then knocked again, stronger this time.

A light inside the apartment came on, illuminating the blue curtains on the window beside the door. A couple seconds later, the door opened and Father Michael peered out at them, half awake and a hundred percent confused. Jackson flashed his badge.

"We need to have a word with you, Father," Jackson said.

Father Michael's eyes widened, but he stepped back and allowed them inside. As he shut the door, he looked at Shaye. "You're the private investigator that I spoke to Sunday."

Shaye nodded but didn't offer him any information.

"I apologize for the mess," he said, waving his hand at the stacks of paper and books on the couch and coffee table. "I was doing some research before bed. We can sit at the table if you'd like. At least the chairs are empty."

They stepped over into the nook off the kitchen and took seats at the tiny kitchen table. Father Michael shoved files and books to one side and looked down at them. "Can I make some coffee?"

"No thank you," Jackson said. "We're in a time-critical situation."

"Okay," he said, looking back and forth between them. "How can I help?"

"Do you know Bobby Fuller?" Jackson asked.

"Bobby? Yes. He's doing the brickwork on the building."

"How well do you know him?" Jackson asked.

"Not well at all. He's been doing the work here for several months, but he was never much of a talker, and I'm not present much during the day. I have my street ministry that takes up most of the daylight hours."

"Did he appear to be a violent man?" Jackson asked.

"What? No!"

Jackson narrowed his eyes at the priest. "Then it would surprise you to hear that he attempted to kill a teen tonight. One of the street teens that skates at the dock. I think you know the place."

Father Michael looked back and forth between them, his expression one of disbelief. As if he were waiting for the punch line. When none was forthcoming, he took a deep breath and blew it out. "Is the child all right? Was he injured?"

"He's shaken up, but he'll be fine," Jackson said.

"If what you say is true," Father Michael said, "it's highly disturbing. You're sure it was Bobby? The child couldn't have been mistaken about his identity?"

"The child isn't the one who identified him. The medical examiner did. Bobby's on a slab in the morgue. A good citizen saw him attacking the boy and put a bullet through his chest."

Father Michael paled. "A bullet…" He made the sign of the cross. "That poor man."

"Which one?" Jackson asked.

"The good citizen, of course. If Bobby was attacking a child, then he left the man no choice. I'll pray for his soul, but my empathy is with the man who shot him and the child who was attacked."

Jackson cocked his head to the side, studying Father Michael. Shaye had been watching him closely during the entire exchange and had found his responses credible, so far, but then more than one disturbed individual had managed to hide in the church.

"Father Michael," Jackson said, "I have a big problem. You see, my problem is someone's been abducting kids and I don't think Mr. Fuller was working alone. I think he was working for or with someone else, someone who knew the kids who were taken."

Father Michael stared. "And you think I am the one he was working for? Is that what this is? You're accusing me of harming children?"

"Is it such a leap?" Jackson asked. "Jinx, Joker, Peter Carlin, Bradley Thompson ...all of those are children who are missing or dead. You know the only person they all had in common?"

"Oh no." Father Michael ran one hand through his hair, clearly panicked. "You've got this all wrong. I swear. I can explain, but you have to promise not to tell anyone."

"I can't promise you anything," Jackson said. "This is a murder investigation."

"Of course. Okay. I understand. I just wish...this is not how things were supposed to go."

"How about you tell me what you know?" Jackson said.

"Yes. I know or knew all of the children you mentioned, but I was sent here to protect the children. Not to harm them."

"I don't follow you," Jackson said.

"The archbishop was worried about the church's reputation. You know, with all the things that have happened."

"You mean things like protecting pedophiles?" Jackson said.

Father Michael frowned. "Yes, that's a big part of it. Anyway, I've known the archbishop since I was a baby. He was childhood friends with my father, who is a policeman. He came to me and asked me to go to different churches and make sure nothing untoward was happening."

Shaye stared at him in surprise. "You were spying on priests?"

Father Michael winced. "It sounds awful put that way. I prefer to think of it as protecting the weak and preserving the reputation and purpose of the church."

"Regardless of what you want to call it," Jackson said, "you want us to believe that the archbishop sent you to all these churches to get the dirt on the staff?"

Father Michael nodded. "He sent me to the churches that he'd heard rumors about."

"Including this one?" Shaye asked. "Is Bradley Thompson the latest victim?"

"Possibly," Father Michael said. "I called the archbishop tonight and let him know my suspicions."

"And what will happen?" Jackson asked.

"The archbishop will visit and conduct an interview. If he feels the indicated is guilty, he'll ask him to leave the church of his own accord and request that the local police begin an investigation."

"How have you managed to hide what you're doing from spreading throughout the diocese?" Shaye asked.

"I suspect when my transfer comes immediately following a police investigation, most assume a cover-up is going on."

"They think you're a perpetrator," Shaye said. "And that doesn't bother you?"

"Of course it bothers me, but it's a small price to pay if I can help save even one child from abuse. My father saw so much on the job…he thought I didn't know, but I overheard things, and sometimes I'd catch him crying. I saw the archbishop's request as a call from God."

"This is all very interesting," Jackson said, "but can you prove everything you're saying? I'm sure you understand why I can't just take your word for it."

"Of course," Father Michael said. He grabbed a piece of paper and pen from the table and wrote down a number. "This is the archbishop's private cell. Given the situation, I'm sure he'll be willing to tell you what I already have."

"There's nothing more you can tell us about Bobby Fuller?" Shaye asked. "Anything at all about his family or friends? Did he have a fishing cabin? Anything that might help us find the missing children before it's too late?"

"He had a cousin that stopped by once to drop him off lunch. I didn't meet him and only saw him from a distance, but his build and movement was that of a young man, possibly even a teen."

"Was he driving a vehicle?" Shaye asked.

"I didn't see one. I saw him speaking to Bobby as I was walking home. He had his back to me and walked away from me and around the corner. He could have had a vehicle parked around the block."

"How do you know it was his cousin?" Shaye asked.

"Bobby told me. He was eating lunch on the front porch when I left. I commented on the aroma of the barbecue and he said his cousin had dropped it off for him."

"That's it?" Shaye asked. "You can't think of anything else?"

Father Michael shook his head, his dismay apparent. "That exchange was the most words we'd ever spoken to each other. As I said before, he wasn't much of a talker. I suppose now I have a good reason as to why."

"While you worked your street ministry," Shaye asked, "did you notice anyone else hanging around? Someone you might have seen watching the kids or working nearby? Anyone that gave you pause?"

"No. I'm sorry. I wish I knew something that could help. The girl, Jinx, is she still missing?"

Shaye nodded.

"She was a kind soul," Father Michael said. "Tough exterior, but she hadn't been hardened by life yet. I hoped to find an alternative for her that she'd accept. I'll pray for all of them, and for you."

Jackson rose and tucked the paper with the archbishop's phone number into his pocket. "Thank you for your time, Father." He pulled a business card out and handed it to the priest. "If you think of anything…anything at all, please let us know."

They left the priest's house and climbed back into Jackson's car. "Do you believe him?" Shaye asked.

"Yes, damn it. Which puts us back to square one."

"Maybe," she said and frowned. "The young cousin that Father Michael mentioned…it could have been Rick Rivette. He's a teen and we know Johnny has interests in the construction business. And I'm certain Rick was lying about knowing who Jinx was. He knew her and he had her skateboard."

"Even so, it's not enough to go after Johnny Rivette, and even if by some miracle of God we could get a warrant, he wouldn't be stupid enough to be holding the kids at his house. There's no telling how much property he owns. It could take weeks to run down all the deeds."

"And we don't have weeks."

Shaye's phone buzzed and she pulled it out.

It wasn't the same man.

"It's from Hustle," she said, and told him the message.

"What does that mean?"

"I think he's saying it was two different men that attacked him."

"They were both wearing a mask. How would he know?"

Her phone buzzed again.

The first man held the needle in his left hand.

Then a second text arrived and panic ran through her.

I'm going to check something out. Please don't be mad.

Shaye showed the phone to Jackson, then texted back.

Where are you? Don't do anything without backup.

She pressed Send and watched as the message was delivered. She stared at the phone, silently willing a response to show, but the message sat, delivered but not read.

"We have to find him."

Jackson shook his head. "We don't even know where to start."

Shaye forced her racing mind to slow down and think. It was possible that the person Hustle was going to check out was someone she'd been in contact with. Someone left-handed. She thought back to her visit with Johnny Rivette. He'd slapped his nephew with his right hand, but Rick had been standing on his right side. She replayed in her mind when she'd pushed her cell phone across the desk to Johnny, and was pretty sure he'd retrieved it with his right hand.

Then it hit her—the man who'd unlocked a padlock with the key in his left hand.

She turned to Jackson. "We have to find John Clancy."

CHAPTER TWENTY

Hustle peered around the corner of the building and across the street at John Clancy's office. It was dark and the padlock was in place, but that didn't mean no one was watching. If Clancy was the man who'd attacked him and taken Jinx and Scratch, then he knew how to remain hidden better than most.

He backtracked a block and a half and crossed the street in the middle, where the light from the lamps didn't meet, then worked his way back up the block to the office, approaching the building from the side. He could pick the lock, but there was a light over the front door. Anyone on the street would be able to see what he was doing, even from some distance.

When he'd been inside the office, he'd noticed a window behind Clancy's desk, on the side wall. If he could get it open, that was his opportunity to get inside without being seen. The side of the building was dark, and he could easily duck farther back down the street if he heard a car approaching.

He crept up to the window and pushed up on it. It held firm, which he expected, so he pulled the long piece of scrap metal he'd taken from the construction site and stuck it under the window ledge, then he pulled down on the metal, using all of his body weight to force it up. He hung there for a moment, then he heard a *pop* as the ancient latch gave way and the window shot up an inch.

He pushed the window up, peered inside, and then jumped up, pulling himself through the opening. As soon as he got into the room, he closed the window and pulled out his cell phone to use as a flashlight. He started with the desk. Maybe he wouldn't find anything, but if Clancy was hiding something, it probably wouldn't be at his house, which is the first place the police would search. At minimum, he might find other projects Clancy was scheduled to work on—buildings that hadn't yet been demolished and provided him a place to hold the kids.

He riffled through the notebook in the top drawer, but it only contained accounting information, and none of the references were other job sites or addresses. The other drawers contained office supplies and coffee mugs. He left the desk and went to the file cabinet, jimmying the lock. The first three drawers held files related to the job—people he paid, instructions for the jobs, and paperwork from the city.

The bottom one had some parts for heavy equipment and a locked metal box at the bottom. He pulled the box out, figuring it held cash, and picked the lock. He opened the lid and his jaw dropped.

It was the mask.

"You're making this too easy." The office light came

on and John Clancy stepped through a doorway that led to the back of the building and office, a gun leveled at Hustle. "I figured after two failed attempts, I wouldn't get another chance at you. Not that it matters. By this time tomorrow, I'll be soaking up sun far away from New Orleans. But since it's your fault I had to close my business early, it will be nice to take care of this loose thread."

"You killed my friends," Hustle said. "Was I supposed to let that go?"

"I didn't kill your friends. I sold them. Unless a buyer screws up, I don't know what happens to them, and I don't care. I supply a product."

Hustle stared at him. He'd seen awful things done to his mother by her ex-boyfriend and he'd seen worse on the streets, but this man was something beyond anything he'd encountered before. "You're a monster," he said.

Clancy shrugged. "I'm sure some will think so. I consider myself a businessman. I saw a need and filled it. And because the business was off anyone's radar, the IRS, state, city, and that piece of shit Johnny Rivette couldn't all take a hunk of it until there was barely anything left for me."

"Where is Jinx?"

"Dead, probably. Or maybe not. She wasn't bad-looking."

"You son of a bitch!" Hustle knew he didn't stand a chance against the firearm, but none of that mattered because Clancy was going to kill him anyway. Hustle launched himself across the room at him.

Clancy fired, and Hustle felt the bullet rip through his side. He leaped at the man, tackling him at the waist, flipping them both backward over boxes. Clancy managed to keep hold of the gun and lifted his arm, trying to get another shot off. Hustle straddled him, holding his arm back so that he couldn't shoot, but he wasn't going to be able to hold him for long.

Clancy, who'd been clutching the firearm with both hands, let go with his right hand and clocked Hustle on the side of the head. Hustle's head exploded in pain and he loosened his grip on Clancy, who managed to yank his arm from Hustle's grip and push himself backward. Clancy leveled the gun at him.

Hustle stared at him, his vision blurred. "I'm sorry, Jinx," he whispered.

Jackson disconnected the call and looked over at Shaye. "Clancy wasn't home."

As soon as Shaye had made the left-handed connection, Jackson called for assistance. A patrol car was only a block away from Clancy's building and had checked it. They'd gotten no answer, then roused the manager from bed and convinced him to open the door. Clancy wasn't there, and by the look of the open, emptied drawers, it looked as if he'd packed in a hurry.

"He's making a run for it," Shaye said.

"We'll find him. At least Hustle didn't get to him first."

Shaye worked to control her frustration, but she was losing ground fast. Would they catch Clancy? He had a head start and probably had been planning his escape for a long time. He had to know he couldn't get away with what he was doing for long. Then a thought ran through her mind, and she grabbed Jackson's arm.

"Hustle wouldn't have gone to Clancy's house. He would have gone to his office."

"Where?" Jackson started the car and squealed away from the curb.

Shaye gave him directions as he wheeled the car around the corner and called for backup to the construction site. She cursed silently, chastising herself for not thinking of it sooner. Sure, at this time of night, a normal person would have been at home asleep, but all signs pointed to Clancy not being normal at all. And Hustle was a kid, not a seasoned investigator. He would have returned to the place he knew Clancy frequented.

Whatever he was, he'd fooled Shaye, and that pissed her off.

"No one told me this job would put me in front of so many sociopaths," she said.

"That's the small print no one wants you to know about," Jackson said. "If you keep taking on criminal cases, you're bound to run up against evil."

"Turn here," she said. "It's at the end of the block on the left."

"There's a light on," Jackson said. He parked halfway down the block and jumped out of the car, his pistol in hand. Shaye pulled her nine millimeter out and followed him down the sidewalk. They were halfway to the building when a shot rang out.

Jackson sprinted for the building, Shaye right on his heels. When they got to the door, they could hear a scuffle going on inside.

"Stand back," Jackson said, and launched himself at the door.

The door splintered and Jackson fell inside. Shaye ran in behind him just in time to see him lift his pistol and fire at Clancy, who had a gun leveled at Hustle. The bullet hit Clancy in the throat and he dropped the pistol, clutching his throat with both hands. Hustle jumped up and ran over to Clancy.

"Tell me where she is!" he demanded. "Tell me!"

Clancy's eyes widened and he opened his mouth, but all that came out was a gurgle, then blood poured from his mouth and his body went limp.

"No!" Hustle pounded on the dead man. "You have to tell me!"

Shaye went over to Hustle and pulled on his arm. "He's gone."

The teen went still for several seconds, then his shoulders slumped and he started to weep. "He said he sold her. Like a fucking dog. He sold her and now we'll never know who it was he sold her to."

Shaye's blood ran cold. Of all the things she'd imagined could be happening, that was one that had never crossed her mind. She bent down to try to comfort Hustle and that's when she saw blood seeping from his side.

"Hustle, you're bleeding," she said. "Were you hit?"

"Doesn't matter," he said.

"It does matter," she said. "Let me see."

Jackson, who'd been on the phone with the police, stepped over to them. "An ambulance is on the way. Let us check you out."

Hustle rose and started to lift his shirt, then winced. Shaye reached over and gently lifted the fabric away from his side.

"It's a flesh wound," Jackson said. "You were lucky."

"Don't feel lucky. Didn't find Jinx."

"We need to search the office," Shaye said.

"I did that," Hustle said. "Found his mask in the bottom drawer of that file cabinet locked in a metal box."

"Where is it?" Shaye asked.

"I dropped it when I tackled him," Hustle said. "Should be over there somewhere."

Jackson scanned the floor, then got down on his knees and looked under the desk. "Here it is."

He rose, holding the box in his hands, and showed it to Shaye.

She looked at the purple and white and was unable to control the chill that ran through her. Leaning closer, she noticed something underneath. "There's something under the mask."

Jackson grabbed a pencil from the desk, stuck it into the eyehole, and pulled the mask out of the box, placing it on the desk. A piece of paper was underneath.

"It's phone numbers," Jackson said. "Five of them."

"You've got to let Detectives Grayson and Elliot know," Shaye said. "One of those people might have paid for Peter Carlin."

"I'll call them now and get a trace on these numbers." Jackson pulled out his cell phone and Shaye heard him asking for the trace. As he was talking, the paramedics arrived and Shaye helped them with Hustle, who cooperated but barely. He insisted on walking himself to the ambulance, and the paramedics cleaned and put a temporary dressing on his wound.

"It doesn't look deep," one of the paramedics said, "but he should have an X-ray done, and the doctor needs to prescribe antibiotics to avoid infection. Do you want to take him yourself or would you like us to transport him?"

Shaye looked back at the building as Jackson dashed out.

"Did you get a hold of Grayson and Elliot?" Shaye asked.

"Yeah. Grayson is thirty minutes out from New Orleans and told me to run with whatever I find. Elliot is going with his men to search Clancy's apartment for more construction locations to see if any of the kids are being held in them or if they provide a lead to where the kids might have been transferred."

It registered with Shaye that even Jackson couldn't use the word "sold" in his description. "What happens here now?" she asked.

Jackson pointed to the patrol car that had just parked

behind the ambulance. "This unit will secure the scene and scour the place for evidence. At the station, they're running a search on construction permits."

"What about the telephone numbers?"

"Four of the numbers were burner cells, but the last is registered to Emmanuel Abshire. He's been dead for five years, but his sons, Jacob and Moses, inherited his farm. Get this—it's smack in the middle of Maurepas wildlife refuge."

"Where Scratch was found?" Shaye said.

Jackson nodded. "And I was thinking—Lake Maurepas dumps into Lake Pontchartrain. That could account for Joker as well."

"Then what are we standing here for?" Hustle asked and started to get off the gurney.

Shaye put her hand on his shoulder and stopped him. "You're going to the hospital. If Jackson has to handcuff you, he will."

Hustle started to protest, and Jackson pulled out his cuffs. Knowing he was defeated, Hustle sighed. "Promise me you'll get her."

"I promise," Shaye said, even though she was afraid she might return with a body bag.

"And that you'll make them pay."

She nodded. That was one promise she could definitely keep.

Jinx hurried through the swamp as quickly as the dim light allowed. She stayed close to the bank of the bayou, but not right by it, as she was sure her alligator friend wasn't the only one in residence. She glanced back every once in a while to make sure Spider was still behind her. Every time she looked, he was farther behind even though she hadn't increased pace. If anything, she was moving slower now because the moonlight kept disappearing and she had no other source of light.

She stopped and waited for Spider to catch up. "Are you all right?" she asked. They'd been walking for an hour already, but it didn't feel to Jinx as though they'd made it very far. She knew Spider was holding her up, but that couldn't be helped.

"Tired." His breath came out in ragged gasps. "Getting dizzy."

She leaned closer to look at his shoulder and could see fresh blood coming out from under the life vest that he had clutched against it. He was losing too much blood. He wouldn't make it much farther without losing consciousness. She rubbed the sides of her face and tried to come up with an alternative plan.

Then upriver she heard a boat engine fire up, and her pulse rate shot up into the stratosphere. Spider's eyes widened and he looked at the bayou, then back at her.

"They're coming," Spider said. "They're going to find us."

She could tell he was starting to panic and grabbed his good shoulder. "They are not going to find us. I sank the boat in the middle of the bayou so they wouldn't know where we got out of it. The dogs can't track us if they can't pick up our trail."

"So? We don't know where we're going. They've got a boat and guns and probably know this entire place. It could be miles to the next house. I can't make it that far and you know it."

The boat engine grew louder and spotlights filtered into the swamp behind them. Jinx pulled on Spider's arm, forcing him down to the ground behind a clump of brush. She peered in between the foliage and watched as the boat made its way slowly past them, the spotlight illuminating the bank all around where they were hiding. She waited until the boat had disappeared around a bend in the bayou before standing.

"It's hopeless," Spider said. "We're going to die here. Your idea was great, and you did your best, but we never had a chance."

"Stop thinking like that. There's always a way."

"Are you going to carry me out of here on your back? How many miles can you manage—probably not even one?"

"Wait here," she said, and crept down to the edge of the bank. A set of tree roots made up an embankment next to a flat spot of marsh grass that led into the water. She pulled a clump of marsh grass from the bank and stuffed it in between some of the tree roots. It wasn't exactly natural, but it wouldn't stand out to anyone but her.

She hurried back up the bank and motioned to Spider.

"Come with me."

"Where are we going?"

"We're going to find you a place to hide, then I'm going for help."

"No! You can't leave me here."

"I don't have a choice. Either you stay here and I get help or we die here together. This is our only option. Now get a move on while you can still walk."

She walked past him and into the swamp directly away from the bayou. She needed to find a place deep enough in that he couldn't be spotted from the bank. The thunder rumbling overhead was getting louder and lightning flashed in the distance. She needed to find him a place that offered some protection from the approaching storm; otherwise he could lose consciousness and drown.

About thirty yards away, she found a cluster of cypress trees that had been uprooted, probably from a tornado. The fallen trunks were covered with thick moss and offered a nature-made lean-to. She convinced Spider to get under the trunks, then pulled some of the moss down the front, creating a drape that hid Spider completely from view.

She went inside and dropped down next to him, looking him directly in the eyes. "I'm coming back for you," she said.

"I believe you."

Jinx nodded and headed back into the swamp. Spider's words and tone had conveyed his belief that she intended to return for him, but his eyes betrayed his belief that she wouldn't be able to.

She was determined to prove him wrong.

When she got back to the bank, she crept close to the water, trying to see or hear where the men were. The hum of the boat engine carried across the water, but it sounded distant. They had probably continued down the bayou, but at some point they would double back, figuring they'd missed her.

Or they'll be sitting at the finish line, waiting on you.

She stepped back from the bank and hurried through the swamp, keeping the water in sight. She knew the score, and no benefit was gained from dwelling on it. When she got close to help, she'd go deeper into the swamp and circle back around. And she'd pray that she saw those dogs before they caught her scent. If the dogs got onto her, it was all over.

She managed fifteen minutes at a decent clip when the storm that had been threatening to break loose dropped upon her. Lightning flashed across the night sky, bolts of it reaching down to the swamp, shattering the night air with its strikes. The rolls of thunder seemed to run one into the other, making it impossible to hear anything at all. Then the rain began to fall in giant sheets, the wind blowing so hard it felt like needles pricking her skin.

She tucked her arms across her chest and bent slightly forward, lowering her head as she pushed forward. She couldn't afford to stop. The rain made progress slow and she couldn't hear the boat any longer, but that also meant the men couldn't see or hear her. The most important part was that it made it much harder for the dogs to pick up her scent, and they probably wouldn't be able to pick up Spider's at all, not after this.

The spotlight flashed right in front of her and she dropped onto her hands and knees and crawled behind a cypress trunk. The light danced on the foliage where she'd just been standing, and her heart pounded as she watched it move past the trunk where she was hiding and farther down the bank until it disappeared into the storm.

She hadn't heard them at all, nor had she seen the light ahead of her. She was going to have to be more careful, maybe move farther away from the bank, then double back periodically to make sure she was still moving in the right direction. If that spotlight had been only a couple of feet farther back, she would have been standing right in the middle of it.

She rose from the ground and peered around the trunk. Lightning flashed and lit up the bayou, but there was no sign of the boat. She looked down the bayou as far as she could see, checking its direction, and it didn't appear to shift. She backtracked deeper into the swamp about twenty yards, then turned to the right and started moving parallel with the bayou. At least, she hoped it was parallel. With the storm, it was hard to tell if she was moving in a straight line.

Ten minutes of travel forward and then she'd double back and make sure she was still on the same track as the bayou. It had to end somewhere, and water usually ended at a lake or a town. Either way, there would be people. And people usually had cell phones.

Or weapons.

At this point, Jinx would probably trade a cell phone for a handgun. She and Spider might get out of this alive, but she really hoped the men didn't.

CHAPTER TWENTY-ONE

Jackson killed the lights on his car and rolled to a stop at the edge of the tree line that surrounded the Abshire farm. He and Shaye climbed out of the car and crept to the gate, peering over the rotten wood fence.

"Lights are on," Jackson said, "but I don't see any movement."

"How far out is backup?" Shaye asked.

"Fifteen minutes, at least."

Shaye's jaw flexed involuntarily. Dispatch had alerted Jackson that a news crew turned up at Clancy's office as they were hauling his body out. Another had arrived at the hospital at the same time as the paramedics and had made a scene as medical personnel worked to get Hustle inside and push the reporters back out. Someone smelled a story, and things were about to be all over the Internet and TV.

That meant if Jinx was here and still alive, she wouldn't be for long.

And the storm moving in only added to her concern. Thunder and lightning boomed just south of them. In a matter of minutes, the whole mess would be right on top of them, making everything harder.

"Did you hear that?" Jackson grabbed her arm.

"I heard thunder."

He shook his head. "I think it was a rifle firing, but I can't be sure."

Shaye stiffened. "At the house?"

"No. Much farther away."

"Could it have been fireworks?" Shaye asked. Kids shot fireworks for days following the holiday, and out in the swamp would be the perfect place to do it.

Jackson nodded. "It's possible, but I don't think that's what I heard. I'm not waiting on backup. I'm going to check out the house."

"I'm going with you."

"No. You're not a cop."

"But I'm here and I have a gun."

Jackson stared at her for several seconds, his indecision apparent. Finally, he pulled out his portable radio and called dispatch to tell them he was entering the property and silencing radio communication.

He put his radio back on his belt and looked at her. "Follow me and don't make a move unless I direct it." He started to move forward, then stopped and looked back at her again. "And since all of this is probably going to go public, promise me you'll tell your mother that I told you to stay in the car."

He turned around and crept down the fence line. Shaye smiled and set out behind him. More than anything, she hoped that tomorrow morning, she'd be sitting at her mother's kitchen counter, listening to her complain while watching the news story of Jinx's rescue.

When they reached the gate, Jackson bent down and slipped between the railings. Shaye followed suit and they headed for the back side of a line of overgrown hedges that ran down the driveway. The hedges offered them a route to the house without being seen. As they neared the edge of the last hedge, Jackson held up his hand and Shaye stopped. He inched forward and peered around the bushes, then looked back and motioned to her to follow. He hurried across the opening between the hedges and the house and flattened himself on the wall next to the porch. Shaye followed suit.

He pointed to a window to their left and ducked past her, then slowly rose until he could see inside. He dropped back down and looked at her, shaking his head, then moved to the next window, repeating the process. Again, he indicated that he saw no one. He moved to the end of the side and peered around back, then motioned to Shaye. She crept up beside him and saw the back door standing open.

"Stay here and cover the door," he whispered.

He slipped around the corner and up the concrete steps into the house. Shaye lifted her arms and clenched her pistol, training it on the back door. Sweat ran down her forehead and into her eyes. Her palms were clammy, and while she wanted to blame it on the impending storm, she knew it was fear. Jackson was right. She wasn't trained for this, but damned if she was going to wait in the car while he risked his life with no backup. And no way was she waiting on backup when Jinx might have only minutes left.

She took one hand off the pistol and wiped the sweat from her eyes, wondering how long he'd been inside. It felt like forever, but couldn't have been more than a couple minutes. She took a deep breath and slowly blew it out, trying to maintain her focus on the back door. Finally, she heard something moving inside and Jackson emerged from the house and hurried down the steps.

"It's empty," he whispered. "Two dirty plates on the table. Two unmade beds. No sign of Jinx."

"So they got out of bed and left?" If the brothers had fled as John Clancy had attempted, would they have taken Jinx with them?

"Hard to tell. The whole house is a pit. I don't think they're the type to make beds. They probably always look like that. Their truck is out front, though, and dispatch said only one vehicle is registered to them."

"That doesn't mean anything. An old farm like this could have another old unregistered vehicle around. Would they have taken Jinx? If they were trying to get away?"

"I don't know." He pointed directly behind the house. "I think I see the roofline of something out there. Let's check it out."

Thunder boomed overhead and lightning flashed across the sky, lighting up the barn, the grounds, and everything on them, including them. Jackson took one look up at the sky and took off running for the barn. They were halfway there when the storm hit. Shaye threw her arm over her head to protect her face from the piercing raindrops. The wind whipped around her so hard it slowed her down, almost stopping her completely with a couple of huge gusts. She bent forward, almost doubled over, and ran for the structure. The rain was so hard and so thick that she couldn't even see Jackson any longer, and it was too risky to turn on flashlights.

She would have run right into the side of the barn if Jackson hadn't grabbed her. She slid to a stop and watched as he motioned to the corner. He crept down the side of the barn and paused, then continued around the corner. Shaye followed him around the corner and eased up beside him, where he was paused next to a door. He lifted his pistol and motioned for her to do the same, then reached around with his left hand and opened the door.

A gas lamp sat on a workbench near the door, the light illuminating a small patch of the large space. Jackson hurried inside and behind a tractor. Shaye waited a couple seconds, and when no commotion was forthcoming, she slipped around the doorway and rushed over beside him.

He held his fingers up to his ears and shook his head, indicating he didn't hear anything. She nodded, but wondered how much they'd be able to hear with the storm raging outside. The rain beating down on the metal roof sounded like a drum corps was performing outside.

Jackson headed for the rear of the tractor then stopped, peering around the giant tire. He made his way back to her and stopped right next to her, leaning over so that his mouth almost touched her ear.

"I'm going to take the lantern and search the barn," he whispered. "Stay here and cover me."

She nodded, and he ran over to the workbench and grabbed the lantern. She moved to the rear of the tractor and peered around the tire, watching as Jackson made his way around the barn. When he reached the rear, the lantern stopped moving.

"Come look at this," he called out softly.

Shaye hurried to the back of the barn and drew up short behind him, sucking in a breath when she saw the cages. "Oh my God." Her hand flew up over her mouth. "Why would someone build something like this?"

"I have an idea, but I don't think either of us likes the answer."

"They're empty," Shaye said. "We're too late."

He reached down and picked up a padlock. "Look."

Shaye leaned over and looked at the keyhole of the padlock where he was pointing and saw the thin piece of metal sticking out. It could only mean one thing.

"She picked the lock," Shaye said.

"Someone did. We don't know for certain it was Jinx." Jackson reached inside the cage and picked up a paper bag and smelled it. "There was one of these in the other cage, too. It smells fresh."

"There were two of them, and they got away. It could be Peter." Then she remembered the shot that Jackson thought he'd heard and the empty house with unmade beds and the parked vehicle in the driveway.

She clutched Jackson's arm. "The brothers are hunting them," she said.

Jackson's eyes widened. "That shot I heard was in the

swamp. We have no way of knowing where it came from and no way to find them in this storm."

"We can't just leave them out there with crazy people chasing them with rifles."

Jackson ran his hand through his hair, looking up at the ceiling. "Let's go back to the car and check GPS. We can't conduct a search without some knowledge of the terrain. Rushing into the woods wouldn't accomplish anything but leaving four people out there at the mercy of men who grew up in this swamp and can probably traverse it blindfolded."

"Okay," Shaye said, and they set out into the storm back to the car. She didn't like the delay but knew he was right. They might be able to move around the swamp for a little while, but in the long run, they didn't stand a chance against the Abshire brothers.

Neither did Jinx or her companion, especially if he was a scared young child.

By the time they got back to the car, they were completely soaked. Another squad car was pulling up behind them and Jackson motioned them into his vehicle. The two cops hopped inside the backseat and Jackson explained the situation. He pulled up the area on GPS and they all studied the small screen.

"The bayou," Shaye said. "If they'd left using the road, we would have seen them on our way here."

"Unless they were hiding, thinking you were the Abshire brothers," one of the cops pointed out.

"I don't think they left this way," Jackson said. "I saw

two bowls of dog food in the kitchen. If they'd gone past the house, the dogs would have seen them. My guess is they went straight around the back of the barn and into the swamp. That's where the gunshot came from."

Shaye nodded. "The brothers might have had a boat on the bayou. Even if there wasn't a boat, if they got to the bayou, they would follow it until they found someone who could help."

"Assuming they were smart enough," one cop said.

"We're assuming at least one is a street kid," Shaye said. "One of them managed to pick two padlocks with something made from tiny strips of metal. That's resourceful."

The two cops looked at each other. They weren't convinced, but Shaye didn't care what they thought as long as it didn't prevent them from taking action.

Jackson pointed to two roads on the map that encountered the bayou from opposite sides near a set of homes. "The shot I heard came from the south. I think we should each take one of these roads. The bayou runs right past this group of houses. If they're following it downstream, then that's where they'll look for help."

The other two cops nodded. "We'll take the one on this side of the bayou. You guys take the other side."

The cops hopped out and headed for their car. Jackson started up his car and turned around, spraying gravel as he went. "There's some paper towels in the glove compartment," he said.

Shaye pulled out the towels and handed a couple to

Jackson, then wiped her own face and the top of her head, trying to stop the dripping. The storm was still raging, and Jackson was driving as fast as he could in the downpour.

"We'd have to be on top of them before we could see them," Shaye said.

Jackson nodded. "It's pretty bad."

"What do you think their chances are?"

"Honestly? Slim at best, and if one of them is Peter Carlin, even worse. The storm will eliminate the brothers' use of the dogs, but the kids are still at a huge disadvantage. No equipment, no knowledge of the terrain…"

"And most likely, no knowledge even of where they started."

"Yeah." Jackson looked over at her. "We're going to do everything we can to find them alive, but no matter what happens, the Abshire brothers are going down. You can count on that."

Jinx made the right turn and counted the steps until she reached the bayou, except the bayou wasn't where it was supposed to be. She cursed silently and continued forward ten more steps until she saw a ripple of water through the trees. The bayou had turned right, moving away from her, which meant she'd wasted several minutes moving in the wrong direction.

She continued forward until she could make out a longer stretch of the bayou and saw that it continued in the direction it had shifted. She headed back into the swamp, but this time, changing her trajectory to match the turn in the bayou, checked her watch, and started walking again. She'd been at this for thirty minutes and still hadn't seen a single light or structure...something that let her know people were nearby, and telephones.

The storm continued to rage, making visibility low and travel time slow. It didn't help that she stopped every minute or so to listen for the dogs or the boat motor. It also didn't help that her attention was divided between finding help and worrying about Spider, not to mention Peter. One more day and he would be turned over to a pervert. She had to get out of here, get help for Spider, and figure out a way to find Peter.

Hunched over and with her hand up over her head, she almost stepped out of the swamp before she realized she'd reached the edge of it. Immediately, she shuffled backward and crouched down, hoping no one had seen her. She waited several seconds, trying to make out the sound of dogs. When only the sounds of the storm reached her, she crept forward until she was at the edge of the tree line and peered out.

The moon slipped behind storm clouds, pitching the open field into darkness, but it illuminated a light in the distance. It wasn't strong enough for Jinx to identify the source, but it was higher off the ground than a vehicle and didn't look like a headlight or a spotlight. She ducked back a couple of steps and started skirting the tree line, bringing her closer to the light. When a burst of lightning flashed overhead, she hurried to the edge of the clearing and looked out as the flash lit up the house with a porch light on.

It was so tempting to run across the field straight toward the house, but the field grass was too short to hide her passage. All it would take is one flash of lightning while the men were looking the right direction, and they could pick her off like a sitting duck. She stepped back into the swamp again and moved forward. The end of the tree line brought her within twenty yards of the house. It was a safer bet.

And at least if the men killed her there on the front lawn, she might have some witnesses. Someone would know what happened.

She picked up her pace, trying to clamp down on her excitement. She wasn't home free yet, and she wouldn't be happy until Spider and Peter were both safe. It took her only a couple of minutes to make it to the end of the tree line, then she stood back in the brush, waiting for the next lightning strike. When it came, she scanned the area to make sure it was clear and took stock of the house, the porch, and the cement steps leading up to it, four of them in total.

When the light disappeared again, she burst from the swamp and ran straight for the one burning light. She leaped up three of the four steps and slid to a stop in front of the door. She banged on it, praying that someone was home, waited a couple of seconds, then banged again.

She backed up and looked up at the second story. No

lights flashed on and she heard no movement inside. Maybe no one was home. She moved to one of the windows and tried to lift it, but it didn't budge. She scanned the porch, looking for something to break the window with. Better to be carried out of here in handcuffs than a body bag.

She grabbed a small table sitting in between two rocking chairs and lifted it, but just as she started to smash it into the window, a shot rang out and buzzed right by her head, piercing the glass. She dropped the table and dived across the chair, knocking it over, then scrambled for the end of the porch and fell over the side. She sprang up and took off for the back of the house.

Lightning flashed across the sky as she ran, illuminating a small barn not too far behind the house. If she could make it inside, she might be able to hide there.

Then she heard the dogs and knew it was all over.

CHAPTER TWENTY-TWO

Shaye stared out the windshield, desperate to catch sight of Jinx.

You're assuming too much.

The thought had lingered in the back of her mind since she'd seen the cages. Based on what Clancy had told Hustle, she definitely believed they'd contained people, but they had no way of knowing exactly who had been housed inside. Jinx wasn't the only street kid still missing and the Abshires weren't the only number on the list that had been hidden in the box. Jinx could have been sold to whoever owned one of the burner numbers.

But despite all the facts, she refused to let go of the belief that it was Jinx they were trying to rescue. Stubborn and optimistic. Eleonore would have a field day with her when this was all over. For this and so many other reasons.

A faint boom carried through the raging storm and Shaye looked over at Jackson, who nodded. "I heard it, too. Same as earlier."

She leaned forward, silently willing herself to see farther and more clearly, praying that whatever the shot had been fired at had been able to dodge a bullet, possibly for the second time that night.

"There!" Shaye grabbed Jackson's arm and pointed to the right side of the road. "I saw a light."

Jackson checked the GPS. "Looks like a house."

Shaye looked at the screen. "The bayou runs by the property in the swamp about a hundred yards away. If they were following the bayou, that's the first house they'd reach."

Jackson nodded and increased his speed, then turned into the long driveway that led to the house. He slammed on the brakes in front of the house and shone his floodlight on the porch. Shaye took in the overturned chair and discarded table, and her back tightened.

"There's a hole in the window," Jackson said and shone the light directly on the window next to the overturned chair. "I hear dogs!"

Jackson cut off the spotlight and they jumped out of the car and ran for the back of the house. The sound of the dogs grew louder with every step and Shaye prayed they got to the Abshire brothers before they got to their prisoners. When they reached the rear of the house, clouds swept over the moon and they stopped and gazed around in the pitch black. The dogs had gone silent and no sound drifted past them except the storm.

Shaye held her arm over her eyes and squinted into the darkness. The kids were here somewhere, and standing here wasn't going to find them. She felt Jackson tug on her sleeve and looked over at him. He handed her the spotlight and motioned in front of them, then held up three fingers.

She stuck her pistol in her waistband and took the light from Jackson. His intent was clear. On the count of three, she'd fire up the light, hopefully illuminating the Abshire brothers and allowing Jackson to get off a good shot. He pulled on her sleeve again and motioned for her to get lower.

She crouched and he dropped his left arm down where she could see his fingers. He stuck the first finger out and she lifted the spotlight, directing it toward the area they'd last heard the dogs. He stuck the second finger out and she tightened her grip and said a quick prayer.

Third finger.

She paused only long enough for him to get his left hand back up and on the pistol before she pulled the trigger on the spotlight, shooting a broad beam across the backyard. All five of them had been standing still, but the light sent everyone into motion.

A small figure bolted for a barn. The man holding the dogs turned them loose and they took off. The second man lifted a rifle and leveled it at the escaping child. Jackson fired and the man dropped the rifle and fell over. The second man turned to face them and fired back.

Shaye heard the bullet whiz past and strike the side of the house. She dropped the spotlight on the ground and rolled to the side. The next shot shattered the light and pieces of plastic hit her face as she scrambled up from the ground and pulled out her gun. She heard Jackson running away from her and lifted her gun in the direction of the second man. All she needed was a little bit of light.

A second shot rang out and she heard Jackson yell, but the words were lost in the storm.

Fear coursed through her and she moved forward, kicking the ground with her feet but never taking her eyes from the spot where she'd seen the second man. When her right foot connected with something hard, she glanced down. At that moment, lightning ripped across the sky and she saw the second man not twenty feet in front of her, his rifle leveled directly on her.

She dropped and squeezed off three rounds as she went. The other man screamed and got off another shot. She flattened herself on the ground and crawled over to where Jackson was lying inert. Panicked, she went to check his pulse, but he reached over and put a finger on her lips.

He lifted himself up onto all fours and crept forward, Shaye following suit. They reached the first man and Jackson checked his pulse, then shook his head. The second man had been about ten feet away when Shaye had shot him. They crept toward that spot and found it empty.

Suddenly, the entire field lit up with lights, blinding them.

"Lamotte!" a voice called out. "It's Detective Forrester. We have your suspect in custody."

Shaye jumped up from the ground and ran for the barn, where the hounds had been baying. The door was wide open and she ran inside, her hand searching the wall for a light switch. She found it and flipped it on, illuminating the space. The dogs stood at the bottom of the hayloft, looking up and barking. Jackson ran in behind her and grabbed the two dogs by the collars and closed them in an empty stall.

"Jinx?" Shaye called. "Is that you? I'm a friend of Hustle's. The police are here. You're safe."

The boards above her creaked and Jinx peered over.

"Are there two of you?" Shaye asked, praying for a positive response.

Jinx shook her head. "I had to leave Spider behind. He got shot in the shoulder and was losing too much blood. He couldn't make it any farther. We need to get to him fast. It's been a long time since I left him."

"He's in the swamp?" Jackson asked.

Jinx started down the ladder from the loft. "I know where to find him. A boat would be the fastest way."

"Looks like the storm is breaking up. I'll find a boat," Jackson said and ran out of the barn.

"Let's get you out of here," Shaye said.

"Wait!" Jinx said. "You have to tell the cops to find Peter."

"You know where Peter Carlin is?"

"No," Jinx said, clearly miserable. "We were held together in the basement of a building, but then they drugged me and I woke up caged in the barn. The guys who took us said they were giving Peter to some pervert tomorrow night. You can't let that happen."

"Come with me," Shaye said, "and you can tell the officers everything you know."

Jinx fell in step beside Shaye. "You said you're a friend of Hustle's."

"Yes. My name is Shaye Archer. I'm a private investigator. Hustle hired me to find you."

"I didn't think anyone would notice I was gone."

Shaye put her arm around the girl and squeezed. "He's paying a lot more attention than you think."

Jinx sniffed and Shaye could see the tears forming in her eyes. She was tough, but even the toughest of people had their breaking point. Now that she was safe, she could afford to let some of her emotions out.

"If he hadn't hired you…"

"Don't even think about that. Let's focus on rescuing Spider and Peter."

"How can we find Peter?" Jinx asked, her voice breaking. "I don't even know where we were, and I never saw their faces. They wore these masks."

Shaye stopped and looked at her. "Both those men are dead. The police are searching everything connected with them. We'll find him."

Jackson whistled. "We got a boat!"

"Let's go get Spider," Shaye said. "You can tell the officers everything you know about Peter on the way to the boat."

Jackson waved them in his direction. "There's a boat tied to the bank just beyond the tree line. We can use that."

"It probably belongs to those monsters," Jinx said. "They shot a hole in the one Spider and I took, but they showed up later in another one."

"Great," Jackson replied. "Then no one will report it stolen."

Jinx relayed what little she knew about where she and Peter had been held to Detective Forrester, then Jackson, Shaye, Jinx, and another officer headed up the bayou in the boat. Jinx sat up front, watching the bank for the twisted cypress roots where she'd stuffed the clump of moss. It didn't take long to find it and Jackson drove the front of the boat onto a sloped part of the shore.

Jinx scrambled up the bank and took off into the woods, Shaye and the others running behind her.

"Spider!" Jinx yelled as she ran. "It's safe! Come out!"

They came to a stop in front of several fallen trees and a pale teen stepped out from behind a clump of hanging moss. He had a piece of a life jacket pressed to his shoulder and from the amount of blood on his clothes, it looked like he'd lost a lot. He staggered as he walked toward them and fell. Jackson caught him and scooped him up.

The ride back to the house didn't take long, but Shaye and Jinx anxiously watched over Spider, who seemed to drift right on the verge of unconsciousness. Shaye was relieved to see paramedics waiting for them when they arrived. The paramedics placed Spider on a gurney and immediately went to work stabilizing him.

"Lamotte!" one of the policemen yelled. "Got a Detective Grayson on the radio for you."

Jackson hurried off and Shaye stood with Jinx at the back of the ambulance, watching as the paramedics secured Spider. The cop who'd been on the boat with them hopped in the back of the ambulance and they closed the doors and took off.

"Is he going to be all right?" Jinx asked.

"I think so," Shaye said, hoping it was the truth. "He's just weak from the blood loss."

Jackson ran back over, a huge smile on his face. "They found Peter in an old house Clancy owned. He's scared and hungry, but he's going to be fine."

Jinx choked back a cry but finally couldn't hold it in any longer. Shaye wrapped her arms around the girl as she collapsed into tears. It was all over. And yet, it wasn't.

Shaye knew that better than anyone.

CHAPTER TWENTY-THREE

The scene at the hospital was like something out of a Lifetime movie. Hustle hugging Jinx. Jinx hugging Peter. Peter's mom and dad hugging Jinx. Corrine and Eleonore hugging a contrite Hustle and a non-contrite Shaye. Eleonore hugging an embarrassed Jackson. And the harried medical staff finally allowing them a fifteen-second reunion with Scratch, who'd finally regained consciousness.

They all waited anxiously for news on Spider and when it came, it set off another round of celebrating. Spider was weak and exhausted, but he was going to be fine. Doctors insisted on keeping all of the injured overnight and when Shaye backed them up, Hustle finally acquiesced, but insisted on sharing a room with Spider.

Corrine and Eleonore finally bowed out, but only after Shaye promised to report the next day at Corrine's house to fill them in on all the details. Shaye, Jackson, and Jinx headed to Hustle and Spider's hospital room, promising the staff that they'd only be a few minutes.

Jackson started filling Hustle in on everything that he'd missed, and Shaye looked around the room until she saw what she'd been looking for—Hustle's skateboard, which she'd asked her mother to bring to the hospital. She picked it up and turned it over, hoping it confirmed her suspicion. She smiled when it did. The one missing piece was about to fall into place.

"You thinking of taking up skating?" Hustle asked.

"No," Shaye said, "I was just looking for an answer to the one question that never got answered to my satisfaction."

"What's that?" Jackson asked.

"How Clancy and Fuller knew where to find you guys. At first I thought they could have watched for a while and eventually put together your night routes, a little bit at a time. But that couldn't account for Fuller being at the hotel waiting for Hustle. No way could he have followed you all the way from the French Quarter without you noticing. And no way could he have followed us from my apartment that morning. But yet he was waiting for you there."

"So how did they find us?" Hustle asked.

"They had help." Shaye flipped his skateboard over and pointed to the small square taped onto the bottom of the board. "It's a tracking device. I suspect Jinx's board had the same thing but it was knocked off when she was attacked."

Everyone stared at her.

"But they were never anywhere near my board," Hustle said.

"I think," Shaye said, "someone in your midst isn't who you think they are. Has anyone asked to try out your board lately?"

Hustle straightened up in his bed. "Reaper did!"

"Mine too," Jinx said.

"That bastard!" Hustle said. "He was working for Clancy? How could he do that? Sell out his own people?"

Shaye shook her head. "I don't think he was like you at all. I think he only pretended to be on the street. My guess is he's related to Clancy or Fuller."

Jackson's eyes widened. "The cousin who brought Fuller lunch."

Shaye nodded. "I'm sure he's on the run now."

"Give me a description," Jackson said. "I'll get people started tracking him."

"I can do better than that," Hustle said and pulled out his phone. "I took this the other day when he was skating on my board." He passed Jackson the phone with the picture of Reaper.

Jackson sent the picture to his phone and handed it back to Hustle. "I'll be right back," he said, and stepped out of the room.

"We need to get going as well," Shaye said.

"Where are you taking Jinx?" Hustle asked.

Jinx's eyes widened. "I'm not going to one of those homes."

"You don't have to," Shaye said. "I'm taking you to your aunt."

"You're driving me to North Carolina?" Jinx stared at her in disbelief.

"No. Your aunt is living right here in New Orleans. She's been looking for you too, but thought you were still in Baton Rouge."

Jinx's eyes teared up. "Aunt Cora is here? For real?"

Shaye nodded. "She's going to be so happy to see you." Shaye looked over at Hustle. "I'll see you tomorrow morning."

He nodded and gave her a thumbs-up. She could see the tears glistening in his eyes.

It was almost daylight when Jackson pulled up in front of Shaye's apartment. It had been a long and exhausting night, but satisfying as well. Reaper had been apprehended at the airport, proclaiming his innocence in everything, but Scratch had awakened shortly after they'd left the hospital with a clarity he'd lacked when they'd spoken with him earlier. He'd immediately called the police and told them he recognized Reaper's voice as the angry voice who had given Fuller orders.

Grayson's crew were still going over all of Clancy's properties with a fine-tooth comb, seeing if they could find information on any other missing persons.

Jackson climbed out of the car along with Shaye and she looked over at him. "Don't tell me you're walking me to my door," she said. "It's ten feet away."

"No. I'm coming inside and making sure everything is secure."

"Jackson, it's over."

"I sure as hell hope so, but it will only take me a

couple of minutes to ease my conscience. Then I can rest with no worries."

Shaye shook her head. "Fine."

She pulled out her key and opened the front door, then walked inside, Jackson trailing behind her. He watched as she disarmed the alarm, and then he did a sweep of the apartment, checking the doors and windows in every room. When he was done, he came back into the living room and looked down at Shaye, who'd slumped onto the couch.

"All clear?" she asked.

"Yep." He hesitated for a second, then flopped onto the other end of the couch. He closed his eyes for a moment, then looked over at her. "You did a really good job on this case."

"Thanks. I think about how many people Clancy could have sold and I feel sick inside. What if there are still more out there?"

"The search for victims is already under way and will have a ton of police resources behind it. All you need to think about now is the people you helped save."

He leaned his head back and closed his eyes again. A couple of seconds later, he was snoring softly. Shaye started to get up and go to bed, but just the thought of standing made her cringe.

"What the hell," she said, and curled up in the corner of the couch.

She was asleep in seconds.

CHAPTER TWENTY-FOUR

Shaye pulled up a stool to the counter at her mother's house. Corrine and Eleonore were still wearing pajamas even though it was close to noon. Her mother poured a round of coffee, then slipped onto a stool across from her, ready to hear all the details.

Shaye filled them in on Hustle's message about his attacker and the showdown at Clancy's office. As the story grew more intense, Corrine grew more awake. By the time Shaye got to the part where Jackson shot Clancy, her eyes were wide open.

"When you called and said he'd left the house," Corrine said, "I almost had a heart attack."

Eleonore nodded. "At first we thought you were wrong, but when we searched the yard we found the chair next to the fence. That one is sneaky."

"He is," Shaye agreed. "And stubborn."

"Sounds like someone else I know," Corrine said. "So finish telling us about the Abshire farm."

Shaye told them about the phone number trace and her and Jackson's search of the house. When she got to the part about the cages in the barn, everyone went quiet.

"I've heard some horrible things," Corrine said, "but nothing like that. Hunting people? I could never even imagine something so evil."

Eleonore sat down her coffee cup. "You said Spider wasn't the first one held there. I assume the teen from Jackson's case was one of the victims?"

Shaye nodded. "Spider ID'd him when Jackson showed him a picture, and ballistics matched the bullet they took out of Joker to one of the Abshire brothers' rifles."

"Were there any others before Joker?" Corrine asked.

"We don't think so," Shaye said. "Based on what Spider got from Joker and the Abshire brothers, they had five hunts scheduled. We figure Scratch was supposed to be one of them but they overdosed him. Scratch heard two men arguing about it during one of his semiconscious states. Since he didn't recognize those voices, we figure he heard Fuller and Clancy."

"And they paid twenty grand each for them?" Corrine asked. "Where did those cretins get a hundred thousand dollars?"

"Oil," Shaye said. "Their great-grandfather built that farm and owned a ton of land south of here that was full of oil. He leased it to the oil companies, and the monthly checks allowed the family to stop farming and live on easy street."

"And become the monsters they are," Eleonore said. "I wonder if the police would allow me access to their property."

"Eleonore Blanchet!" Corrine stared at her friend in

dismay. "You are not going to study those evil bastards and write another one of those horrifying books."

"Those books give law enforcement an advantage in dealing with the extremes of human behavior," Eleonore said.

"I guess," Corrine said, "but no one should spend that much time in such a dark place."

Shaye didn't say anything because she wasn't sure how she felt about it. Her past was one of those dark places and she was trying to uncover it, even though she knew it would probably change her forever to know the truth. Eleonore believed the truth made for a better future. She thought people who could dwell successfully in reality were far better off than those who refused to look behind the closed door because they were afraid of what they might see.

"What about the fake skater?" Corrine asked. "The one who put the tracking device on Hustle's skateboard?"

"The police caught him at the airport with a ticket to Brazil. Apparently, the escape plan was already in place for Clancy. Grayson's men found a fake passport at Clancy's office and a receipt for a charter flight to Indonesia. It doesn't look like Fuller or Reaper were part of Clancy's finale. Jackson figures Reaper and Fuller were two loose ends Clancy was going to wrap up before he left."

"What was the relationship among them all?" Eleonore asked.

"Fuller was Clancy's half brother. According to Fuller's neighbors, he wasn't exactly setting the world on fire. My guess is Clancy's been looking out for him since they were kids."

"And using him for his side business," Corrine said. "What about Reaper?"

"Clancy's son," Shaye said, "and he was an adult, not a teen like he pretended to be."

Corrine's eyes widened. "Really? That's one I didn't see coming."

"Me either," Shaye said. "Clancy was never married to his mother, but police talked to her this morning and she said Reaper took off when he turned eighteen and she hadn't heard from him since."

"She didn't try to find him?" Corrine asked.

Shaye shook her head. "She told the cops she was glad he left because she was afraid of him. Said he was just like his father."

"Sociopaths," Eleonore said. "You can't sell human beings, calling them 'products,' and have any humanity left."

"That was my guess," Shaye said. "Reaper's not talking, of course. He lawyered up and is sitting in a cell. Grayson said when they told him Clancy was planning on leaving without him, he punched the wall and broke his hand."

"Karmic justice," Eleonore said.

Corrine had been frowning down at the counter and finally she looked back up at Shaye. "How many people are we talking about? I figure this isn't the first time."

Shaye shook her head. "Grayson's team found a pile of

notebooks in the back room of the building next to a can of gasoline. They figure Clancy was going to burn all the evidence before he left and Hustle interrupted him. They're going through them now. Jackson said it looks like lists of customers and the amounts they paid, but it's all in some sort of code. Other books appear to be people Clancy paid off, but again, the names are in code."

"People he paid?" Eleonore asked.

"Probably buying babies," Corrine said, clearly disgusted. "Illegal adoption is a big business, and there's plenty of poor people who'd give up a child for a pittance if it meant covering their next meal."

Shaye nodded. "Another team is trying to match the dates of payments with adoption records, but it's going to take a long time. Jackson said the records go back almost twenty years."

"Twenty years!" Corrine stared. "Oh my God. The number of lives that man destroyed is unimaginable."

"Yeah," Shaye agreed. Jackson had told her it would probably take the police years to comb through all the evidence and even longer to track down the people on the lists, assuming they could break the code.

"How did he get away with it for almost twenty years?" Corrine asked.

"Grayson told Jackson that the records contained a sharp uptick in sales recently," Shaye said. "My guess is Clancy was preparing to shut down his business and leave the country and was trying to get the last boost to his nest egg that he could."

Eleonore nodded. "If he was trafficking people at a much slower rate than his recent deals, it wouldn't have been hard to get away with it for a long time."

Corrine stared at them in dismay. "The two of you are beyond depressing. Don't you have anything good to tell us?"

"What about the reunion between Jinx and her aunt?" Eleonore asked.

"That went even better than I'd hoped," Shaye said. "It's obvious how much Cora and Jinx love each other, even though they've had so little time together. I think Jinx has a great future with her."

Shaye felt her eyes mist up as she recalled the teary reunion between Cora and Jinx. It reminded her of her relationship with Corrine.

"I talked with Cora's attorney this morning," Corrine said. "I'm having her case moved to New Orleans and handling it myself from the state's side of things. Jinx is going to get the happy ending she deserves."

Shaye smiled at Corrine. "I have all the confidence in the world in you."

Corrine blushed. "That's the good part of the job, you know? And I don't get to see it enough."

"What's going to happen to Hustle?" Eleonore asked. "He doesn't strike me as the type that would go willingly into four walls and three squares a day—not if it meant following someone else's rules."

"I have an idea about that," Shaye said, "but I have to talk to some people first."

Shaye's cell phone went off and she picked it up. "Speak of the devil. The hospital has cut him loose. I better get over there before he skateboards off into the sunset."

"Let us know if we can do anything," Corrine called after her as she headed out.

Shaye waved one hand over her head and dialed another number on her way out of the house. If he was on board, then she could pitch her idea to Hustle when she picked him up at the hospital. If not, she'd figure something else out.

There was always a way. Corrine had taught her that.

Hustle practically jumped out of the wheelchair when Shaye walked into the emergency room. It had only been half an hour since he'd called her, but cooped up in this place, it had felt like an eternity.

"Give me just a minute," Shaye said and headed over to the aggravated-looking nurse who kept telling him to stay put.

"I'm Shaye Archer," Shaye said. "Do you have release forms I need to sign?"

"Yes, Ms. Archer." The nurse's demeanor changed from aggravated to pleasant. "Detective Lamotte gave us permission to release the boy into your custody."

"Great. What about the bill?"

"It's not prepared, but we can forward it to you if you'd like."

"That would be fine." Shaye pulled out a business card and handed it to the nurse. "You can send it to my post office box. Are there any instructions?"

"The doctor wants him to rest the ankle and change the dressing on his side twice a day. I have a prescription here for antibiotics. If you see any sign of infection, then bring him back in. Otherwise, the doctor would like to see him again in a week."

"Okay," Shaye said. "I'll call and make an appointment."

Hustle held in a sigh. His ankle was already feeling better and the wound on his side was small. It had just bled a lot. This was a whole lot of hoopla over nothing, and he was ready to get out from under the watchful eye of adults.

Shaye signed some papers, then thanked the nurse and waved at him. "Let's get out of here," she said.

"About time," he grumbled.

"You in a hurry to go somewhere?" Shaye asked as they walked to her SUV.

"Anywhere but here—all those people constantly poking at me and smiling all the time. Makes me nervous."

"I can see where being surrounded by pleasant people who are caring for you might be a strain."

Hustle looked over at her. "Please. Like you would be any happier with that setup."

"Probably not, but I am an adult with my own apartment, bed, and cable television subscription. You are not."

Hustle's attitude shifted from aggrieved to panicked.

"Where are you taking me?"

"Where did you think I would take you?"

"I don't know. The docks."

"I see. So Jackson vouched for me, releasing you to my custody, and you think I should just turn you loose back on the streets."

He felt a twinge of guilt that what he wanted might get Jackson and Shaye into trouble, but there was a limit to what he could live with. "I'm not going to one of them homes. You can take me there, but you can't make me stay."

"You told me that when this was over, you'd listen to options, right?"

He sighed. "Yeah."

"I'm calling my marker. You have to listen to my proposal."

Damn. "And if I don't like your idea?"

"Then I'll attempt to keep you in my custody until the doctor releases you, but I can't control your actions when I'm not looking."

Hustle stared at her for several seconds, then nodded. "Fair enough."

Shaye rounded a corner and he looked up in surprise. "This is Saul's hotel."

"Yep," she said, and parked in front of the lobby. "Come on. We've got business to discuss."

Hustle climbed out of the car and followed Shaye inside. Saul was in his usual spot behind the counter and looked up and smiled when they walked in. "There's the heroes of New Orleans," he said.

Shaye laughed and Hustle managed a bit of a smile for Saul. He wasn't comfortable with being called a hero, but the man *had* saved his life.

"I could say the same for you," Hustle said.

Saul waved a hand in dismissal. "All in a night's work."

"Let's hope last night wasn't typical," Shaye said.

Hustle shoved his hands in his jeans pockets, anxious to find out what Shaye had in mind and why they were here at Saul's hotel. Shaye looked over at Saul, who nodded, then she looked back at Hustle and smiled.

"We have a proposition for you. You see, Saul is an approved foster parent, and I have no doubt I can get you placed in his care, at least temporarily."

He stared at them for a bit, his emotions too out of whack to respond. Saul was a good man and Hustle had no doubt he would treat him well, but so many things could happen to change that. The state could change its mind, and even with Corrine's connections, Hustle knew Shaye couldn't guarantee things would remain the way she arranged them.

"I appreciate the offer," he said, "but I can't let Mr. Bordelon take responsibility for me. I can take care of myself."

"Hell, I'm not taking you to raise," Saul said. "You're damned near grown, anyway. But I can give you a room in my apartment out back and three squares a day. In return, you can help me out around this place."

"How can I help you?" Hustle asked.

"My military service left me with a bad knee, and it's getting worse every day. I got a lot of painting that needs to be done here for starters—inside and out. Shaye says you're an artist. I was thinking about doing some of them fancy paintings on some of the walls."

"Murals," Shaye said.

Hustle stared at them, his mind a jumble of emotions. It was almost too good to be true—a place to live, guaranteed meals, and work he would enjoy. "What if the state changes their mind? What if they say I have to leave here?"

"That's possible," Shaye said, "so what Saul would like to do is file for legal guardianship."

Hustle shook his head. "I don't know…"

"With the intention of helping you become emancipated," Saul said.

"What's that mean?" Hustle asked.

"It means," Shaye said, "that the government would consider you an adult. You could hold a job, rent an apartment, get your own cable bill, or buy a car."

"That way," Saul said, "the state couldn't make you leave, and if once you became emancipated, you wanted your own space, you could move into one of the units and I'd pay you wages plus free rent for the work you do."

"What about school?" Hustle asked. "Would I have to go?"

"Once you're emancipated, it's up to you. Until then, Saul can arrange for you to be homeschooled if that's what you'd prefer."

Hustle felt a glimmer of hope. The first one he'd had since his mom died. If he had a place to live and a job that paid him money, maybe he could go to art school, as Shaye had mentioned. It was such an awesome thought that he felt a smile break through.

"You're serious about all of this?" he asked, still not able to comprehend his good fortune.

Shaye and Saul nodded.

"I'll do it," Hustle said, "but I'll earn my keep. You ain't gonna be put out none 'cause of me."

"I have plenty enough to keep you busy," Saul said. "And you'll be helping me a great deal. I might even like the company."

Hustle felt a blush creep up his neck and he looked down at the floor. Finally, he looked at Shaye. "Maybe if you need it, I can help you with another case sometime."

Shaye smiled. "I would love that. But only if you promise me you won't attempt to confront the bad guy without backup."

"That's one promise you can count on."

It was almost four o'clock when Jackson pushed open the door to the police station. He was pretty sure he'd slipped into some form of a waking coma when he'd crashed on Shaye's couch in the wee hours of the morning. He'd awakened to the smell of coffee around eleven and had looked up to see Shaye pouring a cup and looking as worse for the wear as he suspected he did.

They'd split an entire pot, trying to get their tired bodies and minds going, then he'd thanked her for the coffee and the couch and headed for home for a much-needed shower. No one would be expecting him in the office that day, so he'd gone straight to bed again after drying off and hadn't moved for hours.

When he awakened, he felt almost human again and decided to stop in at work and see if Grayson had made any more headway on the case. He nodded at the desk sergeant as he stepped inside the station.

"Big one last night," the desk sergeant said. "I hear congratulations are in order."

"Thanks," Jackson said. "But you may want to keep them to yourself. I have a feeling Vincent's going to make my life hell."

"Probably going to try, but that doesn't change what you did. I've heard some about those records recovered from Clancy's office." He shook his head. "When you're on the job as long as I've been, you think you can't be shocked anymore, but this one…it's something out of a nightmare."

"I couldn't agree more."

"Grayson is in one of the interrogation rooms where they're working on the records. He said if you came in today to send you back there. Something he needed to discuss with you."

Jackson headed down the hallway and spotted Grayson in the largest interrogation room, leaning over the table and looking at a notebook with Detective Elliot. Jackson opened the door and Grayson looked up and nodded.

"Give me a minute," Grayson said to Elliot as he reached for one of the notebooks.

He exited the room, motioning for Jackson to follow him into the smaller empty room across the hall. He shut the door as soon as Jackson stepped inside.

"This is going to get out," Grayson said, "but I didn't want the others to overhear. Right now, me, Elliot, and Chief Bernard are the only people who know, but given the situation, we felt you should get a heads-up before this breaks loose."

"What is it?" Jackson asked, unable to imagine what Grayson could possibly tell him that would make the facts of the case worse, but from the look on the senior detective's face, that's exactly what he was about to do.

Grayson held up the notebook. "This is one of the old record books that we took from Clancy's office. You know they're all in code, but the code in this one isn't the same. We think Clancy might have changed it periodically."

"That would make sense."

"Elliot figured this one out. It was a simple backward alphabet-to-number code. Probably something Clancy used in the beginning before he decided he needed to make it harder to crack."

Jackson felt excitement course through him. "Then you've figured out more buyers?"

"No. This is a payment log. One entry per page, each detailing a description of the 'product,' the date acquired, the person paid, and the amount."

"Well, that's still something."

Grayson frowned. "It's more than something." He opened the journal to a page and pointed. "This page details the sale of an eight-year-old girl."

Grayson looked at Jackson, clearly upset. "The seller was Lydia Johnson."

Shaye uncovers the truth about her past in DIABOLICAL.
Coming Fall 2016.

15088355R10201

Printed in Great Britain
by Amazon.co.uk, Ltd.,
Marston Gate.